RENEGADES

HOTBLOODS 3

BELLA FORREST

$\mathcal{I}$ braced myself against the hard floor, feeling the friction of the rubble and rock beneath my boots, my eyes facing forward. Sweat dripped down my forehead, with rivulets meandering beneath the collar of my military vest, winding their way between my tensed shoulder blades. Everything ached, though I had learned to ignore the constant, dull pain that pulsed through my body. It was part of me now.

Up ahead, appearing from behind crumbling buildings, a swarm of holographic enemy soldiers were gearing up to retaliate. I kept my eyes on them, trying to count how many were approaching, but there were too many. They moved slowly at first, blending into formation, clutching their weapons to their sides. I took a deep breath and waited for the moment we could strike.

To my left and right stood a line of Queen Brisha's coldblood trainees, their focus never leaving the oncoming enemy, each one holding their weapon of choice. Some carried enormous pikes that crackled, while others gripped the leather handles of deadly blades. Guns were too easy for the trainees, since anyone could shoot one and the enemy could disable firearms with a jammer on the battlefield. Close combat was a more revered skill within the coldblood army.

The masked holograms broke into a slow jog, charging at us from over the hills of rubble, the crunch of their boots providing a terrifying percussion to the already-intense boom of the overhead explosion sound effects. My pulse was racing, my hands shaking, even as I reminded myself that this was only a simulation. Still, I didn't want to let anyone down, not when I had come so far. I refused to be the weak link. More than that, I refused to let Pandora be right about me. I needed to prove that I could be as good as the cold-bloods on either side of me. I was just different.

"You ready for this?" Navan shouted from beside me. He was clutching a katana-like sword, the blade glinting as he took a half-step forward, holding the blade horizontal in front of his face.

"Ready!" I adjusted the gear I'd been given. The heavy vest was made of a strange, almost rubbery material that made me feel like I was wearing half a wetsuit, with glowing green piping that ran through every seam, making it blaze with light. Everyone on the trainee side wore one to help monitor performance during the battle, and to indicate when a person was "out."

Around my waist and across my chest was a bandolier of knives, small but perfectly formed, designed to fit my fingers and my skillset. I pulled the straps tighter just to be sure I wouldn't lose any of them in the fight. I'd already been reprimanded for doing that, two days before, and it wasn't an experience I was eager to repeat. My arms still throbbed from the Vysanthean version of five hundred push-ups.

Looking toward the enemy army, which was now mere yards away from where I stood, I refastened the fingerless gloves I was wearing, which were forged from the same rubbery material as the vest, and flexed my fingers, plucking a knife from the side of my waist and preparing to make my first strike.

It had only been a week since we'd started our military training, and this was our first chance to try out the skills we'd learned. There had been a few test runs that hadn't exactly been successful, especially where my knife-throwing was concerned, but this was the first full-fledged battle scenario we'd been allowed to participate in. I could feel the rush of adrenaline in my veins, making me faster, stronger, sharper, but there was no telling how this would play out. All I knew was I had to show I was worthy.

"Not long now!" Navan said, turning in my direction.

I managed a teasing smile. "Then keep your eyes on the enemy!"

The world shifted as the holographic soldiers burst into action. Some sprinted at us, while others extended their mighty wings and took to the skies before plummeting to the ground in death-defying stunts of aerial warfare, launching various forms of artillery. Holographic arrowheads and darts shot from beneath their wings. Other soldiers crashed down in a spiraling movement, the flash of a sword whirling around them, striking at trainees left, right, and center.

I leapt out of the way of a stray dart, watching with regret as the vest of the trainee behind me turned red, signifying he was now out of the game. The coldblood scowled in my direction, clearly blaming me for the blow he hadn't been quick enough to dodge. I'd had to deal with a lot of that over the last week—endless blame for things I hadn't done, because I was the puny Kryptonian, not fit to fight beside these superior Vysantheans. Navan had told me to just ignore it and prove to them I was capable in my own right by getting through the scenarios, but it was hard to push away their endless negativity.

I flung the knife in my hand at the nearest hologram—a giant coldblood with wings twice my size—and watched with satisfaction as the blade struck its heart. A moment later, the figure flickered and sparked before disappearing from the game, the hologram taken down.

Sprinting for cover behind the remnants of a cracked wall, I released four more knives, each one sailing clean through my chosen assailant, prompting them to flicker and disappear, just as the first had done.

I felt a whoosh of air behind me and turned in time to send a knife through the neck of an enemy soldier who had sought to take me by surprise. As it disappeared, I let loose another blade, taking out an identical figure just behind where the first had stood. I didn't know if it was a glitch in the game or not, but I wasn't taking any chances.

Realizing I had used most of the knives strapped across my chest, I pressed the buttons attached to the wrists of my fingerless gloves, prompting them to light up with a silvery glow. There was a magnetic connection between the gloves and the handles of the knives I had thrown, meaning they could be brought back to me at will, but to do that, I had to have a clear path, to avoid accidentally injuring one of my teammates. I had already had close calls with at least three other cold-blood trainees, who refused to let me live it down, even though the cuts to their faces and arms had faded away to nothing thanks to the vials they all took.

They had it easy. I was still covered in bruises and scrapes, unable to ingest the medicines they were using to rapidly heal themselves. Navan had tried to dilute one of the potions so that I could take it, but so far it had only succeeded in giving me cramps.

Focusing on the blades that glinted on the ground, I drew my fingers inward, feeling the vibration of the magnetic force as the knives came hurtling back to me. I moved my hands to the left and right, trying to navigate them through the clusters of coldbloods, and ended up taking out two more holograms in the process.

"Navan, get out of the way!" I yelled, suddenly realizing he had shifted position. One of my knives was heading his way. I tried to stall it, but it was too late—it was moving too fast.

Navan looked puzzled for a moment, then spotted the deadly projectile racing toward him. He ducked just in time, the edge of the knife catching him on the apple of his cheek before shooting past him on its way back to my hands.

"Maybe warn me sooner next time!" Navan panted, returning to his full height.

"Sorry!" I flushed, grasping each knife as it returned to me and placing it back in its slot on the bandolier.

All around me, the sky had darkened with Brisha's coldbloods, their wings flapping majestically as they clashed with the holograms. Although my knives could fly an impressive distance, *I* couldn't, giving me a clear disadvantage when it came to point-scoring. I watched one of the coldbloods, a female named Vizeria, slashing away with a curved saber, taking out hologram after hologram as she rocketed through the air, twisting like a whirling dervish, unrelenting and terrifying.

Navan jogged up beside me, distracting my attention from the formidable air force. He turned his samurai blade with a flourish, taking off the head of an attacker who had sprinted up behind him before settling behind a fallen spire with me.

"How's it going?" he asked, his eyes peering over the lip of the makeshift shield.

"Okay," I replied, flinging two knives through the abdomens of two enemies. They flickered and fell, and Navan whistled, raising an impressed eyebrow.

"Your knife skills are getting better and better. You just need a bit more practice with those gloves," he said, nodding to the offending articles, which had left the deep cut on the side of his face.

"I'm getting there," I promised, taking out another two enemies. "Come on, we need to take out more of these tools. Otherwise, this game is never going to end!"

We picked our way over the rubble, firing at any holograms that crossed our path, though most of them were distracted by the aerial forces above us. I grimaced, realizing I was probably holding Navan back from his full potential, since he seemed eager to stick by me instead of taking to the skies. If I had a set of wings, I knew with practice I could be as formidable as the rest of them. I felt it in my bones.

Just then, my boot caught on a piece of twisted metal, and I stumbled forward, my knees crashing to the ground. As I doubled over, I felt the bite of the blade edges from the bandolier nipping at the vest, though it kept them from piercing my skin. A split second later, Navan gripped my arm and hauled me up, narrowly avoiding a stray arrowhead that shot past, just above his shoulder.

"You okay?" he shouted over the noise.

"Yeah, don't worry." I laughed tightly, not wanting him to see how frustrated I was. Hearing the telltale flurry of air behind me, I dove to one side, twisting in midair before landing heavily on my back. I grasped at two of my throwing knives, sending them hurtling through the body of an enemy, only to catch the arm of one of my own teammates, who had been trying to creep up behind the enemy to take him out.

With a sinking feeling, I watched as the coldblood's vest turned red, his eyes growing stony as he looked down and saw that he was out. Whether you got hit by a holographic or a real weapon, the result was the same: game over.

"Sorry!" I shouted as he angrily grasped at his cut, then turned and stalked away toward the base square, where all "dead" soldiers had to return. I hurried to my feet, knowing there would be more holograms coming for us, especially as the trainee numbers seemed to be dwindling. To my surprise, all around us trainees were landing, their faces angry, their vests glowing a vibrant red.

I stood there, frozen, trying to take stock of what was going on. A moment later, Navan shoved me roughly to the ground as he took out a team of three spiraling enemies, who were shooting down from the skies. I hadn't even heard them coming or seen them in my periphery. All I could think about was the cold-blood I'd accidentally taken out and the rookie mistakes I was making.

Focus, Riley. Get your head back in the game, I told myself furiously as I jumped back up, sending out the rest of my throwing knives in quick succession. The little pep talk seemed to have worked, as my weapons splayed out across the battlefield, taking out enemies, the holograms flickering and sparking before disappearing from the simulation.

Realizing I had no more knives on my bandolier, I pushed the buttons on my gloves once more, feeling the powerful vibration of the magnetic force as it struggled to reach out to the blades I had thrown. To my horror, I realized nothing was happening. A few of the knives wriggled a little, but none of them seemed to want to return.

"They're not coming back!" I shouted, panicking.

"You've thrown them too far," Navan said as he hauled a huge block of stone in front of us, ducking down beside me. "You're going to have to fight hand-to-hand," he added, with a grimace that didn't exactly fill me with confidence. How was I supposed to take on coldbloods in hand-to-hand combat?

A holographic arm suddenly slipped around my throat. I made a small sound of shock that caused Navan to turn sharply, wielding his sword, but there was no way he could slash the attacker away without risking hurting me. Thinking fast, I remembered what I knew of Aksavdo, the Vysanthean martial art. I placed one hand over the enemy's arm and pulled, putting some space between us, before dropping to the ground, causing my assailant to roll to the floor. Navan plunged his sword straight through the figure, forcing it to disappear with a dull fizz.

As I caught my breath and looked around, I realized that Navan and I were now the only two left on the battlefield, with a limited number of enemies still coming at us in waves. For the most part, Navan was doing the grunt work, slashing this way and that with his katana, but I raised my fists and struck at anyone who came too close. I knew I was holding him back, but there was nothing else I could do. We were still too far away from where my knives had fallen, and per the rules, Navan wasn't allowed to fetch them for me, which left nothing but my limited knowledge of Aksavdo to get me through.

I was just glad I couldn't see the rest of the trainees watching us. I didn't need the distraction of their hostile faces, waiting for me to fail.

A circle of enemy soldiers came at us, hemming us in. Navan zigzagged between them, focusing on protecting me from their weapons, but one broke through his defenses and hurtled toward me. I dropped to the ground, managing to duck under the soldier hologram's sword stroke and trip it over its own feet. It reached out for my arm as it fell, but I managed to dodge it. Before I could go another round with the hologram, Navan swooped in behind me, gripping my arm and pulling me away. I opened my mouth to tell him it was okay, that I had this hologram under control, then watched in horror as a soldier emerged from behind him and plunged a knife into his back. A look of shock rippled across Navan's face as his vest lit up red.

In a flicker, the enemy and the knife vanished, the scenery shifting back to black screens, the rubble and texture disappearing beneath my boots. The sky faded away to a plain white ceiling. At the far side of the training room, my teammates were watching through the glass of the observation chamber. They couldn't have looked more unimpressed if they tried.

Navan had fallen, while the puny Kryptonian was the last one left standing—though they'd all seen she didn't deserve to be.

I sighed. The simulation was over.

"Why did you do that?" I asked Navan as I hurried across the black landscape, picking up all the knives I had dropped and using the gloves to quicken the job.

He raised a brow. "Do what?"

"Why did you sacrifice yourself for me?" I replied, feeling disgruntled that he had forfeited his own success to save me from a situation that I had under control. I slotted the last of the throwing knives back into my bandolier, and we headed over to the far side of the room, where an exit sign glowed above the doorway.

"You needed help," he said.

"I didn't need help. I shoved the soldier out of the way. You thought I was falling, but I wasn't—I was fine," I insisted, trying to rein in my emotions. I was sore from days of training, and irritable from lack of sleep. I wouldn't be nearly as bothered by this if I didn't feel like a broken husk of myself.

"What did you plan to do with him on the ground?" Navan asked.

"I'm not sure, but I'd have thought of something."

"And by the time you'd thought of something, you'd have been dead," Navan said pointedly. "Look, Riley, you already have the makings of an incredible soldier, but you're starting at a disadvantage compared to the rest of us. Most of us have been practicing Aksavdo and training with weapons since we were kids. I know I need to leave you to your own devices a bit more, but I can't help stepping in when I see you in trouble."

"And I think you need to stop doing that," I said, the disapproving faces of the other trainees flashing through my mind. "The others already think I'm weak and stupid, and you saving me all the time is making it worse. I appreciate you looking out for me, but you need to let me mess up. Let me figure out where I'm going wrong, so I don't make the same mistake twice."

Navan sighed. "I just don't want you getting hurt."

"It's a simulation, dude. How much harm can it do? Plus, I'm already in pieces after the assault course and training grounds. There's nothing these simulations can do to me that I haven't already suffered through. And what are you going to do if we find ourselves on an *actual* battlefield, where there are real risks and real lives at stake? You can't be running around playing the hero and watching my back all the time. *That* is likely to get people killed."

"The goal is to make sure you never see a real battle, remember?" Navan said.

Before I could respond, the throng of trainees descended from the stairwell that led up to the observation chamber, the hum of their chatter echoing through the hallway beyond as they streamed out toward the armory. Navan pushed open the door to the training room, leading me into the corridor, and we followed.

A few of our teammates looked back at us with cold stares—well, at me. Navan wasn't doing himself any favors by fraternizing with the puny Kryptonian, but they didn't seem to have the balls to snub him directly. It was just me they had no problem ostracizing.

When we reached the armory, I wandered over to my locker and waved my bracelet over the lock. We had each been given a bracelet when we'd started our training; it contained our food tokens and let us into otherwise restricted areas. The bracelets also ensured we were assigned to the correct weapons, and they recorded our daily training performance, which could be viewed if we flashed our bracelets in front of the performance log. The bracelets themselves were made of a strange metal that almost looked like hematite, with a small ruby in the center. It was this small jewel that seemed to hold all of our personal data.

The locker sprung open, revealing the drawers where my knives and other items belonged. Slipping awkwardly out of my military attire, I pulled on the white t-shirt and navy-blue trousers I had left in my locker and instantly felt more comfortable.

"I'm serious about what I said before. You can't fight in a real battle," Navan said, once the rest of the cold-blood trainees had left, their laughter ringing down the hallways.

I sat down on a nearby bench and leaned my head back against the wall. I was hot and sweaty, and my stomach was grumbling. "Yeah, I know that. I don't exactly want to fight in a real battle either. But what if things don't go according to plan? I want to be prepared, in case I don't have a choice. If Queen Gianne's soldiers ambush us, or Queen Brisha orders it, I might have—"

He shook his head. "Nope. Not while I have breath in my lungs. A real battle is nothing like these simulations. You would be dead in an instant, Riley. Your knives are exceptional, but they won't protect you in a true battle." He sat down next to me. "Plus, the training will never prepare you for the psychological damage that taking the life of another person causes. *Nothing* can prepare you for that."

I glanced at him, surprised by the emotion in his voice. His expression was hard to read—he was good at hiding his suffering from me—but I sensed a well of pain flowing behind his gray eyes. He had described some of that pain to me before, but in that moment, I felt I had only scratched the surface. To be honest, it seemed he could distance his mind without a problem once his temper took hold. He had killed Jethro easily enough, and he'd spoken openly about how it had felt to murder his best friend... but the flicker of regret in his voice told me that killing had been hard for him once. Was there someone else he had killed, earlier in his life, whose death had caused him untold damage?

"What?" he said, making me realize I'd been staring at him for way longer than I'd meant to. Not that I minded staring at him. He was nice to stare at.

"I just... I'm wondering what it might be like to actually take a life. You know... could I do it if I had to? It's not something I ever thought I'd have to think about," I said, and even as I spoke, I was hit by a sudden wave of doubt. *Could* I do it, if such a moment came? I was the kind of girl who had trouble swatting flies and wasps; how would I cope if faced with killing a being so similar to myself?

"It's not something I ever want you to think about," Navan replied, taking my face in his hands and planting a firm kiss on my lips. In the safety of the empty armory, I let myself sink into the moment, only for him to pull away a second later. In Vysanthe, there was no such thing as a safe place.

We'd managed to keep the true extent of our relationship a secret from our fellow trainees—Brisha knew about it, but there was no point in everyone and their mother knowing if we could help it—but they were starting to suspect, more and more each day, that there was something amiss between Navan and me. Having someone walk in on us while we were kissing would only fuel their animosity.

"It's still something I have to consider, Navan," I said. "What if the day comes when I have no choice but to defend myself... to kill... and there's nothing you can do to prevent it?" It was something I'd been thinking about more and more recently. Proving myself here in Queen Brisha's army was a double-edged sword. If I *could* prove myself, then the queen would deem me useful and very possibly send me out in the field. If I didn't prove myself, then I had failed, and shown just how weak and vulnerable my species was. It wasn't exactly a simple situation.

Navan scowled. "We'll cross that bridge *if* we come

to it. Right now, all you have to focus on is getting through training, okay?"

"And you'll take it easier on the hero front?" I asked, nudging him in the shoulder.

He sighed. "If you want me to back off, I'll back off, but if you want me to help, I'm here," he said, brushing strands of my hair behind my ears.

"Okay, deal," I said.

I was still desperate for a shower, but the loud growl of my stomach took precedence. I hadn't eaten for hours, and we'd already agreed to meet Angie, Lauren, and Bashrik for a late lunch.

"I suppose we should get going," I murmured, stretching out my tired arms. "Wish I had time for a shower first, though. I feel gross."

At the mention of the word "shower," Navan dropped his gaze, running an awkward hand through his short dark hair. My cheeks flushed too, as I remembered just how close we'd come to taking things to the next level, over a week ago. Before we'd even reached the bathroom, where the enticing promise of a hot shower had beckoned, we'd fallen onto the sofa, tangled up in one another, making out like our lives depended on it. It had gotten pretty heated by the time I finally suggested that we continue things under the tumbling water. He'd scooped me up like I weighed nothing and carried me across the room—only for the devastating sound of a knock at the door to interrupt us.

A moment later, Bashrik had burst into the room, coming to find out where Navan had run off to, since there were things that still needed to be discussed, brother to brother. Seeing me in Navan's arms, he'd immediately announced his disapproval, though I suspected that was more out of embarrassment than true condemnation. Bickering between the brothers had followed, with Bashrik insisting that we were taking too much of a risk by allowing ourselves to be an item here, and the moment had been ruined. Since then, we hadn't really had the chance to pick things back up where they'd left off, with the brutal training regime, the early starts, and the unexpected calls to additional sessions.

"Well, you don't *look* gross," Navan said, breaking the silence. Smirking, he dipped his head and caught my lips in his once more, though his eyes flicked cautiously to the door. After the arguments Bashrik had made, and the cold stares of the other trainees, I was beginning to worry Northern Vysanthe wasn't quite as liberal as I'd hoped when it came to interspecies relationships.

Once we drew apart, I took my fur coat from the locker and we left the training room, the oddly sweet taste of his kiss still lingering on my lips. Coldbloods definitely didn't sweat the same way humans did.

The hallways were silent as we headed through the now-familiar network of corridors that formed the training center. It was a large, silver-domed building, the majority of it built into the rock of the mountain range that nestled behind Nessun, the capital city of Northern Vysanthe. As we hurried out of the main exit, the biting wind nipped at my cheeks, prompting me to pull the coat tighter around my face. Even though the sun was high in the sky, it did nothing to warm the world below.

I shuddered, breaking into a jog. My eyes were fixed on the palace up ahead, on its three gleaming minarets standing proud, on the crystals and rubies that adorned it flashing in the sunlight. Even after more than a week in Nessun, I still hadn't gotten used to the striking building, with the twisting statues of male and female coldbloods seeming to dance off the very sides of the palace walls. It might not have been as exquisite as Gianne's, but it was darn close in my opinion. The gardens were my favorite part of the palace, with their frozen water features, beautiful blooms, and delicate trees, and though I could just about see them from the apartment I shared with Navan, I sadly hadn't had the chance to visit them properly since training had begun.

We reached the relative warmth of the palace and headed toward one of the smaller dayrooms, where we'd arranged to have lunch and discuss what we were going to do about Orion and his cruel provisos. I had let training distract my mind from falling to pieces at the potential consequences of failure. If we couldn't deliver the intel the rebel leader wanted, he would kill my parents and other innocent humans. A chill coursed through me, fueling my fear and rage. As much as I hated the idea of sending Orion information that could make him stronger, I *couldn't* let the alternative happen.

We had yet to come up with a solution to delivering the intel, once we obtained it. The disc Navan had procured from Gianne's Observatory, along with the black box that could transmit the information, had been abandoned in Southern Vysanthe with no hope of retrieval. Now, we needed a new way to get intel to Orion without arousing the suspicions of anyone in Queen Brisha's kingdom. It wasn't going to be easy, since Navan didn't know the landscape of Northern Vysanthe like he knew the South, but I was hopeful we'd be able to get far enough away to at least send something. My parents' lives depended on it. Countless human lives depended on it.

"How do we get information to him if we're only allowed between the palace and the training center?" I asked in a low tone, a wave of concern rippling through me. A week had already passed, which gave us just under three weeks to get Orion what he'd asked for.

"I've been thinking about it," Navan said, "and I still think the queen's control room is our best bet, when the time comes. I can't see any other options."

I bit my lip, wanting to agree but unable to shake the feeling that it was simply too risky. We'd had this same conversation a few times over the last week. "If anyone caught us, that'd be it, Navan. Game over."

"They won't catch us. Not if we're careful," Navan said.

I sighed, still unconvinced. "I guess we still have a bit of time to think about it. We need to gather information first anyway, before we even attempt to send it. Bashrik, Angie, and Lauren should have something for us today. Even if it's something small, it'll be a start." Bashrik had asked Navan to give them all a week to try to piece something useful together.

A figure emerged from one of the side corridors that led off from the main hallway. With her purple-tinted hair woven through with golden ornaments, and her imposing stature, I recognized her in an instant.

"Hello, Pandora." I smiled politely as Navan and I made to press on past Queen Brisha's advisor.

She stepped in front of us, blocking the way, though it wasn't an aggressive motion. "Riley, I hate to interrupt your afternoon, but the queen wishes to see you right away. I was just coming over to find you at the training center, but it seems you've saved me the trip," she said brightly, gesturing for me to follow her.

"Has she requested my presence, also?" Navan asked, his hand instinctively closing around my wrist.

Pandora shook her head. "Not today, Navan. I am certain she will call for you when she requires you." She smiled softly, but there was a firmness to her voice that brooked no argument.

"I'll catch up with you later," I promised Navan, loosening his hold on my wrist and squeezing his hand. He looked at me with a worried expression, but I turned my back on him, trying to act confident as I hurried after Pandora, who was already most of the way down the hallway, her impressive strides far larger than mine.

As I walked, however, I struggled to push down the ominous feeling that always came before a meeting with one of these regal sisters. I had no idea why Brisha wanted to see me so urgently. All I knew was that these exchanges rarely ended well for me. I still had a small scar where my blood had been taken the last time we'd met.

3

I caught up with Pandora, determined not to fall behind, though by the time we reached Queen Brisha's library I was out of breath, my lungs burning.

As we moved toward the huge carved doors to the library, Lauren emerged.

"I thought we were meeting for lunch," she said, pushing her glasses back up onto the bridge of her nose and looking at me with surprise. "Wait, did I get the time wrong?" A flutter of panic settled across her features, making me smile. I knew how Lauren got when she was deep in study mode, losing hours, and sometimes days, to piles of books and essays.

"Queen Brisha has asked to see me. I think everyone else is still going to lunch, though," I replied.

"Oh, thank God. I'll be honest, I wasn't even sure what day it was." She laughed, then flashed an anxious look back into the room behind her and clutched my shoulder. "Be careful, Riley. I'll see you later?"

I nodded. "Once I'm finished here, I'll come find you all."

Pandora beckoned at me to hurry, and I stepped through the door to the library, leaving Lauren to head in the direction of the others without me. I could feel her eyes on the back of my head, her worry palpable, until the very last moment before the door shut.

On the walk over, I'd been wondering what the queen might want to talk to me about. My first guess was that it would involve my blood sample and the immortality elixir, since that was all any of these Vysanthean leaders seemed interested in where I was concerned. They were obsessed. I just wished the queens could see how idiotic it made them look, squabbling for the prize of being first. Saying that, I had no idea how the research was coming along in terms of synthesizing the blood, especially since the alchemy lab had been razed to the ground.

I found Queen Brisha sitting by the roaring fire, her feet tucked up beneath her, a book open on the side of her armchair. It was an oddly normal sight, the kind of thing I might do with a Sunday afternoon to spare. I'd forgotten that, underneath everything, Queen Brisha was still a young woman, no doubt with passions and hobbies outside ruling queendoms.

She looked up as I took the seat opposite her. "Ah, you came! How wonderful," she said.

I tried not to frown. Hadn't she invited me? I looked to Pandora for confirmation, but the advisor merely shrugged, an amused expression on her face. "I did, Queen Brisha," I replied uncertainly. "Did you... want to speak to me about our blood, or something?"

The queen shook her head, chuckling. "No, no, nothing so grim. For now, the blood you and your friends have given is ample. If I need more, I'll ask. Honestly, you'd think this place was all doom and gloom, the way you talk," she said with a coy smile. "I brought you here for far more pleasant reasons, if you can believe such a thing." Her silver eyes glittered with playful irreverence. It was a side of her I hadn't seen much of, and I didn't know whether I liked it or not.

"Pleasant reasons, Your Highness?"

"Indeed," she said warmly, folding up her book and sitting up in her chair. "The reason I've asked you here is to award you with a prize! I must say, it's extremely unexpected that you should be its recipient, but I'm always happy for pleasant surprises."

"A prize, Your Highness?" I asked, utterly baffled.

"You were the last soldier standing in the combat simulation, and such a feat of skill must be rewarded.

By all accounts, you lasted far longer than any previous recruit has done in their first simulation. Very impressive, little Kryptonian. Perhaps I misjudged the strength of will your race possesses!"

My cheeks heated at the praise. "I, uh... I only lasted that long because Navan helped me out," I muttered, wanting to rectify the situation. "Honestly, Navan deserves the prize, not me."

Evidently mistaking my blushes and words for modesty, the queen chuckled. "Oh, nonsense! You continue to show a bravery that nobody anticipated, Riley, and from the report, you were doing just fine by yourself. Besides, my interest in you lies in more than your performance in the simulation."

"Oh?" I wasn't sure where this conversation was headed.

"Nobody made you sign up for the military. You did that yourself, even though your physical makeup is inferior to that of a Vysanthean. Nobody forced you to train alongside those who have been preparing for years, and yet you push through every trial and obstacle," the queen gushed. "Nobody urged you to excel, but you are proving your capability with each day that passes. I must say that not even Pandora has seen knives thrown with such precision! That sort of bravery and tenacity must be rewarded."

"There's no need to—" I began.

"Indeed, I see much of myself in you, Riley," Queen Brisha continued, as if I hadn't interrupted. "You might not agree, but we are similar souls, you and I. And I have decided to make it my objective to help you become more than merely Kryptonian. I would see you stronger, faster, smarter, sharper..."

I frowned, letting her words sink in. Even with a body that felt like it was giving up, and training sessions in which I mostly ended up splayed on the ground, wishing someone would put me out of my misery, I had somehow managed to impress Queen Brisha.

"I don't understand, Your Highness," I admitted, not knowing what kind of prize Vysantheans even gave out. If it was blood or slaves, she could keep it.

With a smile, Queen Brisha leaned over the left side of her armchair and picked up a small wooden box inlaid with gold and jewels. An opaleine clasp shaped like a pair of coldblood wings held the lid closed. She opened the box with a flourish of her fingers and took out three medium-sized silver vials that were sealed with an emerald stopper.

"Here is your prize, Riley," she said, handing over the vials, and I took them warily.

"Um, thank you. What is it, Your Highness?" I asked, shaking the first vial and hearing the swish of liquid inside.

"It is a serum that will enable you to grow wings," she announced. "I thought three would suffice for now."

I gaped at her, my jaw slackening.

"Only on a temporary basis, of course," she added, smiling at my expression. "The effects tend to wear off after a few hours, though it varies from species to species, especially as it's still fairly experimental. With this, you will no longer have to remain on the ground while your fellow recruits take to the skies. This will level the playing field and allow us to see if you truly have what it takes to be exceptional."

I stared at the queen. "It... It grows wings," I repeated. "How does that even work?"

Her dismissive laugh hardly eased my nerves. "You wouldn't understand the science behind it. *I* hardly do. That's what my alchemists are for. But rest assured, it works."

"Though, you said it's... fairly experimental, Your Highness?" I repeated, those words echoing in my head, sounding alarm bells.

She nodded. "It was invented as a means to repair and regrow broken wings that had been ripped or fully torn off during battle. So far, we have had an excellent success rate, though it's still in the testing phase," she explained animatedly. "We have tried it on several test subjects of differing species also, just to make note of certain outcomes, and we are happy with the progress. We don't know all the side effects, but nobody has died yet, which is always an excellent sign!"

I wasn't sure whether that made me feel better or worse, and yet, now that I'd gotten over the initial shock of the idea, I couldn't help feeling intrigued by the thought of having my own set of wings.

My own set of freaking wings.

As a kid, I'd *dreamed* of being able to fly, and I remembered how it had felt to rush through the air in Navan's arms, marveling at his ability to go where he wanted, when he wanted. Now, Queen Brisha was offering me that same opportunity. Who the hell was I to say no?

"Thank you, Your Highness. This is beyond kind," I said, a broad smile spreading across my face.

"And that's not all," Queen Brisha noted, her tone still girlish and excitable. "I've got a few other surprises in store for you as a reward for your excellent work."

"Really, Your Highness, you don't need—" I began, but she cut me off again.

"I've had some special delicacies shipped in for you and your Kryptonian friends to enjoy. These have all been delivered to your apartments," she said, clapping her hands.

"That's incredibly generous of you, Your Highness." My stomach rumbled at the thought of a new cuisine. I had a feeling it was probably pillaged from some poor planet at an unknown edge of the galaxy, but it would admittedly be great to eat something other than plain fruit and vegetables or powdered astronaut food. Pickings were slim here on Vysanthe, and I didn't have the luxury of being fussy.

"Oh, and one more thing," Brisha said, picking up another box from behind her armchair. With a shy smile, she handed it to me. "I... I have this for you to give to Bashrik, since I know you all enjoy meals together sometimes. I would have given it to him myself but... never mind." Her eyes grew strangely wistful. "Hopefully, this will encourage him to continue all of his hard work on the new alchemy lab. I must say, I am enjoying the designs I've seen, and the swiftness with which he has managed to corral the best builders and masons in the region. I mean, I knew he was good, but I didn't know he was *that* good."

The queen's voice had taken on a curious tone whenever she spoke of Bashrik lately, which both amused and disturbed me. It sounded almost like affection, but there was no way a woman of Brisha's standing would be interested in an underling like Bashrik. He came from a high-class family, sure, but he was still far inferior to *her*. But Queen Brisha seemed to value superior skill, so it was probably just admiration for his talent. I'd seen the alchemy lab designs myself, and she was right: they were *very* impressive.

"Thank you again, Your Highness. I'm sure Bashrik will be pleased with whatever is in here, and I know the girls and I are definitely in need of a good meal," I said, patting my stomach.

"Don't mention it," the queen said, brushing me away. "It is the least I can do after the opportunities you have offered me. You have renewed my sense of spirit and defiance! Indeed, in the days since my sister's foolish assault upon my queendom, I have been carefully planning my counterattack, as payback for her ruination of my alchemy lab. She killed many of my soldiers and citizens, and I won't stand for it. I shall prevail, if it is the last thing I do. Already, the tools of her destruction are being built." A cold smile crept upon Brisha's dark lips, her eyes glittering.

I shuddered, feeling uneasy at all this talk of vengeance. If Queen Brisha launched an attack on her sister, that meant Navan could be sent off to battle at any moment. Whether or not she would send me too remained to be seen, but I wasn't looking forward to such a terrible event either way. In a game of war, there were no winners.

More than that, Queen Brisha's hospitality made me feel unsettled. We were being treated far better than I had ever expected, with all these special gifts being thrown in for good measure. The apartments we were staying in were luxurious, with our every whim catered to at the push of a button. We wanted for nothing, the kitchens always stocked with vials and blood stews for Navan and his brother, and bowls of fruit and vegetables for me and my human friends. We were permitted somewhat free rein of her dominion, as long as we didn't step outside the walls of Nessun. And here Brisha was, opening up to me, telling me of her battleplans.

My stomach turned at the realization that all of this would come crashing down around us, if—or when—she discovered our betrayal. There would be no coming back from that.

4

*G*ripping the serum and the box for Bashrik in my hands, I left Queen Brisha to her books and her vengeance and walked quickly through the palace until I reached the dayroom we were supposed to be meeting in for lunch. I'd been in the library for what felt like hours, though the clocks on the wall told me it had barely been thirty minutes.

When I entered, my friends looked up at me from a circular table that was laden with empty plates. Behind them, floor-to-ceiling windows opened out onto a wide balcony overlooking the tumbling waterfalls that cascaded from the mountainside beyond, the water frothing a pinkish white at the bottom. The color had something to do with a red sediment found in the rocks, but its resemblance to blood troubled me.

"About time!" Angie said, though it was clear that both Navan and Lauren had filled the others in on my whereabouts. I could see in the relieved expressions on their faces that they were happy to see me in one piece.

"How did it go?" Navan asked, standing to pull back one of the chairs so I could sit down.

I shrugged. "A lot better than expected, to be honest," I replied, as Navan sat back down in the chair beside me.

Lauren frowned. "How so?"

"I thought she might want to talk about the blood sample or the elixir, but she didn't. She just wanted to give me a gift," I explained, knowing how strange it sounded. Seeing the empty plates in front of everyone, I glanced at the food that remained in the bowls, but I'd lost my appetite.

"The queen wanted to give *you* a gift?" Bashrik remarked, almost disdainfully.

I placed the vials of wing serum on the table. "She gave me these."

Navan picked up one of the vials and turned it over in his hands. Just as I'd done, he shook the small bottle, listening to the sound of liquid within.

"It's a serum that can give me wings for a few hours at a time," I continued, feeling increasingly excited at the thought of taking to the air by myself. "She wants to even the playing field for me in battle scenarios. It's still a little bit experimental, but apparently it's safe enough."

Navan's expression darkened. "There's no way this stuff can be safe for humans to use," he announced, lifting the vial up to the light. "You're not seriously thinking about taking it, are you?"

I shrugged. "I'm still deciding," I hedged.

"You're going to have to use it at least once," Bashrik interjected, flashing his brother a knowing look.

"She doesn't have to do anything she doesn't want to," Angie cut in, giving Bashrik a pointed glare. I almost laughed, wondering how they'd been getting along recently, working together in such close quarters on the new alchemy lab. It seemed they were still fully capable of getting on each other's nerves.

"Angie has a point," Navan said.

Bashrik rolled his eyes. "Am I the only one with any common sense around this table?" He sighed, exasperated. "You're going to have to use it, Riley, because if you don't, Queen Brisha will see your refusal of it as a personal slight. She has given you a gift that, even by Vysanthean standards, is pretty exceptional. If you don't use it she'll be beyond offended, and, seriously, we can do without that kind of trouble—"

"It's too dangerous," Navan said, only to get another savage eyeroll from his brother.

"This whole planet is too dangerous for them,

Navan," Bashrik replied. "Somehow, against all odds, the queen has taken a liking to your beloved Riley, and I suggest we use that to our advantage. If the queen says the stuff isn't going to kill her, then what's the harm? There are a million things on this planet that *could* kill her, but I don't see you worrying about those."

"I do worry about those, actually," Navan muttered.

"By the way, the queen had something for you, Bashrik," I said, wanting to break up their argument before it got too heated. I handed the box over to the astonished Bashrik. "She hoped it might help you continue with all your hard work on the alchemy lab," I explained, though I had no idea what the box contained.

Bashrik took the box tentatively before lifting the lid and peering inside. Immediately, his face paled, his cheeks flushing a deep shade of pink. Through the ashen skin of his throat, I saw his Adam's apple bob as he gulped.

"An arakar heart!" Navan burst out laughing, clutching his stomach. Bashrik looked on, utterly mortified. Every time Navan looked up, he started laughing again, descending into hysterics as Bashrik scowled in his direction. Whatever the queen had given him, it clearly wasn't something he'd been expecting. "She gave you an arakar heart!" Navan managed between laughs, smacking a hand down on the table. "Looks like Riley isn't the *only* one who has won the queen's affections!"

"It's not funny!" Bashrik snapped, punching his brother in the shoulder.

"An *arakar heart*?" I asked. Glancing at Angie and Lauren, I could see that they were just as bemused as I was.

Navan nodded, wiping his eyes. "It's a Vysanthean gift of courtship," he explained, still chuckling through his words. "I've seen you humans give roses or chocolates, but we give arakar hearts if we *really* like someone," he added, grinning at his brother.

"Where's Riley's arakar heart, then?" Bashrik countered, evidently intending to claw some of his dignity back. My outburst of laughter made his face fall again. I didn't care about arakar hearts, or roses, or chocolates. I knew Navan's feelings for me, and that was all I needed.

"Queenie loves you!" Angie chimed in, her eyes glittering with mischief. "That's why she keeps sending all those vials when we're working! It all makes sense now. She thinks you're *gorgeous*. She wants to *kiss* you," she cackled, clearly thrilled with her new ammunition.

"And you'll be out of a job if you don't shut it!" Bashrik warned sourly.

Angie laughed. "I'd like to see you *try* to fire me. You wouldn't have gotten those foundations built if it weren't for me, and you know it. I am captain of measurement, and without me pointing out that the builders were off by almost an entire foot, you'd have a wonky base and your beautiful building would topple over before you even got it finished."

Bashrik scowled. "Yeah, well, you're skating on thin ice right now. I can find someone else to be my captain of measurement if you're going to step out of line," he said, though the fight had gone from his voice. Instead, his features softened as he lifted the lid again to stare at the item inside. "I can't believe she sent me this," he said hoarsely. "What am I supposed to do if she expects something in return?"

"Avoid her like the plague," Angie suggested. "I used to have a million ways to avoid boys I didn't want to speak to. I'll teach you a few tricks, and I can always run interference if you need me to." Her grin broadened.

I smiled too, that world of high-school boys seeming impossibly far away. This wasn't where our lives were supposed to end up. In all the chaos, I'd lost track of time, but I knew it couldn't be long before Angie was supposed to be in Paris taking on her big internship at a trendy sports fashion brand, and Lauren was meant to head off to start pre-law. We'd had such big dreams, but had fallen into this whirlwind of madness instead, with no end in sight.

I could only begin to imagine what everyone back home would think when we didn't return home as promised. Police would get involved, missing persons cases would be filed, and our loved ones would endure untold heartache.

"As wonderful as your blossoming romance is, dear Brother, we have other things to attend to now that Riley is here," Navan said, clearing his throat and finally managing to wipe the smirk off his face. "We thought we'd wait until you got back before we started discussing Orion," he explained, turning to me.

I nodded, drawing in a breath. "Has anyone managed to gather any intel on the elixir?"

An awkward tension spread through the group.

"With all the plans for the alchemy lab being drawn up, and eyes on us all the time, we haven't really had a chance to sneak out and do any Sherlocking," Angie said apologetically, flashing a glance at Bashrik.

"It'll be easier once the first floor starts to go in, but I think everyone was worried we'd run off while the foundations were being built," he said. "Since we're still here, and the foundations have been laid, the security around us should ease up."

"I've been buried in books for a week, to no avail," Lauren added. "I've been absorbing as much as I can about Vysanthean lore and alchemical compounds to see if there's anything that can help us, but I haven't come across anything to do with the elixir that we don't already know. Not yet, anyway."

"And with us in training all week, that leaves us with nothing." Navan sighed.

"Well, actually, not nothing," Bashrik returned, a thoughtful expression on his face. "There's this alchemist who keeps bugging Angie and me about the status of the new alchemy lab and the proposed completion date. He's pretty antsy to get back to his work—"

"And he makes Oscar the Grouch look like a pussy-cat," Angie cut in, pulling a twisted, angry face that I presumed was meant to look like this mystery guy.

Bashrik frowned. "While I have no idea who 'Oscar' is, this particular alchemist is the very definition of a grouch. Yorrek is definitely not the kind of guy you want to have pestering you all the time. However, he could be pretty useful if we could capture him and interrogate him."

Angie nodded. "He lives in a village nearby, though he comes into the city to bother us pretty much every day. If we can intercept him on his way into the city, we could try to squeeze some info out of him."

"It'll be risky, but since he doesn't live in the city, and nobody likes him, nobody will miss him," Bashrik continued, glancing at Angie for confirmation. "He doesn't really have any friends as far as I can tell, and keeps to himself—when he's not bothering us, that is. And, with the alchemists mostly out of action until the new lab is built, he could disappear for days and no one would know or care."

Angie grinned. "I think we'd be doing them a favor."

"And what about putting him back once we're done with him?" I asked, seeing several holes in this risky scheme. "Surely he'd tell everyone what happened to him, but then, we can't lock him away forever, or... kill him. Somebody would notice, eventually."

"We can always use a vial of Elysium to wipe his memory once we're done," Navan replied. "I'm sure there's some lying around the palace interrogation rooms or medical wing that we could get our hands on. This Yorrek guy probably has the ingredients in his house, if he's the kind of alchemist I think he might be —the kind who takes his work home with him, if he doesn't like to be around other people. My concern is that he won't give up any useful information in the first place. He has no reason to."

I hadn't thought about that. If Yorrek was as obsessed with his job as Bashrik made him seem, there was no way he'd give up his secrets. He would never put his position as a royal alchemist at risk, even under duress.

"We can always create a serum from the poroporo

fruit," Lauren said suddenly, as though a bulb had just flashed in her mind. "It's a fruit I've been reading about in the library. It's indigenous to Northern Vysanthe. It has hypnotic qualities when ingested or injected and puts a person in a state of extreme susceptibility. It would give us a chance to ask questions and receive honest answers... if we can administer the right amount."

"Never heard of it," Navan and Bashrik chorused.

"Of course you haven't! You're southerners," Angie remarked. "Go on, Lauren. Ignore these dumbos."

Lauren smiled. "Apparently, they had a few problems with it a couple of decades ago. People were using it recreationally, and they used so much of it that they nearly harvested it into extinction, so it doesn't really grow in many places anymore. One book said it still grows in some areas of Northern Vysanthe, though I can't remember whereabouts off the top of my head... I'll double check and get back to you as soon as I can."

"Riley and I can track it down if you pass us the information," Navan said. "We have a day off a week, where the rest of you don't. If we tell the queen we want to leave the city on a romantic outing, I'm sure she'd let us. Especially since she seems to be in a romantic mood herself." Navan's smirk returned as he gave Bashrik a pat on the back.

His brother scowled; he had evidently hoped the

arakar heart incident had been forgotten. "No matter how we get around her security, we'll need to work quickly," he said tersely. "We're running out of time."

I swallowed, my heart sinking like a stone at the reminder. There were only three weeks remaining until Orion carried out his threat to kill my parents. Now, more than ever before, the pressure was on.

This was a deadline we couldn't afford to miss.

5

I hit the deck, my lungs burning as the impact forced the air out of me. Already, every single muscle in my body hurt and ached beyond anything I'd ever felt before, but it didn't matter. I *had* to get up. I *had* to keep fighting.

Grimacing, I dug my fingers into the floor and pulled myself back up, raising my fists to my face as I prepared for another onslaught. I had been paired with a coldblood female named Iskra who seemed hellbent on knocking me to the ground every five seconds. Even so, I was determined not to stay down. There was no way I'd give any coldblood the satisfaction of seeing me surrender.

My legs were shaking as I faced Iskra once more. Her face was a mask of fury as I squared up to her.

With each defiance of her blows, I knew I was annoying her more, getting under her skin. It was exactly as I'd planned. She would slip up once frustration set in.

With her teeth bared, she lunged for me, offering me the opportunity I'd been waiting for. It was a clumsy assault, her muscles not quite braced for my sudden burst in speed. Sidestepping swiftly, I stuck out my foot, and she stumbled over it. With her knocked off balance, I brought my elbow down hard against the softest part of her shoulder, adding the last bit of weight I needed to send her sprawling forward on the ground. She fell with a grunt, her eyes flashing back at me as I knelt against the small of her back, pinning her there for a moment as she flailed, trying to swipe at me. I knew it wouldn't last, considering her superior strength, but I was happy to have floored her, even once.

I sprang back as she twisted around, her eyes burning with hatred. All around me, the other recruits were watching, amused expressions on their faces, as Iskra leapt back to her feet. It would've been embarrassing for any of them to have been knocked down by an inferior species, and I could see they were glad someone else had taken the fall.

"You'll pay for that, leech!" she snarled, the muscle rippling beneath her ashen skin. This time, I knew she'd be better prepared when she came for me. In truth, I wasn't sure how many more knocks I could take before I was forced to stay on the ground. I was already feeling pretty broken, and we were only halfway through the day's training, with sixty circuits of the brutal assault course to look forward to after lunch.

"Your embarrassment will last longer than my bruises," I taunted, lifting my fists again. I was getting better at preempting the movements of my opponent, though it took each beating to learn the motion she was going to use next, and my mind was starting to get foggy with all the blows I'd taken to the head.

Before Iskra could spring at me again, a voice cut through the dull acoustics of the training room. "Take five minutes!" Pandora shouted, bringing the training to a sudden halt. I hadn't seen her watching the proceedings, nor had I seen the figure who was descending the stairs to the observation room, walking a few steps behind Pandora.

The coldblood recruits bowed low as Queen Brisha swept through the group, then dispersed to fetch water, gathering in smaller clusters so they could discuss the events of the morning. A few looked over in my direction, but I ignored them. The queen came to a stop beside my training square. I followed Iskra's lead, dipping low from the waist as the queen waved her hand, dismissing my opponent.

"Very impressive, Riley," she remarked with a smile.

"I didn't realize you were watching, Your Highness," I replied politely, trying not to grimace against the throbbing pain in my elbow, where I was pretty sure I'd cracked something.

She nodded. "I occasionally enjoy observing my new recruits unawares. I feel as though trainees try too hard if they know they are being watched."

"I might have tried a little harder if I had known, Your Highness," I joked, wiping my brow with a towel I'd left to one side.

"Nonsense, you seem to be doing marvelously!" she said. "Although, I haven't seen you use your wings, even though other trainees are attempting aerial combat. Have you tried out your gift yet?" A curious flicker of emotion glittered in her silver eyes as she awaited my answer. I felt as though I was letting down an aunt whose present I had pretended to like.

"I have taken a few sips, Your Highness, but nothing seemed to happen. Maybe it just doesn't work on me," I replied, hoping she couldn't see through my lies. In all honesty, the vials of wing serum had worried me so much in the end that I had simply chosen to ignore them. Navan's nerves had gotten to me. I didn't know how it might affect me, given that it was still in a very experimental phase of production, and, after my last struggle with Vysanthean potions, I didn't feel like risking my health on it unless I could be more hopeful about the outcome.

"A few sips?" The queen narrowed her eyes at me.

I nodded, though I couldn't meet her gaze.

"Impossible, Riley. A few sips and you would have wings as strong and wide as anyone in this training room. Why are you lying to me? Do you know the punishment for lying to your queen?" she asked, though her tone didn't seem angry. It was something closer to disappointed. It didn't take a genius to see that she was offended by my rejection of her gift, just as Bashrik had warned she would be.

"I'm sorry, Your Highness. I didn't mean to lie to you. It's just that I'm... Well, I'm embarrassed," I replied, thinking quickly. "I'm embarrassed because I'm worried I won't be any good. I'm nervous about how difficult it will be to learn to fly."

For a moment, Queen Brisha said nothing, her face a blank mask. Then, a burst of laughter erupted from her throat. I was off the hook. I didn't know how, but I was.

"Have you not offered to teach your lover, Navan?" she chided, gesturing toward Navan, who had been standing not far from my training square. "You surprise me. I thought you would have been eager to teach your partner how to be more like one of us!" She smiled

coyly, making me wonder if she was thinking about
Bashrik.

Meanwhile, I found myself looking around the
training room, hoping nobody had overheard Brisha
revealing our relationship in such a carefree, open
manner. I was pretty sure everyone already suspected
by now, but I didn't want to give them any more ammunition than they already had against me.

"I would have offered had she told me she'd
received such a gift, Your Highness," he replied coolly,
snaking his arm around my waist. "How come you
didn't say anything?" he asked, frowning down at me.

"I wanted it to be a surprise," I said. "I was going to
try to learn on my own, but then I got scared, and just...
never got around to it."

Navan smiled warmly, looking deep into my eyes.
"Well, now I can teach you without you having to
worry about dropping out of the sky. If you fall, I'll be
there to catch you," he said in a low tone, stroking a
strand of hair behind my ears. With every word, I
wanted to burst out laughing, the whole thing feeling
like something out of a cheesy rom-com. And yet, the
queen seemed delighted by it, her eyes gleaming with
the magic of romance.

"Love's young dream, the pair of you," she sighed,
showing her approval. "Instead of continuing here,
why don't you head out to the training fields to try out

your gift? I give you my permission to skip today's scheduled sessions in favor of learning to fly." She winked, ushering the pair of us out of the door, leaving no room for a refusal. I knew it wouldn't go down well with the other trainees, but I found I just couldn't bring myself to care anymore. They were going to hate me no matter what I did, so I might as well learn something useful in the process.

With me bundled up in my fur coat, we took the long hallway that led through the middle of the training center, going in the opposite direction of the entrance and not stopping until we reached the very end. It was a lengthy trek that ended in a vast hangar, with various ships stowed against the walls. They were practice vessels, for when the trainees reached that stage of their journey from recruit to full-fledged soldier. Beyond the hangar stood two large doors that opened onto vast, empty fields that were used for battle scenarios involving gunships and other armored vessels. Nobody was out there today, giving us the perfect opportunity to practice flying.

Without drawing attention to ourselves, we slipped out of a smaller door that was embedded in the larger one and headed into the bitter cold. It was a clear day, the sky a pale, almost lilac hue, the icy sun beating down upon the landscape. Barely a cloud spoiled the perfect calm above, though I could still smell the tang of ozone in the air that usually came before a storm. I kept forgetting that smell was always here on Vysanthe, whether it rained or not.

We paused in the center of the second field over, the brisk breeze restoring me after the tiring morning of training I'd endured. I already had a vial of wing serum in the pocket of my coat, stowed away there for safekeeping, while the other two were safely hidden away in the apartment. But the thought of it still made me nervous. What if it all went wrong?

"Are you sure you want to do this?" Navan asked as I lifted out the vial of serum.

I nodded stiffly. "She'll be watching, and I don't want to offend her any more than I already have."

"I've got no idea how this is going to work, but you'll have to take your coat off," he muttered.

Dreading the sensation of the Vysanthean wind on my skin, I shuffled off the protective layer of the fur coat and cast it aside, instantly regretting it as I began to shiver. I ignored the cold as best I could and took the emerald stopper out of the vial, then lifted it to my lips. The metal of the bottle was cold against my skin, and a sour aroma rose up from within.

I allowed a few drops of the surprisingly thick liquid to trickle down the back of my throat. It was done before I had a chance to think too hard about it.

"So... nothing's happening," I said, tapping my shoulders to see if anything was growing.

"Give it a minute. I doubt it will be instantaneous," Navan said encouragingly, though I could tell he was worried.

"How did you learn to fly?" I asked as I waited for the serum to kick in. I needed to do something to take my mind off what I'd just done.

He smiled. "My mother taught me when I was two. You start out with the basics, with lifting and falling and soaring techniques, then move on to sweeping and wing control. It's all about currents and pockets of air, as well as the force you can create by flapping them together," he explained. Normally, the image of Navan as a flapping, bumbling two-year-old would have brought a smile to my lips, but right now, all I could focus on was the serum inside me. I still couldn't feel anything.

And then, it started.

It began as a burning sensation in the pit of my stomach, searing shocks of electricity shooting through my nerve endings. I winced, trying to brace against it, but the pain was too intense. It rocketed through my body, taking hold of every sense and cell, until I could only feel the white-hot agony of it. Navan put his arms around me, and I gripped his shoulders, using him as an anchor to get through the wave of torture.

A moment later, the pain moved away from my limbs and settled beneath the hard edges of my scapula. A strange sensation followed, like something was pushing violently against my skin, trying to burst through. I thought of all the sci-fi horror movies I'd ever seen, and worried that something alien and disgusting was about to explode out of my skin. The idea made me feel queasy, forcing me to grip harder at Navan's shoulders for fear of collapsing.

I felt something split and tear, like someone had sliced my back open with a razor blade. I screamed out in pain, squeezing my eyes shut against it. It *hurt*. It really hurt. I remembered the way Ronad had struggled through the loss of his wings, his brow feverish, his cries echoing through the Texan night, and realized how idiotic I'd been—I should have known it would hurt.

On the grass in front of me, I saw two strange shadows spread out to either side of me, but my eyes were too clouded by pained tears to see the silhouettes properly. There was a weight, too, that I wasn't used to. Most surprisingly, however, was the fact I didn't feel cold anymore. Whatever the serum had done, it had made me less vulnerable than before.

"Are they there?" I whispered as the pain subsided.

Navan nodded slowly, his eyes wide. "They're

there... and, whoa, it is super weird seeing you like this."

I sucked in a breath and waited a few moments before daring to pull away from Navan's grasp, feeling the strangeness of the wings for the first time. They were bigger and heavier than I'd expected, the shift in balance almost making me fall over. Managing to keep upright, I focused on trying to flap them, but nothing happened.

"Let's start small," Navan suggested as he unfurled his own majestic wings. He wrapped his arms gently around me and lifted me up off the ground. I held him tight, taking a moment to enjoy the feel of his body pressed against mine, now that I wasn't in a world of pain.

"It's going to be hard to concentrate," I whispered with a shy grin.

He smiled. "Focus, girl," he chastised. "I want you to think of your wings like muscles. Think about what you want to move, and move it." His hands strayed along my back to where the wings had emerged.

I did as he asked, picturing the new lines of muscle and sinew that had been created and focusing on getting them to move. To my surprise, the left wing flapped slightly. I shrieked in delight, trying it again. This time, it gave a full flap that almost encompassed the two of us entirely. Focusing even harder, I flapped the right, then the left, before bringing them both together, giving me my first sight of both wings together. They were dark and sleek, though not nearly as leathery as regular coldblood wings. Mine had an almost green sheen, like the feathers of a magpie whenever they caught the sun in a certain light.

"Good. Now I want you to try soaring on an air current," Navan said. He held my waist and flew me toward a pocket of warmer air. He paused as he felt out a suitable current, before holding me over it. "Open your wings and let the current push you upward."

I obeyed, feeling elated when my wings caught the rush of air, my body shooting upward. It was only when the current ebbed that I began to panic, as I started to plummet to the ground. I flapped frantically, but I couldn't get both wings to move at the same time, causing me to jolt from side to side. Navan swept down and grabbed me before I got too close to the ground, his laughter sounding sweet and comforting in my ear. He turned me around in his arms and held me close.

"Not bad," he whispered. "And I have to say, now that I've gotten used to it, there's something about Winged Riley that is incredibly sexy." He dipped his head and kissed me full on the mouth, one hand locked around me, his other holding the back of my neck.

"Likewise," I managed. There was something about

being so close to him, in such a dangerous setting, that made me want to tear his clothes off.

I hadn't thought about the prospect of sex with Navan in too much detail since Bashrik's interruption just over a week ago, but right now it was something I couldn't ignore. All I could think about was his body against mine, his lips exploring every inch of my skin, his hands discovering every secret I held. It wasn't really something Navan and I had spoken about, though our bodies had said plenty on the subject.

"How much longer do we have to stay out here?" I asked, breathless. There was only thin material between us as we hovered in the air, clutched against one another.

"As long as you want," he murmured, dipping his head to kiss my neck.

"Maybe we shouldn't... We might have an audience," I gasped, little shivers of electricity rippling up my spine.

Navan grinned. "Then think fast," he chuckled, before dropping me out of his arms.

I yelped, my stomach turning as I fell. I forced my mind to focus, and, to my surprise, my wings flapped in unison, stirring up gusts of wind beneath them that carried me safely upward, keeping me away from the ground below. I giggled delightedly, my cheeks still hot from Navan's kiss, and soared through the cold air, feeling the rush of it against my bare skin as I swept this way and that.

"You're doing it!" Navan cried. He flew in underneath me, wrapping his arms around me so we began to corkscrew through the air. I had never been so exhilarated in all my life. Together, we flew across the sky, racing one another, twisting and turning in each other's arms.

We flew until I felt an ache beneath my shoulders, telling me that the serum was wearing off. Not wanting to risk being in the air when it happened, I flew downward, landing with a thud on the ground. Walking off my less-than-graceful touchdown, I felt a rush of wind as Navan landed beside me. I could already feel my wings receding, their magnificence fading away, though the pain of their disappearance was nothing compared to the pain of their arrival. It was a dull ache, followed by a few sharp jolts, then nothing more.

"Are they gone?" I asked sadly.

"For now." His hand slipped into mine, and we headed toward the back entrance of the training center. On the way, I picked up my fur coat and put it back on, shivering against the Vysanthean cold, the heat from my wing serum all but gone. Instantly, I felt warmer, especially since the fur covered the two holes that had been torn in the back of my shirt and revealed the bare skin of my shoulder blades.

"Do you think we can get back to our chambers without being interrupted?" I wondered, flashing him a knowing look.

He smiled, staring at me with such desire I thought I might burst. "I think we can try," he whispered, his voice low and thick.

Still holding hands, we sprinted through the hangar and into the main hallway of the training center, our minds on our chamber and the bed that beckoned to us. We tore across the gap between the center and the palace, feeling smug that we had managed to get away without anyone noticing, or anyone calling us in to do something else, when a sight in one of the windows of the gleaming building distracted my attention. I skidded to a halt, knowing it wasn't accidental. There, written on a rectangle of paper stuck in the pane, was the word *LIBRARY*, written in big, bold letters.

"Rask," Navan muttered.

"Rask," I concurred.

It looked like the promise of some alone time would have to wait.

6

We hurried toward the library, knowing the note had to be for us. It was written in crude, bubbly lettering that I couldn't imagine a Vysanthean using. I had seen Lauren use it before, though, as she sprawled over school textbooks and secret journals.

Reaching the familiar door, I knocked. Lauren answered a moment later, ducking her head out into the hallway before yanking the pair of us inside. The armchair Queen Brisha usually lounged in was empty, though the fire was still roaring in the grate. In fact, it was absolutely roasting in the library, and beads of sweat started to form on my forehead. Realizing the thick layer of fur wrapped around me probably wasn't helping, I shuffled it off my shoulders, putting it to one side.

"You got my message, then?" Lauren asked conspiratorially as she led us through a network of bookshelves, heading for the back of the vast room.

I nodded. "On the window."

"Good. I was worried you might miss it. I didn't think it was big enough, and when hours passed and you still hadn't arrived, I figured you hadn't seen it," she explained rapidly, pulling us down a long passageway of particularly tall stacks filled to the brim with dusty tomes. At the end of it stood a strange circular nook, which appeared to be hewn from the inside of an old tower. There, a circular banquette hugged the nook's outer rim, and a table sat in the center, though both things were difficult to make out, given the quantity of books scattered across every surface. Lauren had certainly been a busy bee.

"Nope, we saw it," Navan muttered, flashing me a look of remorse.

"I'm glad. I wasn't sure it could wait until I saw you this evening." Lauren sighed anxiously, ducking into the nook. Navan and I followed, taking a seat wherever we could.

"How are you even reading all of these?" I asked, picking up one of the nearby tomes. The writing was in a language I couldn't decipher, though there seemed to be texts in several languages lying about. Hardly any of them were uniformly one kind or another.

She smiled shyly, tapping the side of her purple-rimmed glasses. "When I first showed an interest in the books here, Queen Brisha installed a device in the lenses of my glasses. It links up to the language center in my brain and transforms the writing into words I can understand."

Navan looked stunned. "She gave you one of them?"

"I think she saw how desperate I was to read this entire library," Lauren said, glancing around with an expression of contentment.

"And I bet you will! So, what've you got for us?" I asked, gesturing to the texts that lay in haphazard piles all around me.

"Oh, sorry about the mess," she mumbled, picking up a large, cream-colored book. "*This* is the one we're going to need," she explained, flicking to the right page. "So, I was doing some research, as you can see, and I came across this. It's not a textbook, per se, but the journal of some horticulturist here in Northern Vysanthe. No idea who he is, but he seems to know his stuff. Now, he says that the poroporo fruit I was talking about still grows in remote ice caves up in the Fazar mountain range. They're pretty much at the pole of

Northern Vysanthe, but they're reachable, by his understanding."

"How come they're still there, then? Surely, those addicts would just have harvested it all?" Navan asked dubiously.

Lauren smiled. "That's where it gets interesting. In order to protect the fruit, the old royal family put safeguards in place. They used to do that a lot, apparently. There are loads of instances of it happening with precious gemstones, ancient relics, sacred sites..." She trailed off, flipping to another page in the book.

"What kind of safeguards are we talking about?" I wondered. "Are there actual guards, or some sort of barrier?"

Lauren shook her head. "Nothing so simple, I'm afraid. The horticulturist describes beasts of some sort, though he didn't stay long enough to find out what they were. All he says is there were 'vast shadows in the darkness' that killed his two partners soon after they ventured into the caves, judging by their screams. He muses, later on in the passage, that these creatures might have been bred for the purpose of security."

Navan and I exchanged a look. "What, so they're like guard dogs?" he asked.

"Not dogs—think bigger than dogs," Lauren replied, giving a reluctant shrug. It seemed like, whatever these beasts were, we were going to have to discover them ourselves. "Like I said, it's hard to tell from the horticulturist's notes, but they sound pretty massive, whatever they are, and even more dangerous."

"Does he say anything else about them?" I pressed, the thought of vicious, unknown Vysanthean creatures filling me with dread.

"He says that, whatever they were, they took his partners unawares. The horticulturist ran before he could be captured, too. He mentions a strange sound, and a sudden feeling of immense heat and extreme cold, both at once, but that's all he describes," Lauren said apologetically, closing the book. "But he says the fruit is still there, ripe and ready for the picking. You'll just need to get past whatever is lurking there."

I frowned, envisioning a coiled dragon nestled atop piles of gold and jewels, or a troll with a wooden club standing in front of a gaping cave mouth. Whatever it was we had to face, it sounded like something straight out of a fable. Saying that, nothing surprised me anymore. Vysanthe was full of things that wanted to kill me, so why not these mysterious creatures, who crept out of the dark and made strange sounds? It wouldn't be the weirdest thing that had happened to me this summer.

"Anything else we need to know?" I asked anxiously.

Lauren tapped a passage. "The poroporo fruit only

ripens at certain times of the year, and always at night. From what I've gathered, it happens during what is known as the Alignment of the Queens, which is when eight stars align every other month, for a week or so."

I sighed. "Let me guess, that's weeks from now?"

"No, actually. That's this week," Navan cut in, his tone intrigued.

"You're right," Lauren confirmed. "In fact, it started two nights ago, but the sooner you can harvest the fruit, from the beginning of the Alignment, the more potent the juice will be. That's why, when it was used recreationally, there was never anything left to replant by the end of the Alignment. Whole crops would be destroyed by desperate people tearing off the fruit."

"Okay, so we need to go tonight then," I said firmly, looking to Navan. We didn't have to be in training again until tomorrow evening, for night combat training and night flying simulations, which gave us plenty of time to leave Nessun and get the fruit.

"If we want the good stuff, then yeah. I've drawn out a map for you to follow," Lauren said brightly, handing me a folded piece of paper.

"Wait, how are we supposed to get all the way to the pole of Northern Vysanthe?" I asked, the thought coming to me in a burst of panic. "We don't have a ship anymore, and I doubt we can hitch a ride."

Navan smiled. "The serum, Riley. It makes you less

vulnerable to the cold, and you'll be able to brave the harsh air."

My heart thundered at the prospect. "We're going to fly there?"

"We're going to fly there," he repeated, "but we'll have to leave as soon as everyone in the palace is asleep. It'll be too risky in daylight. People will see us leave and wonder where we're going."

"Tonight it is, then," I said softly, forcing a smile onto my face, though I felt nothing but trepidation inside. The prospect of coming face-to-face with some unknown creatures wasn't exactly comforting, and that was only if we managed to get out of the palace without being spotted. Even then, there were no guarantees we wouldn't be tailed.

It was going to be a long night.

———

As darkness fell, I stood on the balcony of our apartment and stared out at the twinkling lights of the city below. Navan joined me, handing me a glass of something sparkling that Queen Brisha had sent to our room, while he sipped from a glass of something thick and red. My drink wasn't alcoholic, as far as I could tell, but it refreshed me in a way no other liquid ever had, tasting faintly like apple, though a little sourer. I drank it down in one gulp, my nerves getting the better of me.

"What do you think these creatures are?" I asked, my eyes drawn to the silver dome of the training center.

Navan shrugged. "Something savage. If they're anything like the guard beasts we have in the South, they'll be trained killers."

I frowned at him. "Aren't you worried?"

"I doubt it'll be anything I haven't fought before," he said calmly, though I could see a flicker of doubt in his slate eyes. Once again, I realized he was putting on a show of bravery to ease my nerves. "We'll be fine, don't worry," he added, sipping from his drink.

As the hour grew later, we stole out of the apartment and headed down to the lower floors of the palace, thinking we might sneak out through the gardens. From our balcony, I'd spotted a sheltered grove at the back of the beautiful building. It seemed overgrown and forgotten about, like somewhere we could take off under the cover of darkness, undisturbed by prying eyes. Once in the air, we could fly low, sticking to the shadows of the mountainside. Navan had already warned that, if we flew from the balcony itself, we would be spotted immediately, given the bright lights that shone onto the sides of the palace to show off its grandeur, even at night.

Navan led the way as we crept through the empty hallways, ducking into doorways whenever a guard passed by. I knew the overgrown grove had to branch off from one of the older rooms at the farthest edge of the palace—it was just a case of figuring out which one.

"Are we going the right way?" I asked as we entered a gloomy corridor that smelled of dust and decay. It was clear nobody came this way anymore.

Navan nodded. "If this palace is anything like Queen Gianne's, then all the old halls and galleries will be closed up. They're a reminder of bygone days, when the planet was unified, and neither queen particularly likes to dwell on that," he muttered, squinting against the dim light. "In Gianne's palace, these halls and galleries were on the first or second floors, where they could easily be accessed by the public, in the old days. Royalty didn't want members of the public snooping around their private quarters, so everything intended for normal citizens was on the lower floors."

"There!" I whispered, pointing at a door at the end of the hallway. It still bore the first four letters of the word "gallery," though the last three seemed to have been swallowed up by years of abandonment.

As we walked toward it, we froze. A figure emerged from the doorway. Her eyes snapped in our direction, narrowing with suspicion.

"Riley, Navan, what in Rask's name are you doing down here?" Pandora barked, covering the gap between us in a matter of strides. I looked to Navan, my mind racing a mile a minute, yet unable to come up with a suitable excuse.

He smiled sweetly. "You caught us," he said, with a note of apology in his voice. "We were hoping to sneak out for date night. With training and everything, we haven't really had much alone time. I overheard one of the guards talking about taking his wife to the midnight artisan market, and I thought I might do the same for Riley, as a little surprise," he explained, not missing a beat. Even I believed him.

Pandora frowned, though her features softened a moment later. "The midnight artisan market in Paloma Square?" she asked.

"If that's the one near the old university building, then yes," Navan said. "I'm still getting used to where things are around here."

"That's the one. Do you need directions?"

"Bashrik already gave me some," he replied, brandishing the folded piece of paper that contained the map to the Fazar Mountains. What if Pandora tried to take a closer look at it? My heart hammered in my throat.

"Fair enough. After all, who am I to stand in the way of true love?" She smirked, although the humor didn't quite reach her eyes. "While you're there, do you think you could do me a little favor?"

"Sure, what can we do for you?" I asked, knowing it was better to stay on Pandora's good side, given her standing with the queen.

"Could you get me a list of ingredients that the queen has requested?" she replied.

I looked at her curiously, realizing that she was essentially passing off her responsibility to us. Maybe she couldn't be bothered? Then again, it was probably a tough job being the queen's advisor, constantly at her beck and call, doing her bidding. In Pandora's position, I might have been tempted to do the same.

"Of course. Do you have the list on you, or do you want me to write it down?" Navan asked, patting down his pockets for a pen he didn't have.

"Everything you'll need to get is on here," she replied, flashing Navan an almost derisive look as she handed over a small black device. When she tapped the center, a hologram flickered to life, listing all the items the queen desired. "Don't you have these in the South?" she asked, narrowing her eyes again.

Navan grinned. "We do, Pandora. I was just teasing. I can't even remember the last time I wrote something down." He took the device and slipped it into his pocket.

"You'd better get going. You shouldn't be out too

late," Pandora said brusquely. "If the queen finds out you're gone, I won't be able to cover for you." She dipped a hand into her pocket and pulled out a ring of keys, removing a small silver one and placing it in my hand. "There's an old emergency exit in the storage closet at the back of this galleria. This key will let you out."

With that, she strode off and disappeared into the gloom. Navan and I let out a sigh of relief. I liked Pandora, but there was something about her that set my nerves on edge. Whether it was her impressive stature, her brusque manner, or her position as Brisha's right-hand woman, I wasn't sure. Whatever it was, I found her intimidating.

"We'll have to be quick if we're going to get all of this stuff." Navan sighed, still looking toward the spot where Pandora had disappeared. "I hadn't planned for us to stop by the market, but I guess we're going to have to now."

"Will we have enough time to do both?" I asked, worried.

Navan grimaced. "We'll have to be fast, especially if we want to be back before dawn, but it should be okay," he said, though he didn't sound sure.

He took my hand and led me through the door of the ancient gallery, where dustsheets draped countless ghostly shapes and motheaten tapestries hung from moldering walls. I wondered what this place might have looked like in its glory days, though it was clear they were long gone.

We found the storage closet and descended the rickety staircase hidden at the back of it. Navan unlocked the door at the bottom, and a second later, we were stepping out into the cold night, into the forgotten garden I had seen from the balcony. From the shadows of the overgrown bushes and the boughs of skeletal trees, I could have sworn there were eyes watching me.

Shaking off my fears, I plucked the wing serum from my pocket. I still had two thirds of the first vial left, but I had the second one with me just in case.

"Take a long sip," Navan said. "It needs to last longer than the first time."

Letting out a breath, I placed the vial to my lips, tipping the liquid onto my tongue. I swallowed quickly, letting the viscous liquid get to work. This time, knowing what to expect, I sat down on the frost-tipped grass and waited for the pain to come. It did a moment later, ripping through my body like a blazing tornado. Clutching my stomach, I felt the familiar razorblade sensation of the wings pushing through my skin. I gritted my teeth against the searing agony, knowing it would pass.

As my wings spread out behind me, tearing

through the fabric of my shirt, the pain ebbed, leaving me with the strange, weighted sensation. I got to my feet, feeling a little unsteady. Navan stepped up beside me, putting his arm around my waist, letting me lean against him until I felt balanced again.

"I think Brisha's going to need to buy me a whole load of new shirts," I chuckled. This was the second one I'd ruined with my wings.

"You'll have to ask her for some like mine," he replied with a smile, turning to show me the flexible gaps in his shirt fabric, which opened to allow his wings through, causing no harm to the shirt itself. "Now, before thoughts of ripping your shirt off distract me entirely, might I take you on a quick date, you beautiful creature?" Navan teased, turning back around and bending his head so he could kiss my shoulder blades.

I laughed. "I'd be delighted, you handsome devil."

With that, we took to the skies, the Vysanthean night rushing past me, its icy fingers in my hair, twisting through my wings, filling my lungs with its bitter freshness. A grin spread across my face despite the dangers to come. With Navan by my side, the wind beneath my wings, and the world stretching out ahead of me with its endless possibilities, I knew I could get used to this.

"*D*own there," Navan said, pointing to a peculiar structure in the distance.

I frowned, squinting at it. The place didn't look like any city square I had ever seen. It stood next to a curved building with golden spires that I presumed to be the old university Navan had mentioned. A high stone wall formed the square, a crosshatched net of tangled bronze rods rising above and across it, like spun sugar cupped over a dessert in a fancy restaurant. Lights glowed through the strange domed roof of bronze branches, reminding me of stars seen through a canopy of trees.

As we landed, the hubbub of voices rose from within the covered piazza. It was a comforting sound, filled with chatter and laughter, and the telltale bark of bartering stall-owners. I threaded my fingers through Navan's, smiling up at him. We had never been on a real date before, and if this was the closest to one we were going to get, I was more than happy to take it.

A gateway was embedded in the high stone wall of the square, though the two heavy metal doors were swung wide, allowing the public to pass in and out of the piazza with ease. As we stepped through, joining the steady stream of coldbloods entering the market, my eyes went wide with awe.

Flickering candles and glowing string lights twinkled all around, draping from the fronds of willow-like trees. Stalls lined the square, selling all manner of unusual wares. At the center, a band was playing a lively tune on instruments I had never seen before, though some looked vaguely drum-like, and others resembled violins, but these were made from dark metals that glinted in the low light. They still sounded like their Earthen counterparts, making me feel like I was at an Irish jig. As the music enveloped us, I almost felt tempted to take to the floor and lose myself in the melody.

There were other people dancing, a few young couples swinging each other around, but I couldn't see Navan indulging me in a dance or two. I flashed him a look all the same, nodding in the direction of the music.

He shook his head. "No way," he said, smirking. "I've told you before, I'm a terrible dancer. You'd run away from sheer embarrassment."

"I'll get a dance out of you before the night is out," I said, narrowing my eyes at him, though of course it was an empty threat. As much as I wished we had longer to peruse the stalls and enjoy the atmosphere, I knew we couldn't spend much time at the market. For one thing, we didn't know how long it would take to find the poro-poro fruit, and we were going to need as much time in the Fazar Mountains as possible to seek it out. Because if we didn't manage to find the fruit, then we'd have to choose a different method of getting answers about the immortality elixir from Yorrek, a method that probably wouldn't leave us with clean hands or a clean conscience... I shook the thought from my mind.

Hand in hand, listening to the music drifting through the square, we walked along the outer edges, peering at all the wondrous stalls. Everything was new and exciting to my human eyes. The stalls held everything from strange Vysanthean technologies, to hand-made arts and crafts, to curious vials containing rare blood. I wasn't as interested in the latter type of shop, but the rest had me enraptured.

"This is beautiful," I murmured, peering down at a dark metal bracelet with a pale gray gem in the center that seemed to be calling my name.

Navan frowned. "You like that?" he asked, pointing at the bracelet that had caught my eye.

I nodded. "Gorgeous."

"The lady has fine taste," the shopkeeper purred, picking up the bracelet and lifting it toward me. I held out my wrist to receive it, almost on impulse, my blood rushing in my ears, my pulse racing in anticipation. The ashen-faced woman was about to place it on my welcoming wrist, when Navan snatched my arm away.

"Not today, thank you," he said sharply as the shopkeeper flashed her fangs at him.

"It would seem your lover doesn't care for your desires, beautiful mistress," she snarled, clutching the bracelet to her breast. "A shame. A real shame."

I frowned as Navan pulled me away from the jewelry stand and pressed me on along the avenue of stalls. I could still feel the almost magnetic pull of the bracelet calling me back, though I couldn't explain why.

"What *was* that bracelet?" I asked, still sensing the way my blood had longed for it. "It made me feel all funny."

Navan glanced around at the stalls. "Some Vysanthean stones hold that power. It's believed that only certain types of stones work on certain types of people. The way a body responds to that power depends on who, and what, you are," he explained.

"Arcadium is particularly strong to most people, but I've never seen anyone respond quite as quickly to its pull before."

I flushed, remembering the warning I'd been given after ingesting the silver root. It had been a long time since I'd thought about it. So long, in fact, that I'd almost forgotten about the very real issue of how I might react to things, in the future, now that the root was in my system—how it might make me more prone to addictions and vices, my body craving things it wouldn't normally have wanted, or needed.

"We should hurry up and get the stuff on Queen Brisha's list," I said, wanting to change the subject. Even now, the pull of the Arcadium made me feel antsy to return to the stall and have the shopkeeper clamp that bracelet on my wrist.

"We can pick up a few things for our mission too," Navan replied, running his fingertips absently across the edges of my folded wings. "I know the serum keeps you warmer in our bitter climate, but the northern-most mountains are going to be a different challenge completely. While we're here, we should get you a better fur and a few other bits and pieces, if I can find them."

"What sort of things?" I asked as we walked along, my eyes drawn to every sight, sound, and scent that filled the air.

"Yes!" Navan said suddenly, lifting his fist in triumph as he came to a halt beside a stall filled with a confusing array of bric-a-brac. I didn't know what any of it was, save for a few lamps and a braided rope with a horn on the end that dangled from a hook at the edge of the shop. Navan, however, seemed thrilled by something in the middle of the mess, his hand grasping at a palm-sized amber stone that was buried under scraps of leather and a few motheaten books.

"What is it?" I marveled, peering at the flat, smooth stone.

"This is an emberstone," he explained. "Basically, it heats up and warms the person who holds it, though it can also be used to make fires, which is why it's banned in the South as a hazard. Fortunately for us, the North is a little more reckless." He handed over some money and slipped the stone into my hands.

He was right. A minute or so later, the warmth penetrated my skin, seeping into my veins. Glancing down, I saw that the stone was glowing dimly as I held it between my palms, and its delicious warmth radiated through me.

"Where have you been all my life?" I murmured, reveling in the sensation.

"On a planet, far, far away," Navan quipped.

I grinned. "I meant the stone."

"Hey, I can keep you so much warmer than that stone ever could." He pouted.

"I don't doubt it, but if I came to you every time I needed to be warm, I'd never get anything done," I replied with a wink.

"Then we'd better get this list purchased before we get sidetracked," he murmured, slipping his arm around my waist. We continued along the line of stalls.

He picked up a thick fur next, which I wrapped around my shoulders, and as we continued walking, he kept stopping here and there, picking up items that were listed on the black device Pandora had given him. Apparently, the device was also a payment system that the merchants could scan. With each purchased item, Navan double-clicked the center of the device, making it light up red. I listened to the names as he asked for each ingredient, though they didn't mean much to me: serotite shavings, parokium ore, maram root, garovian winterberries, liquid romjal. It was all completely alien, in every sense of the word.

"Last thing, then we can get out of here," Navan promised, checking the list once more. "A vial of aged Ephranian platelets."

I had no idea who, or what, Ephranians were, but I knew what platelets were, and the thought of such a thing being an easily bought-and-sold commodity made me feel slightly queasy. Once again, I was reminded how cruel Vysanthean trade could be—not that there was much in the way of actual trade. Barely anything was natively grown or produced here, with the majority of items stolen and pilfered and snatched, all at the expense of others.

Navan paid for a small silver vial, plucked from the shelf of a trader who seemed to deal in exotic kinds of alien bodily fluids. As he placed it in the burlap sack he was carrying, Navan suddenly froze. His eyes narrowed as he went over the list again. With anxious hands, he checked through the items in the sack, his mouth moving in silent thought.

"What's the matter?" I asked, alarmed by the expression on his face.

"I hope she isn't making what I think she's making," he muttered, his brow furrowing.

"Why, what do you think she's making?" I pressed.

After a moment of stony silence, he shook his head. "Forget I said anything. I'm probably wrong. It's this place—it makes me paranoid," he replied, flashing me a smile, though I didn't quite believe him.

"What do you think she might be making, Navan?" I insisted, but he shook his head again.

"Honestly, I was just being silly. I thought it was something, but I don't think it's made that way. Anyway, let's forget about Queen Brisha. There's something I want to show you," he said, taking my hand and pulling me down the avenue of stalls, to one in particular. I wanted to ask about the ingredients again, but I let it go for now, the sight of the items in front of me distracting my attention.

"What are they?" I asked, letting my fingertips trail across the pairs of small gemstones that gleamed on the table in front of me. Within each one, a strange light brightened then died every few seconds.

Navan smiled. "These are climpets," he said. "They're tokens that Vysantheans give to their loved ones to wear above their hearts. They feed off emotions, and myth has it that the light only goes out if one person ceases to love the other—though, I think they're just meant to be a sweet gift, these days." He picked up a set of pale gems, the color of his slate eyes. "I thought I might buy a pair for us, if you'd like that?" His gaze rested on mine, filled with such warmth that I couldn't possibly refuse.

"Of course, but I don't want you spending your money on me," I said shyly, knowing he didn't have much to fritter away, since whatever wealth he did have was locked away in the South. We only had the credits we'd earned from our military training, which wasn't a massive amount, and I didn't want him to waste it on me, not when he could use it on something more practical.

"There's nothing I'd rather spend it on," he

announced, holding one of the gems out to me. "Come on, let me buy these for us."

I smiled, knowing he wasn't going to back down. "Okay, sir, if you insist." Navan grinned and paid for the climpets, then handed one to me.

"Thank you... Um, what do I do with it?" I asked.

"Watch." He took his climpet and lifted up the edge of his t-shirt, revealing the rippling muscles of his torso, and placing the gem against his chest. It remained there when he took his fingertips away, clinging to the skin, the gemstone glittering as the light within glowed steadily.

"Does that *hurt*?" I asked, staring.

He shook his head. "Nope. Not one bit."

Taking my own gem, I pulled down the collar of my t-shirt, stretching it all the way across my collarbone, until I had enough flesh exposed that I could place the gemstone where Navan had placed his without having to lift my shirt completely. I wasn't quite as much of an exhibitionist as Navan, though he seemed disappointed by my discretion.

"I'm not going to lift my shirt up for you in public, so you can get that thought out of your mind," I joked as I fitted the gem into place. Weirdly, it seemed to sink into the skin, gleaming there. I couldn't take my eyes off it, and neither could Navan.

He stepped closer and put an arm around me. His

other hand came to rest beneath my chin, tilting it upward. I smiled, my eyes gazing into his, relishing the closeness of him, and not caring in that moment who saw or tutted.

"May our light never go out," he whispered, leaning in to kiss me deeply.

"I hope it never does," I breathed, smiling against his lips as I kissed him back. My arms looped around his neck, pulling him closer to me.

Not for the first time, I wondered what it would be like, if the moment actually came for us to make love. If we were committing ourselves to one another like this, then surely *that* had to be in our future somewhere? I wanted to know what I was in for, on a physiological level more than anything else. I mean, what if Vysantheans had different equipment that I had no idea what to do with? Not that I exactly knew what to do with human equipment, either, but even so, I couldn't help worrying about it. We existed on opposite ends of the universe. We probably weren't ever supposed to meet, fall in love, and reach those kinds of desires. What if we weren't... compatible?

As I broke away from Navan's kiss, knowing we had to leave soon if we were going to reach the Fazar Mountain Range and get back before dawn, I felt an impulse to talk to him about it. I wanted to broach the subject

we had been skirting around for weeks, but, once
again, it wasn't the time. It was going to have to wait.

"We should go before it gets too late," he said,
clearing his throat.

I nodded, catching his hand and leading him out of
the magical square, with its fairy-glen lights and beautiful music. Taking one final look around, I bade the
band goodbye, knowing it would be the last warm sight
I'd lay eyes on tonight.

*A*s we took to the skies once more, the landscape of Nessun disappeared beneath us, rushing away into the distance. There was a gap in the mountains on the far side of the city, where it gave way to the rest of Northern Vysanthe's territories, the sparkling lights of the city dimming as we passed through.

The temperature dropped as we flew through the crevasse between the ragged peaks, and I was immediately grateful for the emberstone Navan had bought me, feeling the warmth ripple through my veins as I clutched it in my hands. It was strange to fly so fast and so far, considering the last time I'd done this I had been confined to the training fields. It felt nice, like I could go anywhere, if I wanted to.

Beyond the mountains, our winged bodies weaving in and out of narrow cracks and fissures, the terrain shifted, giving way to vast expanses of flat darkness. With the temperature dropping, we sank lower to the ground, skimming across it, in case we suddenly needed to land and rest. Now and again, I'd see the glint of lights in the distance where a township was clustered, or a hamlet lay on the outskirts of a barren field.

Almost two hours into the flight, a dank, pungent scent crept into my nostrils, smelling of death and decay. I lifted my hand to pinch my nose against the overwhelming aroma, the emberstone tumbling from my hand as I did so. I watched as it fell to the ground. Cursing under my breath, I swooped down to retrieve it. I knew I probably needed to take more of the wing serum anyway; I could feel the strength in my wings ebbing, alongside a dull pain that throbbed beneath my scapula—a sure sign that the serum's effects were fading.

As my feet touched the ground, I heard Navan call out.

"Riley, no! Get back in the air!" he yelled.

But it was too late. My wings no longer felt strong enough to fly, and while I was down here, I really needed to grab that stone. I scrambled over the dirt and grime, the rancid stench getting worse the closer I knelt to the ground. Just then, something rose from the earth, moving toward me at a rapid pace. At this distance, it looked like a black mist or a fog, flitting through the air. My mind jumped to the monsters the horticulturist had spoken of in Lauren's book—shadow creatures that crept in the darkness. Only, there was a noise too. It sounded like paper flapping wildly in a breeze.

"Riley, get back in the air!" Navan bellowed again.

"I can't!" I shouted back. I caught sight of something smooth and shiny in the dirt. Reaching for it, I plucked up the emberstone, just as Navan swooped low, grabbing my arms and lifting me back up into the air.

All around us, the black fog swarmed, the fluttering sound growing louder. I squinted into the darkness, determined to see what was crowding us, though the light was dim. It was only when a strand of the black shadow touched the side of my hand that I realized what it really was—a column of tiny, navy-winged butterflies, all working together like a hive to surround us. When the first fluttering creature bit into my flesh, realization dawned on me.

"Horerczy butterflies?" I gasped, snatching my hand away from the biting insect.

Navan nodded grimly, his arms gripped around my waist. "If we don't get out of here now, we'll be bones in five minutes flat," he said, his eyes turning upward as I struggled to keep my hands and limbs away from the biting butterflies. I could feel their tiny teeth sinking into my skin, each one like a pinprick.

"They're biting me!" I hissed, and I flailed wildly, hoping it would do some good.

"Stop wriggling, or you'll fall!" Navan barked, readjusting his grip on my waist. It took me a moment to realize, but I couldn't see my wings stretching out behind me at all anymore. They were retreating.

Thinking fast, I reached my free hand into my pocket and pulled out the two-thirds-empty vial, trying to juggle keeping the vampiric butterflies away, holding the emberstone, un-stoppering the vial, and not flailing around. I took a deep sip, draining it down to the last drop. Immediately, I felt the burn of it in my stomach, though the pain wasn't nearly as bad as it had been before. Even so, I knew I wouldn't be much use against the butterflies for at least a couple of minutes, until the searing agony subsided. It was all I could do just to cling to the emberstone, and not get eaten alive by the insects.

I felt the air around me lurch as Navan spun around, his arms holding me even tighter than before. My stomach plummeted with the movement as he built up speed, moving like a tornado, twisting through the cold air and sending the Horerczy butterflies scattering all over the place as they whacked into his rapidly turning wings.

Then Navan shot upward like a rocket, putting as much distance as possible between the swamp and us. He didn't stop until the swamp was no longer visible beneath us, the flat expanse of savage marshland branching out into a wooded area, where something howled, and shadowy birds flapped across a dark canopy. It wasn't the most comforting of places, but it was definitely better than a murderous swamp.

"That was close." Navan sighed, slowly releasing me, and my newly unfurled wings took my weight.

"Too close," I said, knowing I had to be more careful about losing my wings while midflight. It was easier while Navan was around to help me, but I couldn't count on him always being there. If he got called away, or I ended up in a true battle scenario, without him to come to my aid, and I lost my wings in midair... I would be utterly screwed.

"At least we know where the swamps are on this side of Vysanthe," he said, shuddering. "I hate those things. Ugh. Give me huge frostfangs or saber-toothed jakous any day."

"What are *those*?" I wondered aloud, envisioning mythical beasts with snarling fangs and snouts that spewed fire.

"Creatures that live in the mountains. Frostfangs

are these huge, hound-like beasts, though they can camouflage to hide in the ice and snow. A much nastier version of the icehounds you saw down in the South. Saber-toothed jakous aren't much better. They're probably closest to what you call polar bears, but they have bigger teeth, and their fur is spiny and filled with poison that paralyzes their victims."

"Well, that's something to look forward to," I muttered, glancing toward the mountain range that was appearing on the horizon, the frosted peaks gleaming beneath the Vysanthean moonlight. "And you think they'll have these things where we're going?"

Navan shrugged. "We'll soon find out."

We set off toward the mountains in the distance, where the poroporo fruit supposedly grew. I just hoped we'd avoid whatever else lay out there.

Less than an hour later, we arrived at the gaping mouth of a cave that was hewn into the side of the mountain, which Lauren had marked on the map. It was the tallest one in the mountain range, its peak glittering almost blue in the darkness. Icicles dangled down like jaws, and the ground was slippery as we landed. In the dark of the tunnels and passageways beyond, everything was deathly silent. We knew the passageways were there because the horticulturist had said so, but nobody knew how far the labyrinth went, or where the poroporo fruit might grow along the way.

"So we have to go in there?" I whispered, wrapping my arms around myself. Even with the fur and the emberstone, I couldn't help but shiver.

"If we want that fruit. Though I'm starting to wonder if there might be another way to drug Yorrek," Navan joked drily.

"Let's get looking. We've got a long journey back, whether we find this fruit or not," I murmured, steeling myself against what was to come.

Holding the emberstone in my left hand, I took his hand in my right. We entered the cave system, and the silence descended on us with a vengeance. It was eerie and disorienting, the quiet so intense it was almost unbearable. Even when we spoke, the sound came out muffled, as though the cave itself wanted to smother it.

Using the faint blue light of the bioluminescent lichen that clung to the icy walls, we picked our way through the tunnels, squinting into the shadows up ahead to make sure nothing was creeping toward us. I turned to look over my shoulder a few times, too, just to be sure there wasn't anything approaching from behind.

Eventually, we reached a cavern within the mountain where glacial pillars spiraled upward and frozen bridges of ice traversed the echoing ceilings above. They were so high, I couldn't see where they ended, the darkness stretching away into oblivion. Somewhere in the vast cave, the sound of rushing water susurrated, but all I could see was a frozen landscape. Wherever that sound was coming from, it had to be deep below us, where the rock was slightly warmer.

And then, I saw it.

It caught the light from a shaft of moonlight that had crept in through a fissure in the stone, the outer flesh glowing with a purple hue that was instantly enticing. The shape was round and plump, shot through with golden veins that seemed to pulsate within, drawing my eye, making my mouth water. On top, there were waxy green leaves that seemed to hold small bowls of frozen dew in their concave valleys, never spilling a drop.

"There," I whispered to Navan, nudging him.

He turned, his eyes going wide. "Well spotted!"

Slowly, we moved toward the fruit. The golden veins acted like a beacon, calling us forward. I wondered how a fruit like that managed to grow in such harsh conditions. Would it even taste good? I supposed that wasn't the point of it. It was the high it gave, and the hypnotic effect it had on people. Remembering the pull of the Arcadium, I made a mental note to let Navan handle the fruit, just in case I got the sudden urge to take a bite.

Suddenly, my arm shot out, grasping Navan and

pulling him back. He looked at me in surprise as I dragged him behind one of the glacial pillars.

"What's the matter with you?" he whispered.

I pointed at the fruit. "Look at it—look at what's under it!"

Navan did so, his eyes narrowing in scrutiny. "It's just rocks and ice," he replied quietly.

I shook my head. "No, it's not! Look closer."

Underneath the plump, glowing fruit was a ragged dome of what looked like ice, stone, and the same bioluminescent lichen that clung to the walls of the mountain caves. However, on closer inspection, my eyes having grown more accustomed to the gloom, I realized that they were, in fact, scales... and those scales were moving up and down very slowly, stirred by the breath of some hidden creature. There was no monster guarding the fruit. The fruit was growing *on* the monster, the way barnacles grew on whales.

"How are we supposed to—" I began, but a tremor beneath the earth cut my words short. It juddered through the rocks all around us, and icicles fell from the cavern above, forcing us to duck out of the way as they came crashing down. They splintered on the ground, smashing with a sharp sound that ricocheted up my spine.

A moment later, the enormous beast rose from its slumbering spot, ice sliding from its scales as it shook off the evening's frost. It was about the size of an elephant, though it was lower to the ground, a stout neck giving way to a bulky head that was somewhere between a wolf's and an anteater's. Icy fangs glinted as it yawned, its beady green eyes surveying the cave for signs of a disturbance. Lifting its oddly long snout, it sniffed the air, drawing in great puffs, scenting out anything that didn't belong. I clung to Navan, holding my breath, hoping it wouldn't smell us.

It opened its mouth wide and let out a curious sound, partway between a wail and a song, which seemed to float across the cavern in a slow, melancholic melody that made me feel unexpectedly sad. Coming from any other creature, I might have thought it was a sweet sound, but this beast was anything but endearing. There was malevolence in its eyes.

Navan went still beside me, his gaze frozen on the monster.

"We need to get out of here," I whispered, tugging on his arm. "Let's regroup, figure out how we can fight this thing," I continued, trying to make him turn around. I didn't want to be nearby if that hulking beast decided to charge us.

"Navan?" I tugged at his arm again, but he wouldn't budge. A strange noise rippled through the air toward me, a kind of growling hiss. At first, I thought it was coming from the scaly creature, but its mouth was shut now, its nostrils no longer sniffing at the icy air. With a shiver of dread, I realized it was coming from the back of Navan's throat, his shoulders rising and falling rapidly with each grunt. He was panting like a frantic hound.

I lifted my hand to his shoulder. "Navan! Are you okay?" I asked, though I knew something was wrong. All I wanted was for him to turn and look at me, but his focus was fixed ahead. It was like I wasn't even there. "Can you hear me?" I whispered, keeping one eye on the creature, who seemed frozen too, at the far side of the cavern.

As Navan's shoulders relaxed, his growling easing, the creature opened its mouth wide and sang its curious song once more. The effect was instantaneous. It was like something had taken hold of Navan, making panic ripple through his veins, speeding up his breath. I could feel his pulse through his shirt, pounding like mad. Whatever song that creature was singing, it had a hypnotic effect on Navan. Somehow, it was controlling him.

"Navan, listen to my voice," I said, hoping to soothe him back into reality.

His head whipped toward me, his eyes a strange, milky white, their gaze unfocused. I snatched my hand away, staggering back, but he just stood there, his muscles tensed. Drawing back his lips, he flashed his fangs at me. A growl rumbled from his throat. It was a warning.

"It's me... Riley," I breathed, praying that part of him would recognize my voice. There had to be a way to snap him out of this trance. "If you can hear me, reach out for my hand," I said, lifting my own hand in his direction, though I was careful to keep enough distance between us.

His unfocused eyes glanced at my outstretched hand for a moment, but it was clear he had no idea who I was, or what I was doing. As his gaze flicked back up, meeting mine, a second growl emerged from his throat, louder than the last, and his lips curled in a savage snarl.

"Navan, you have to—" I didn't get to finish. Without warning, he lunged at me, his wings spread wide, his fangs flashing hungrily. Before I had a chance to back away, or make a run for the cave exit, his hands grasped me by the shoulders, his fingers digging in until I thought my bones might shatter.

"Stop!" I shouted, but he couldn't hear me. I was speaking to a stranger who didn't recognize me as anything but the enemy. I could see the hatred burning in his white eyes, his mind and body under the influence of the beast's strange song. This was the creature's defense mechanism: it got the encroacher to do the dirty work. It made the attacker become the attacked. I didn't know why the song wasn't affecting me. I could only assume it had something to do with my human genetics.

"Let go!" I yelled, trying to fight against his fierce grip. "Navan, you're hurting me!" I grimaced as his grip tightened, my whole body screaming out against the pain.

As tears of agony pricked my eyes, I lifted my leg and kicked him in the shin as hard as I could. It made no difference. Panic flooded through me, and I tried to slap his face with my tortured arms, but the impact barely made him flinch. I wasn't strong enough, especially not with the sapping effect his savage grip was having on my muscles.

"NAVAN!" I roared, knowing I was running out of options. He wouldn't listen, he couldn't feel anything, and I wasn't powerful enough to force him off me.

Thinking quickly, my arms feeling as though they were about to break in Navan's grasp, I shoved the emberstone against his stomach, gripping the smooth edges as hard as I could, knowing it would heat the stone up to the burning point. I hated to do this to him, but I had no choice. As sparks erupted from within, burning up the fabric of Navan's t-shirt and searing his flesh, I felt his grip on me loosen. His eyes flickered for a moment, a look of recognition passing across his face, just for a second. His mouth opened, as if he wanted to say something, but the moment disappeared as quickly as it had come.

Seizing the opportunity, I slipped out of his grasp before he could grab me again. The emberstone's shock to his system had worked in snapping him out of his trance, but it hadn't been applied for long enough. No, if I was going to snap him out of it completely, then I needed that shock to last longer.

As his eyes went blank again, the white fog intensifying, I turned and ran, wracking my brain for an idea. There *had* to be something I could do to stop him. My feet pounded the hard floor of the icy cave, my mind ever-conscious that I could slip at any moment. If I did, I knew there was every possibility that Navan would actually kill me. He didn't know who I was. To him, I was a faceless enemy, and his only duty was to end me. Even so, I didn't let the slippery terrain slow me down as I sprinted for the cavern's exit.

Behind me, I could hear his wings as he took flight, setting my pulse racing. There was no way I could outrun him for long—but maybe I wouldn't have to. In my head, a desperate idea was forming.

Sprinting out of the cavern, following the sound of rushing water, I turned left, into a tunnel we hadn't been through before. At least Navan wouldn't be able to fly in the narrow tunnel. He'd have to get back on his feet, giving me a momentary advantage. My lungs burning in my chest, I continued to run, keeping the sound of water at the forefront of my focus. I knew it had to give way to actual liquid at some point. If it didn't, I was doomed.

Glancing over my shoulder, I saw that Navan was only a few paces behind me, his eyes terrifyingly blank. I peered farther down the tunnel, and the sight that met me filled my heart with hope. Just in time, I skidded to a halt on the edge of a glittering lake, forcing my body to twist off to the side as Navan barreled past me, plummeting into the ice-cold water below. Panting heavily, I crawled up to the lip of the lakeshore, peering into the dark water, watching the center of the ripples that flowed outward.

"Navan!" I shouted, my voice echoing off the walls.

A splash followed as Navan rose to the surface of the black lake, spluttering as he swam upward, his teeth chattering. If he was cold, I knew the water had to be utterly freezing. He turned as I called his name again, his slate eyes no longer shrouded in that peculiar, milky white veil.

"It's f-freezing!" Navan gasped, his whole body shivering as he swam to the edge of the lake.

"I'm sorry!" I said. "You were in this crazy... trance. It was the only way to snap you out of it."

"It's okay. I just need to warm up," he said shakily. Finding a suitable grip on the lake's shallow ledge, he pulled himself out of the water, his body dripping as he stood.

"Here," I said, handing him the emberstone.

"Thanks. What'd you mean by 'trance,' anyway?" Navan asked. He looked around at the tunnel, obviously noticing that we weren't in the same place we'd started. "Was I *chasing* you?"

"Yeah, but... I got away."

His expression darkened. "I didn't hurt you, did I?"

"No, I'm fine," I said, resisting the urge to rub my shoulders where Navan had gripped me. My skin would probably be a little black and blue, but I didn't want him feeling guilty about something he couldn't have controlled.

We sat on the ground together, Navan holding the emberstone between his hands, until he felt ready to attempt the cavern again. Now that we knew what we were up against, we at least had a chance of stopping it.

Plucking two small wads of moss from the wall of the cave, Navan shoved them into his ears, hoping it would help to block out the siren song of the monster. It was a good idea. I just prayed it would work. I didn't think my nerves could cope with the stress of another hypnosis.

As we reentered the cavern, the monster was ready for us, its beady eyes turned in our direction. It immediately lifted its head and sang its sad song, but this time, it fell on deaf ears. I glanced anxiously in Navan's direction, but the sound didn't seem to be affecting him. I doubted the moss cut the noise out entirely, but it must have been muffling it enough.

Spurred on by this success, we stretched out our wings and lifted into the air. Navan went first, dive-bombing the creature as a distraction, while I plucked the fruit from its back.

The creature wasn't stupid, however. Each time I swooped low to try to snatch up the fruit, it lashed its long tail, or turned suddenly, keeping it just out of my grasp. It was only as Navan skyrocketed downward with all his might, landing on the creature's head with a dull crack, that I got the moment I'd been looking for. With the monster utterly bewildered, I grasped for the fruit, plucking it away in one fell swoop before turning and rushing out of the cavern, my wings beating rapidly. Navan followed in hot pursuit as a sad cry rose from the beast.

The song followed us out into the fresh air as we came to land on the ridge at the edge of the cavemouth, catching our breaths before we took off again. I looked down at the plump fruit in my hands, noticing that the golden veins had ceased their glowing. But it didn't matter now. All that mattered was we had it, and we could use it. We had succeeded.

*T*he journey back to Nessun was far simpler than the journey to the Fazar Mountains. I took a sip from the second vial of wing serum before we left the cave entrance, to make sure we didn't end up landing in a vampiric butterfly-infested swamp on the way, and put the fruit in the burlap sack Navan had slung across his shoulders.

We landed in the warped garden at the back of the palace just as the sun was coming up and casting its faint, cold light across the city. I was exhausted, my wings hanging limply behind me as I caught my breath. I might have had Vysanthean wings on my back, but I didn't yet have Vysanthean stamina.

"You okay?" Navan asked, putting his arm around me.

"Just tired," I said, suddenly aware of eyes on us. Knowing exactly who that burning stare belonged to, I quickly slipped my arms around Navan, as if I were cuddling him to me. Delving my hands into the burlap sack, I grabbed the poroporo fruit and stuffed it down the front of my shirt, under my armpit, before turning back around. I knew my arm looked strange, dangling stiffly by my side, but I hoped Pandora would put it down to the weakness of my species, thinking me unable to handle a simple flight to the midnight market and back.

Navan kept his arm around me, shielding the fruit from sight. We looked up at Pandora, who was lingering in the doorway of the forgotten palace exit. It wasn't clear how long she'd been waiting there, but she looked almost happy to see us.

"Good night?" she asked as we moved toward her.

"Pretty good," Navan replied, with a shy smile. I grinned in response, looking up at him with loving eyes, both of us playing the mood just right.

"Must have been, if you're only just getting back," she said, with a hint of a nudge and a wink in her words. "Anyway, spare me the details. Did you get the things I asked for?"

"It's all here." The strange expression on Navan's face worried me. It was the same one he'd had at the market, when he'd frozen, purchasing the last item on the list.

"Thank you. Really, I appreciate you going to the trouble, even if you did bring it back a little later than I was expecting," she remarked, her tone not exactly warm. Then again, I wasn't sure a woman like Pandora knew how to be warm. She always seemed to be on guard, her mind always on the job. I almost felt sorry for her, hoping she found time to let her purple hair down once in a while.

"Sorry, we got carried away," I chimed in.

Pandora smiled, though it seemed forced. "You two should be getting back to your apartment. If you'd be so kind as to return my key, I'll leave you to run along before someone catches you," she said, holding out her hand.

"Could you do one thing for Riley, if it's not too much trouble?" Navan asked as he handed over the silver key, the black device, and the sack of ingredients.

Pandora frowned. "You're asking me for a favor?"

"In a manner of speaking," Navan replied evenly. "With her new wings, she keeps ripping her shirts. I was wondering if you could ask Brisha to send some with wing-slits since you'll see her before we do."

"That is a favor I can do," she conceded, shouldering the sack of ingredients.

With an awkward nod of goodbye, we ascended the

interior staircase, coming out through the abandoned storage closet. I kept expecting Pandora to follow us, but no echo of footsteps sounded on the stairwell. In the courtyard, she had seemed off somehow, in a way I couldn't pinpoint. Maybe our lovey-doveyness had made her uncomfortable. Interspecies romance wasn't a crime in Northern Vysanthe, but that didn't mean everyone approved.

Pushing the negative thoughts away, knowing they were coming from a tired mind, I slipped my arm through Navan's and leaned against him as we returned to our chambers. With the coast clear, I removed the fruit from my armpit and held it tight, keeping it tucked under the edge of my shirt. Only when we got back to the room did I set it down, hiding it in the drawer of the side table next to our bed for safekeeping.

Never in my life had a bed looked more appealing. After the long journey, exhaustion finally hit me, my shoulders burning, my back twinging, my neck stiff and aching. And yet, as Navan snuck up behind me and slipped his arms around my waist, his lips nuzzling at the curve of my neck, I wondered if I might find a second wind somewhere inside me... Where the trip had sapped me, it seemed to have reenergized Navan.

I turned around in his arms and stared up into his heated gaze. He leaned down to trail kisses along the sensitive skin of my neck, sending shivers all the way to my toes. His hands rested on my hips, his fingers wandering along my waistband. A flood of warmth filled me, and I pressed closer to him, until our bodies were flush against each other. I could feel how much he wanted me, could imagine us undressing and moving onto the bed. This was it. We were really going to do it.

My stomach fluttered with nervousness at the thought. A million questions raced through my mind, and, for an instant, my body tensed.

Navan pulled away, the heat in his eyes replaced with a questioning look. Without saying a word, he wandered over to the fireplace, adding more silvery logs to the blaze. He crouched there, staring into the flames, lifting one palm to check the heat. Somehow, I felt both disappointed and relieved.

"Is this how it's always going to be?" I whispered. "We get so far, and then... we stop?"

Navan didn't turn as he replied. "I don't want to rush into anything because you think it's what I want."

He sounded almost guilty, as if he'd been pressuring me into it—even though that couldn't be further from the truth. "But I... I want it, too," I said, a blush heating my face.

Navan looked over his shoulder at me, his eyes darkening as they flicked down my body, making me blush even harder. The feeling of his attentive gaze made me crave more.

He stood and shook his head, as if to clear it. "You're not quite ready yet. I can see it in your eyes. There's something holding you back."

I swallowed hard, amazed that he could read me so well. "It's just that... I have no idea what I'm doing."

"Riley." Navan stepped toward me, and my heart pounded. He rested his hand gently on my cheek. "I want it to happen when the time is right. I want it to happen when *you* are ready for it to happen. When there are no reservations left in your mind. And if there's ever anything you want to know, just ask." His voice was low and full of understanding.

"I have a million questions," I whispered, beyond grateful for his patience. It was true: a hint of resistance sparked in me whenever things got too heated between us. Throughout my teenage years, I'd tended to ignore those thoughts, knowing a day would come when I'd want to sleep with someone... but then that day just hadn't arrived. Not until the moment Navan entered my life. Angie had always called me a prude, but I didn't care. I knew I would never do something with someone until I was truly ready, and it made me happy to know that Navan felt the same.

"I'm all ears," Navan murmured, kissing my shoulder. I gave a playful yelp as he scooped me up in his arms and carried me over to the bed. He lay me down on the covers and snuggled in beside me.

I smiled sleepily. "I think the questions might have to wait for now." I yawned, my eyelids growing heavier. "If I say another word, I'm pretty sure I'll fall asleep on you."

He chuckled, pulling me up onto his chest as he wrapped his arms around me. "I don't mind you falling asleep on me," he said, kissing the top of my head. As my eyes closed, he mumbled something else, but sleep claimed me before I could hear the words.

* * *

After grabbing a few hours of rest, Navan and I dragged ourselves out of the apartment and went to visit Bashrik and Angie. We had until the evening before training began again, and we figured we should spend our time wisely.

We found them standing to the side of a small hut that had been set out on a patch of sparse grass beside the building site for the new alchemy lab, which seemed to be coming along nicely. Naturally, they were in the middle of a spat, Angie jabbing her finger at a blueprint that Bashrik was holding out in front of him.

"If you put the load-bearing pillar there, then the

whole thing will be unstable," she said. "I thought *you* were supposed to be the architect?"

"Yes, but if we don't put one here, then the building won't be balanced. One side will slope down like a bloody avalanche!" he snapped back. "What I'm suggesting is, we put one here *and* one there, to stabilize the whole building."

Angie rolled her eyes. "That's what I've been saying all morning. Do you just not listen to a single word I say?"

They stopped bickering as we approached, though I couldn't wipe the smirk off my face. I flashed Angie a knowing look, as it was beginning to dawn on me what was really going on here. She blushed, turning sharply away, pretending to look at something off in the distance. She couldn't fool me, though. I knew this side of Angie. I had seen it enough times before to recognize when she was harboring a secret crush on someone. Most of the boys I'd seen her fall madly in love with had barely survived her preamble to dating.

"What's it going to look like?" Navan asked, stepping up beside Bashrik to examine the blueprint.

"Here, I'll show you," he replied, gesturing for us all to come into the hut.

Dutifully, we all stepped inside. My jaw dropped as I saw the miniature model of the new alchemy lab. It rested on a table and had clearly been mocked up in a short amount of time, but the effect was no less impressive than if he had spent weeks on it. A towering, silvery behemoth of glittering spires shot up like shards of splintered glass, fracturing at the top and curving back under themselves like frozen ocean waves. In fact, the whole thing reminded me of a frozen ocean scene, with the translucent walls that glinted both blue and silver, depending on which way the light hit. At the top was a platform of hexagonal greenhouses, presumably where rare fruits and plants could be grown onsite, as well as several massive structures that looked like generators. To maintain a lab that size, I supposed they had to handle a lot of power.

"It's beautiful," I murmured, ducking down so I could better see some of the details.

"Well, it is my magnum opus," Bashrik replied proudly. "It better be the most beautiful thing *anyone* has seen."

"Listen to him—'magnum opus.' Who do you think you are, Leonardo da Vinci?" Angie muttered.

"I don't even know who that is, Angie," Bashrik replied dryly. "You might think you're hilarious, and where you come from, your jokes might get a polite clap, but they're pointless on me."

Angie grinned at me. "He's just mad because I made fun of his magnum opus, and you must *never* do that."

Navan put an arm around his brother's shoulder. "Hey, um... I might need your help with something."

Bashrik frowned. "What?"

"I'm about to get started on a concentrated serum from the poroporo fruit we picked up last night," Navan began, only to be cut off by Angie.

"You went? You got it?" she said, her eyes wide. "Lauren said you might be going, but we didn't hear anything from you, and Bashrik told me we couldn't swing by to call on you this morning, though I've got no idea why," she said, flashing Bashrik a look.

I smiled, my cheeks flushing pink at the memory of Bashrik walking in on us. I knew exactly why he hadn't wanted to swing by, but I wasn't about to say anything in front of him. "Yeah, we went, and we got it, and now we need to figure out a way of making it into a potent serum, strong enough to get Yorrek to tell us what we need to know," I replied.

"You run into anything bad?" Bashrik asked, his voice tensing as he turned to his brother.

Navan shrugged. "The usual suspects, but nothing we couldn't handle," he said casually, sparing Bashrik's nerves. He gave me a conspiratorial glance. "Anyway, I need to get my hands on a few things. A centrifuge, a Veracian extractor, and a black diamond compressor. I thought I might be able to get some of them at the market last night, but it was slim pickings where tech was concerned."

"I think there are some things like those lying around, from the ruins of the old lab. Some of the underground storage chambers were relatively unharmed, so I should be able to get that stuff to you. I'll do it as soon as I can," Bashrik said. "Actually, I might have to send *you* on an errand for them later," he added, looking reluctantly at Angie.

"You know it's anything for you, Bash," she replied sweetly, giving him a saccharine smile.

He frowned. "You know, you look really creepy when you smile at me like that. Like you're plotting my death or something."

Angie's smile widened.

"Has Yorrek been back at all?" I asked, distracting their attention away from one another. He was the most important piece of this puzzle.

Angie gave me a strange look that made me feel suddenly nervous. "About that... Yorrek used to come to the site every day, to check up on things and give us a daily earful about how slow and useless we are, but he hasn't been around in a few days. Whether he's decided to wait for information, or he's just being lazy, we don't know. What we do know is, he's not going to be as easy to kidnap if he's not around here to kidnap.

You know what I mean?" Her expression turned apologetic, and she wrung her hands.

I almost swore out loud. The journey to the Fazar Mountains hadn't exactly been a breeze, but I should've known all of this was going too smoothly. There had yet to be a real hiccup, but here it was, as imminent and expected as a bus not arriving when it was pouring down rain.

"It makes it harder, but not impossible," Navan cut in. "If he's not coming to us anymore, then we'll have to scout out his house, in the village outside Nessun. There might be a reason he doesn't want to come into town anymore, and if there *is* a reason, we should find out."

"That's not a bad idea," Bashrik said. "Plus, it might give us a better chance of discreetly snatching him, if we try to take him from his house later on. If you know the exits and entrances, and what the old man likes to do during the day, we'll be in a better position once the serum is ready."

After a momentary dip into optimism, I realized all wasn't lost after all. It was a slight change in plans, but nothing too extreme. No, this was still going to work, I was sure of it. As soon as Navan had the hypnosis serum concocted, we'd be back on track.

"Why don't Angie and I go, since Bashrik and you will be busy with the lab and the serum?" I suggested.

Navan immediately frowned at me. "You two go, alone? I don't like the sound of that."

"Well, I have no idea how to make potions, and neither does Angie. Our skills will definitely be better suited to the task of scoping out Yorrek's place, and we need to utilize our time as efficiently as possible. I promise we'll be careful." Besides, it had been ages since Angie and I had had any alone time to catch up on things. If nothing else, I was intrigued to know exactly what was going on between her and Bashrik. It would be the perfect opportunity to ask.

"I still don't like it," Navan grumbled.

"They'll be okay," Bashrik said firmly, and I couldn't help but gawk at him. I hadn't expected him to back me up on this, given that he was usually the bundle of nerves. Then again, I was guessing he was probably motivated by the prospect of getting some headspace, being apart from Angie for an hour or two. "It's not going to be that dangerous a task. They're just scoping out the area. Riley's definitely done more dangerous things. As long as they keep their faces covered and their intentions vague, they'll be absolutely fine."

Navan's expression was still sour, but it was clear he wasn't going to argue. He needed to get used to the idea that he couldn't always be around to protect me, shadowing my every move, and I needed to develop a sense of self-reliance here on this alien planet.

Saying that, I knew I'd take my knives along with me, in case anything unexpected happened. I had learned to be cautious, my mind always expecting the unexpected.

After all, that seemed to be Vysanthe's motto.

10

*N*avan and Bashrik joined us as we returned to the palace chambers to grab a few things. Much to my delight, I found that a stack of shirts had been delivered. They were waiting for me on the bed, each bearing the flexible wing-slits in the back. I knew I wasn't likely to need my wings on the journey to Yorrek's house, but I couldn't help myself. I threw one on eagerly, knowing it would make my life a whole lot easier. It was the closest to coldblood I'd ever felt. Suitably dressed, I moved over to the big trunk in our apartment's living room. I couldn't access the bandolier of throwing knives I kept in the training center, but I had a spare one stowed away in the trunk, ready for occasions like this.

"Where did you get those?" Bashrik whistled as we

entered the chambers that Lauren and Angie shared so Angie could pick up her jacket. Bashrik had his own room, farther down the same hallway.

I smiled, feeling proud of my bandolier and the personalized blades slotted along the length of the leather-like material. "It was a gift from Queen Brisha," I explained, fastening my coat around myself to keep the weapons hidden.

Bashrik paled. "You should see the pile of things that keep coming to my door from her. There's more and more of every day," he groaned, gesturing toward a mountain of objects that stood against the far wall of the living area. "I even had to ask the girls if I could put some stuff in here. It was getting ridiculous in my chambers."

I walked over to the pile of gifts. There were gems and jewels, cuffs and bracelets, all still in their packaging. There were vials too, though the majority looked untouched.

"Has Queen Brisha actually talked to you about this?" I asked, turning back to him.

"Not yet. I'm dreading she'll make an appearance, one of these days," he muttered darkly. "There is one thing I've been eager to try, however..." He walked over to the pile of gifts and plucked a small blue vial out of a wooden box. "In fact, I've been looking forward to this all day."

"What is it?" I asked, frowning at the little glass bottle.

"The blood of a Haligon. It arrived this morning, with a note for me to have an enlightening breakfast," he explained. "It's supposed to be some of the finest blood in the universe, though it's super rare. How she got her hands on it, I've got no idea. Though, I suppose she *is* the queen." He shrugged. "Anyway, I was saving it for this evening, but I might have it now, to get me through the rest of the day," he said, removing the stopper and lifting it to his lips.

Navan rushed past me in a blur, swiping the vial out of Bashrik's hand with a violent shove. The glass bottle crashed to the ground and shattered into a thousand pieces, a deep purple liquid oozing out.

"What the hell, man!" Bashrik yelled, his expression shocked.

"I *knew* that's what she was up to," Navan said, dipping a finger in the liquid and bringing it up to his nostrils, sniffing it intently.

"Care to tell me what's going on?" Bashrik asked, his tone still tense.

Navan flashed his brother an apologetic look. "We were asked to get some things from the market last night, for the queen. Pandora caught us sneaking out, so we couldn't exactly say no. Anyway, I thought nothing of it, until I read the list again. It reminded me of something, but it had been so long since I'd made one, I couldn't be sure of the ingredients. I just knew something felt off. Now I know why. She made you a love elixir, Bash. That's what's in that vial."

Bashrik looked aghast. "I knew she'd come for me eventually," he whispered, horrified. "I kept thinking I could keep her at bay... but this? This is taking things to another level! How am I supposed to fend off the advances of a *queen*, for Rask's sake!" he cried, much to my amusement. I couldn't help it—it was too comical not to laugh. Even Navan looked like he was struggling not to chuckle. Angie, however, remained stony-faced, strangely not amused at all by the events.

"You be a man, and tell her you're not interested," she said firmly, before turning from the room, flipping up her hood and pulling it tight around her face.

I shrugged, then followed, leaving the two cold-bloods speechless in the apartment. I guessed it was always good to keep them on their toes.

Angie and I set off on foot to find Yorrek's house. I kept thinking about the wing serum in my pocket, wanting to feel the power of the wings behind me, but knew they would be pointless with Angie here. I didn't want to risk carrying her without Navan present. I wasn't quite that confident yet.

"I can't believe she's sending him all these things. Doesn't she have anything better to do?" Angie muttered as we walked along. "Honestly, as queen of half a nation, you'd think she'd have something more important to keep her busy. I'm sick of hearing Bashrik knock at my door every morning, and then having to deal with whatever gift she's sent because *he* can't fit it in his place."

"Methinks the lady doth protest too much," I said, nudging her arm.

She scowled. "I'm not protesting. I just think, as leader of half a planet, she should be able to prioritize. I hardly think chasing after some nobody coldblood is a good use of her time, not when she should be focusing on bringing about peace, or war, or whatever it is she's doing in this stupid conflict with her sister," she said, folding her arms across her chest. "Plus, I don't think it's fair to Bashrik. I mean, sending gifts is one thing, but making a love potion? It's borderline pathetic, and frankly immoral. Bashrik doesn't like her, so she should let it go."

"The lady definitely protests too much." I chuckled, knowing my teasing was infuriating her. And yet, I could see the truth in all of this: she had feelings for Bashrik. She just couldn't admit it to herself. As her friend, it was my duty to get an honest answer out of her. "It's okay if you like him, you know," I said, softening my tone.

"I don't like *Bashrik!*" She snorted, as if the idea were ludicrous.

I grinned. "I think you do. Why else would you be so bothered about what Queen Brisha does? I mean, we've all been that girl, pining over a boy who doesn't like us back. I would've expected sympathy from you, but instead, all I see is jealousy," I prodded.

"I am *not* jealous of the queen and Bashrik," she insisted tersely. "The queen can do whatever she wants. I just don't think she should be forcing Bashrik to like her. I'm not interested in who he *does* like. I'm just interested in seeing injustices stopped, that's all," she added vehemently, her cheeks turning a bright shade of scarlet.

"'Injustices stopped.'" I smirked. "Really, now. You can't fool me, Angie. I know what it's like to have feelings for one of these coldbloods, and I know how weird it is to admit. Once you do, you'll feel better," I said encouragingly, though Angie wasn't having any of it.

"I don't like him, Riley! How could I?" she ranted. "He's so full of himself! I don't think I've ever met a man so arrogant. Yes, his drawings and buildings are some of the most beautiful I've ever seen, but that doesn't give him the right to brag all the time. And he's always so condescending, like I'm this useless little creature that has to be protected. Whenever I step up onto the building site, he puts his arm around me, as if he's expecting me to trip on a pebble or something. I tell him off, but he keeps doing it! Not to mention the fact that he thinks he's right all the time, and he never backs down when he's wrong. Besides, he's way too tall for someone like me, and I wouldn't even know what to do with muscles like that. It must be like cuddling a block of cement. No way do I like him—not a chance!"

I sighed, holding up my hands in surrender. "Okay, if you say you're not interested, then I believe you," I lied, knowing full well that she didn't believe my words either.

As we continued on through the city, I let the topic rest, talking about less incendiary subjects instead. We discussed how the building was coming along, and how she was enjoying her peculiar apprenticeship in architecture, while she asked about my military training and the adventure in the cave the night before. It was nice just to wander and chat, the way we would have done if we were back home. Glancing at her, I realized I missed it. Navan was handsome and charming and wonderful, but sometimes a girl just needed her friends. If Lauren had been here too, I knew it would have felt complete.

It was a fairly short walk to the Vysanthean equivalent of a train station. The station itself sat beneath a concave glass roof that curved upward. Coldbloods were rushing in and out, their eyes staring up at blinking boards that showed a number of platforms and destinations. The oddly domestic, banal scene made me laugh. It seemed that, no matter where you went, there were always commuters trying to beat the rush.

We entered, pulling our hoods up around our faces as we went to the ticket machines and pressed what I hoped were the right buttons for two tickets to Pala-mon. Navan had instructed me on how to do it, since the machine was all symbols I didn't recognize, but sure enough, two silver discs clattered out. I picked them up and handed one to Angie, and we went in search of our platform. In the end, I had to ask a passing coldblood which one it was, but he answered without a hint of derision, too preoccupied with dashing away to observe the color of my skin, so pink and human beneath the hood of my fur coat.

With barely a minute to spare, we jumped onto the train and sat down, just as it pulled away from the station. Catching our breath, we both sat back, though my eyes trailed toward the window, where the Vysanthean world was flashing past in every shade of gray, white, black, and silver imaginable. Now and again, flashes of dark green blurred by as we passed a patch of woodland, but there was little color to this planet.

A few other passengers dotted the train, though nobody seemed eager to speak to one another. The sight reminded me of the subway in New York City, where it was pretty much a crime to make conversation. I wondered just how similar humans and Vysantheans were, at their very core.

Fifteen minutes later, the train pulled into Palamon station. We got off as quickly as we could, but the doors almost closed on us. Glaring at them for almost taking my hand off, I turned and walked toward the gates, with Angie following after. We waved our silver discs over the flashing beacon and exited into a strangely suburban world.

Everything was quiet, with quaint houses in the near distance, complete with low picket fences and boxed-off gardens that grew what they could in the harsh flowerbeds. Coldbloods walked hand in hand with their coldblood children—a weird sight, in truth, though it was undeniably cute to see them open out their small wings and flap them enthusiastically, only to be pulled down by a stern-faced parent.

Checking the map for Yorrek's house, Angie gestured to the right. We walked away from the station and headed down a silent main road. We kept going—past shops, a park, a glittering lake—until we reached the edge of a forest. The leaves swayed in the cold breeze, whispering secrets. Ahead, bathed in the shadow of the woodland, was a single house. It looked like a fairytale cottage, with a slate roof and white-washed walls, and a small garden out front that bore cream-colored roses in a flowerbed protected by glass.

And yet, there was something strange about it.

"Is this his house?" I asked, as Angie checked the map again.

She nodded. "This is the one."

The windows, rather than being aesthetically pleasing like the rest of the house, were boarded up with thick steel panels. Where a pretty door might have once been, now stood a solid metal shutter, with various panels. Flashing an uncertain look at each other, we pulled our hoods closer to our faces and opened the front gate. I felt for my bandolier of knives, readying my hand to unzip my jacket.

As we walked through the garden, Angie stumbled, her foot sinking into one of the stone slabs that formed the pathway. An alarm shrieked, the sound piercing through the air, splitting my eardrums. Angie looked up, terror in her eyes. A split second later, small openings in the side of the house slid up.

"Get down!" I yelled. Flying missiles shot from the openings. Angie managed to extricate her foot just in time for us to duck and roll out of the way. The missiles were sharp, barbed arrows with blinking tips, one of which whizzed right past my ear, making my heart stop. I lay there, panting on the ground, willing the howling siren to cease so I could get my mind to think clearly.

"Yorrek, turn off your alarms!" Angie bellowed, her voice echoing across the garden. "It's me from the build site! Turn your alarms off. I want to speak with you. I've got an update about the lab!" she continued, her voice loud, even above the alarms.

A moment later, the alarms stopped abruptly, followed by the grate of scraping metal as the shutter of the door rolled up. Relieved, I got up and headed toward it, only to find another shutter behind it, just as solid as the first. Angie stepped up beside me, both of us evidently expecting Yorrek to emerge... but there was no sign of him anywhere.

And then, a bluish image flickered in front of us, the picture solidifying to show an old man with wispy gray hair and a steely black stare. His shoulders were hunched, his features pointed and chinless, giving him the appearance of some sort of vulture.

"Don't you have anything better to do than come and harass your respected elders?" the hologram barked. "Look at you, dressed up like lesser-furred mangolins. You look ridiculous. Take your hoods down!"

We did as he instructed, though I wasn't sure how he'd react to two underlings being sent to his door. He made his thoughts known as soon as we revealed our faces.

"Oh, of course they'd send *you!*" he snapped, looking at Angie. "What, is everyone too busy? They had to send their little slaves to do their dirty work? I suppose you're going to tell me it'll be months until my lab is ready. You expect me to wait around here, with all these eyes on me? You *want* them to get me, don't you? Yes, that's it, isn't it? They've sent you to check if I'm still alive? Well, I am, so you can go and tell whoever sent you that they need to try a little harder if they want to get rid of me!" he cried, violently flailing his thin arms around.

"Yorrek, it's me. It's Angie, from the building site," Angie repeated. "Bashrik sent me. You haven't been around in a few days, and he thought it might be nice if I came and invited you to check on the lab's progress, in case you felt he'd been too harsh with you last time," she explained softly, though they were difficult words to believe. I couldn't imagine anyone wanting this guy around.

"So you think me to be a little child who can't handle a bit of banter between males?" Yorrek snorted.

Angie sighed. "No, not at all, Yorrek. He just wanted you to come and give your opinion, since you're going to be working there the most," she replied, trying a different tactic.

Yorrek shook his head angrily. "Nothing will induce me to go outside, so you can turn around and forget about it!" he muttered. "I'm going to stay in the safety of my house, with every security measure I can get my hands on, and conduct my experiments here until the alchemy lab is complete."

I frowned. "Why would you want to do that? Isn't that awfully lonely?"

He scoffed. "It might be a solitary existence, but at least I'll stay alive!"

"What do you mean?" I asked.

"There is someone stalking me, trying to gain intelligence on the immortality elixir. They think I'm not onto them, but I am," he murmured, his holographic eyes flashing left and right, checking every angle for approaching danger. He had apparently judged us to be safe, given our inferiority. "Now, before I get my missiles out again, I'd like you to get off my porch and scram! You're drawing attention to me, you idiots!" he snapped, startling us into backing away.

Even so, his hologram didn't disappear until we had stepped out of the garden. I looked to Angie, seeing my own disappointment reflected on her face. It was clear now that we had no way of capturing Yorrek, even if we had the serum ready. I had my knives, and the others had their strength and skills, but what good were they against a solid metal door and an ultra-high-tech security system? Even with everyone's forces combined, we'd be dead or brutally injured before we pried Yorrek out of that shell.

Realization dawned on me like a punch in the face. We were running out of ways to gather intel for Orion, and time was running out.

11

*L*ater that night, with the Vysanthean moon glowing above me, its silvery surface tinged with the faintest hint of red, I dragged myself away from the training center, with every muscle aching, feeling like the walking dead. Navan had been asked to stay behind for some one-on-one coaching, and I was secretly glad of the time alone.

The training session had been just as tough as I'd feared it would be, with us performing aerial assaults on one another in the darkness. Even with the wing serum, I was at a disadvantage again. The coldbloods could see better in the dark than I could, meaning I'd been battered and thrown in every direction, from all angles. I could see my fellow trainees were relishing it, being able to exact their revenge after the prize I'd been given by the queen. They wanted to take me down a peg or two, which was to be expected. I just wished they could do it in a gentler way.

It had been relentless, with us moving on to flight simulators in some of the small vessel replicas they kept in the huge training hangar. Half of us had been out of the ships, while the other half were in the cockpits. Obviously, I had been outside of the vessels, getting annihilated by the simulated gunfire of the training ships. We were supposed to find a way on board without getting shot out of the sky, but I hadn't managed it. Everyone else had. That fact stuck in my throat as I made my way back to the palace. So far, I'd managed to keep up with the coldbloods, to some extent. This was the first time I'd felt like an actual failure.

Knowing I needed a pick-me-up, I decided to visit Lauren in the library, to update her on the status of our intel efforts. I'd promised Angie I'd do it before I left for training, but a last-minute nap had eaten up my time. It didn't matter, though. Lauren would still be nose-deep in books, having forgotten the outside world even existed.

As I followed the familiar route to the library, the unsuccessful excursion to see Yorrek weighed on my mind, with Orion's name glowing like a neon sign in my head. It was always there, a constant reminder of what he could do if we didn't get him what he wanted. I thought of Roger and Jean and felt a shiver of dread run through me. No matter what, I couldn't let anything happen to them.

I knocked on the library door, praying it wouldn't be Queen Brisha who answered. A minute or so later, the door creaked open, and Lauren's bespectacled eyes peered out, like she was a mole emerging from its hole for the first time in months. A chuckle rippled from my throat, and a smile spread across Lauren's face.

"Riley!" She grabbed my hand and pulled me inside, where a blast of stale, fierce heat hit me full in the face. The fire was blazing, but the evening's training had left me hot and sweaty, to the point where such warmth felt almost unbearable.

"I thought I'd come and give you an update, since we haven't seen a lot of you lately," I said, wiping beads of perspiration from my brow.

She shrugged. "What do you expect when you put me in a library like this? There are so many books! I can't help myself." I knew exactly what she was like, where books were concerned. If she was buried in an interesting book, the sexiest man in the world could walk past her and she wouldn't notice.

"Hopefully you're doing a lot better than the rest of us, then," I replied. "Which is kind of why I'm here. We've had a little hiccup with gathering information from Yorrek. He's got this insane security system set up because, for some reason, he thinks somebody is following him and wants to squeeze him for information... someone other than us, that is," I explained, trying to rein in my frustration.

She grimaced. "He's definitely a bit of a weirdo. I've run into him a couple of times at the building site, when I've gone to see Angie and Bashrik," she explained. "If he's not going to come out of his house, that's no good at all. Has anyone come up with another way we might get some information about the elixir?"

"Not yet, no, though we're all working on it. Do you think you could have a look through some of these books, see if there's anything else we might use? Maybe there's a book on disarming intricate security systems in one easy move," I muttered.

"I'll see what I can find, but, yeah, I don't think it'll be that easy," she said, her eyes already sweeping over the shelves.

"I'm surprised the queen isn't here," I said, glancing around, just to be sure.

"Well, she was here, but she left about an hour ago," Lauren said, grimacing. "She was really upset about something, but I didn't dare ask her what was up. I'm not really sure what you do with weeping queens, so I thought it best not to say anything. Anyway, she was sobbing by the fire for a while, and I couldn't just leave her all alone, but when I came over to offer her a cup of tea, she got up and ran off."

"You're... You're sure she was crying?" I asked.

Lauren nodded, a sad look on her face. "It was that big, ugly crying you do when you're really upset, you know?"

I did know, but I also knew there were only two reasons for tears like that: death and love. With the odds narrowed down, I had a feeling I knew *precisely* what—or rather, who—was responsible for Brisha's tears, and if we were going to stay on her good side, it struck me that this might be an excellent opportunity. After all, she was just a young woman, like the rest of us, trying to make her way in the world.

"Do you mind if I head out for a while?" I asked, flashing Lauren an apologetic look. Even though we were all so busy, I felt as though I'd been neglecting her. "I promise I'll come back to chat some more, and we can talk about things other than doom and gloom, but there's something I have to do first."

"No problem." She shrugged, though I could tell she was a tad disappointed. "Got plenty of books to keep me company."

"You'll have me to keep you company later, I promise," I assured her, before heading to the door and stepping out into the hallway.

I hurried toward the main hall, knowing there

would be someone there who could take me to the queen. Her private chambers were top secret, undoubtedly hidden away in some far corner of the beautiful palace, but I was determined to track her down.

"Could you escort me to Queen Brisha, please?" I asked, striding up to one of the guards on duty.

He shot me a dirty look. "Not a chance."

"She'll want to see me," I insisted. "And, if you don't take me, I'll let her know precisely who it was who kept her personal aide from her," I added, pursing my lips.

"You're that Kryptonian girl, aren't you?" he asked, his features darkening. "The one the queen's so fond of?"

"That's me."

"Well then, I wouldn't want to keep her pet away from her, now, would I?" he said coldly. I wanted to smack him for calling me that, but knew it would get me nowhere. In Vysanthe, I had to play along.

"No, you wouldn't," I remarked sweetly.

"Fine, come with me." He sighed bitterly, then marched up the main hall, where he disappeared through a side door. I followed, running to keep up with his stride, through a network of hallways and corridors, until I was completely disoriented. Only the mountain ranges, visible through the windows, gave me some idea of how high up we were.

At the end of a narrow passageway, he paused,

bundling me into an open elevator. He passed his bracelet—which resembled the ones we'd been given at the training center—over a sensor. The doors slid closed, and the elevator shot upward. It opened onto a wide foyer, where a pleasant-faced young coldblood male sat behind a desk, his eyes going wide in surprise as I appeared, creeping nervously out of the elevator doors.

"Can I help you?" the coldblood asked, arching an eyebrow.

I smiled. "I'm looking for the queen. I think she might be in need of some assistance," I said in a low voice, flashing him a conspiratorial look.

He nodded in understanding. "Ah, yes, I believe she may need some help," he replied solemnly, gesturing toward the large silver double doors behind him. They were two of the grandest doors I'd ever seen, embellished with glittering diamond patterns and rose-gold filigree. "She's in the bathroom. If you go through those doors, past the sitting area, and down the corridor up the black steps, you can't miss it," he instructed, though it sounded pretty complex to me.

"Thank you," I murmured, before skirting around the desk and pushing on through the elegant doors.

I was met by an apartment that made my jaw drop. The left and right walls housed giant windows that seemed to be forged from one-way glass. They had to be, because no such windows were visible from the outside. From here, I could see all of Nessun stretching away toward the mountains. A sunken seating area lay in front of me, with plush sofas and loveseats arranged around a stone fireplace.

I walked across the vast sitting area, past bookshelves filled to the brim with tomes, and made my way toward a small set of black marble steps that led into a wide hallway. I heard something echo from a room at the end of the corridor. It sounded like soft snuffling, as though a hedgehog were rustling through leaves, only more human than that. Well, more cold-blood, anyway.

Tentatively, I knocked on the door of the last room.

"Who is it?" Queen Brisha asked, in a muffled voice.

"It's Riley, Your Highness. I wanted to come and see how you were doing. I swung by the library, but Lauren said you weren't there," I explained, hoping she didn't blame Lauren for spilling the beans about her tears.

"Come in," the queen said, her tone surprised.

I almost froze at the threshold when I saw the bird's nest piled high on top of Brisha's head, with flower-encrusted barrettes shoved in at random. Her beautiful pale copper hair had been backcombed to within an inch of its life, and there were bright blue streaks in it that did nothing for her coloring or her appearance. It looked like a child had been at her with a magic marker, playing a prank while she was asleep.

"What do you think of it?" she asked, looking at me through the huge looking glass of her vanity. "Tell me the truth," she added, her face twisting into an uncertain grimace. It was a look I knew myself, from my many teenage faux pas: the crimper, cornrows with glittery butterflies in them, pigtails past the age of six, thick streaks of blond—there had been too many to list.

I walked across the enormous bathroom, in which everything seemed carved directly from slabs of exquisite marble, and sat down on a chair beside her. It was a bold move, but I had a feeling that what she needed was a confidante, a friend she could be herself with. In a position like hers, I doubted she had anyone she could trust, which almost made me feel worse, since she couldn't trust me either.

"It's not a great look, Your Highness," I said reluctantly. "I would lie to you, but I know that's not what you want. And, I don't want to hurt your feelings, but you're such a beautiful woman, and this does nothing for you." I gestured toward the mess, hoping she didn't send for her guards and have me executed for my impertinence.

She smiled as she took out the flowery barrettes, one by one. "I appreciate your candor, Riley. Most people would have stood in this room and lied to my face, allowing me to look like a fool in front of everyone. Tomorrow, you'd have seen this hairstyle in the streets, even though everyone would know it looked idiotic," she murmured, with a tight chuckle.

"It's not the hair that's upsetting you, though, is it, Your Highness?" I pressed, emboldened. "We could sit here and pretend everything is okay, but the truth is, I heard something was wrong and wanted to check on you. I don't like to hear of anyone being sad, least of all a woman as fierce and strong as you."

Queen Brisha looked as though she were about to cry again, her eyes glittering, her hand clutching at a handkerchief that lay out on the vanity surface. And then, to my surprise, she seemed to rally, her gaze fixed on mine through the mirror. "Riley, do you believe love to be a force stronger than any species in the universe? Do you think it might be the one unifying thing that ties us all together—a supernatural wonder that nobody can explain?" she asked, her face almost childlike in its uncertainty.

I sat in silence for a moment, not knowing what to say to something like that. Queen Brisha definitely wasn't the person I thought I'd ever have a discussion like this with, either. To me, love had always seemed like some intangible, powerful thing, just out of my grasp. Even with Navan, there was no certainty of our love. I could look down and see the flashing light of the climpet I wore above my heart, but did that explain the connection between us? No, that was something else entirely—something that no gemstone could ever represent or encompass.

"I think love is inexplicable. It makes no sense, and yet it can be the sincerest thing in the world," I replied, trying to feel out an answer. "It makes fools and heroes of us all, Your Highness."

She smiled. "I like that... It makes fools and heroes of us all," she repeated.

"It's just a silly thought that came to me, Your Highness, though I think it's probably true," I said, trying really hard not to look at her ridiculous hairstyle. In this scenario, love had definitely made a fool out of her.

"It is very true." Queen Brisha struggled to brush out the backcombed knots in her hair. "Tell me, Riley, how would you go about seeking love, if you desired someone? How did you and Navan end up together? Your romance is so heartwarming. One can see how extraordinary it is, simply from the way you look at one another. If I found somebody who made me feel like that, do you think the same could happen? Do you think love could blossom?" Her expression was both anxious and earnest.

"I think love can only blossom if it's reciprocated, Your Highness," I replied, knowing she was speaking about Bashrik. She was clearly besotted with him, but it would do her no good. She needed to move on before it crossed the line into a true, worrisome obsession.

She frowned. "And if I wasn't sure of their feelings?"

"Your Highness, if somebody loves you the way you deserve to be loved, then they will let you know," I explained kindly. "If you're not sure, chances are there is nothing there to seek out. Don't settle for mediocre, Your Highness. Find someone you can be extraordinary with," I encouraged, hoping she caught my drift. The last thing I wanted her doing was slipping Bashrik another love potion.

"That's it!" she cried, a grin spreading across her face. "I need to make my love known! How else can he be sure of my affections, if I keep it to myself like this?"

"Wait, Your Highness, that's not—" I tried to cut in, but she was on a roll.

Giggling in delight, she turned to me and grasped my face in her hands. "Thank you, Riley! This is the most wondrous advice you could have given me. With the seasons about to change, it's the perfect time. I'll announce a national holiday and open up the gardens to everyone I know. Oh, and I'll invite the public along too, and insist upon street parties and a carnival to celebrate. *There*, I will reveal my feelings to my beloved. Then, he can't possibly fail to realize what I'm trying to say. I see it now, where I have failed. Of course, he would never think that I loved him, given our positions. Oh, Riley, how can I ever thank you?" she squealed, planting a kiss on my forehead.

"Really, Your Highness, I wasn't—" I tried to insist, but she had stopped listening to me a long time ago. Her thoughts were entirely on the garden party and how she might woo poor Bashrik.

"Perhaps I could even propose marriage?" she muttered to herself, tapping her chin thoughtfully. "Tell me, Riley, do you know if Bashrik is in love with anyone else? You seem to spend a great deal of time with him, so if anyone is going to know, it'll be you," she reasoned, looking me dead in the eyes.

I opened my mouth to speak, but nothing came out. The queen had left me speechless. I didn't know what had brought on this infatuation she had with Bashrik so quickly, but all I could think was, what had I done? Angie liked Bashrik, and I wouldn't be surprised if Bashrik was secretly harboring feelings for her, too. If I let the queen do this, then that fledgling romance was doomed. Bashrik's happiness was probably doomed, too. And yet, no matter how much I wanted to dissuade the queen from making any kind of advance toward Bashrik, I couldn't help thinking that it might just be the opportunity we were looking for. If she opened up the gardens for a party and invited everyone she knew, then Yorrek would be on that list. He was one of her best alchemists, and he certainly wouldn't be able to ignore an invitation from the queen, regardless of his fears. I already knew how sensitive Queen Brisha could be about that kind of slight, after the debacle with the wing serum.

Angie, Bashrik, please forgive me, I begged silently. *This might be the only way we can get our hands on Yorrek.*

"I don't think he's shown any interest in anyone, Your Highness," I replied, the half-truth coming out stiffly. Bashrik *hadn't* made his interest known, but that didn't mean he wasn't interested in Angie. I had a sixth sense about those kinds of things.

"Oh, thank Rask for that!" Queen Brisha cried. "I think my heart would have broken if you'd told me he liked someone else."

I tried not to grimace, comforting myself with the knowledge that it was all part of a bigger picture. "Would you be inviting all nearby members of the queendom to attend, Your Highness, or would it just be the elite, who live in the city?"

"Oh, everyone! I would have all my most treasured individuals there. I think the people could do with cheering up, after that battle with my sister," she said with a bright smile.

"The alchemists, for sure, Your Highness," I chimed

in subtly. "They are very downcast after the wreckage of their lab."

She laughed delightedly. "You have an excellent mind, dear Riley! I would not have thought of it if you had not been here to suggest it. Of course, the carnival shall be in celebration of the new laboratory, and the work of the alchemists!"

It was all falling into place, slotting together like pieces of a puzzle. Queen Brisha was too wrapped up in her love for Bashrik to realize she was being manipulated. And, while I felt bad about playing with her feelings, there was more at stake than a broken heart... or two. My planet was counting on me, and I wouldn't let them down, even if it meant breaking a few regal eggs.

12

"We'd better hope Yorrek *does* come," Navan murmured as we stood in one of the small annex rooms that looked out over the gardens. It had been three days since my bathroom visit with the queen, and preparations were well underway for the garden party, with coldbloods running around like headless chickens, carrying crates of lights and boxes of glittering decorations. The national holiday had been announced the morning after I'd spoken with Queen Brisha, to a truly joyful reception from her people, and now the day had come.

In the streets, brightly colored ornaments were being strung up, and lanterns hung from every available space. Once darkness fell, it would look beautiful. Even now, it looked like something out of a fairytale, with Vysantheans rushing around, calling to one another, smiling broadly. Musicians set up in the squares that connected streets together. Everyone seemed happy, and part of me wished I could be out there among the common folk, enjoying the evening without a care in the world.

Instead, the group of us had been asked to attend the queen's private garden party, where the alchemists had all been invited as honored guests. A high table had been arranged at the end of one of the sprawling, deep green lawns, where they would be required to sit for speeches and drinks. It was this table that my eyes were set on as I gazed from the annex window.

"There's no way he'll refuse her invite," I replied. "If he does, he could lose his job, and I think that scares him more than any potential stalker."

Navan nodded. "Do you think he might be right?" he asked after a moment, his eyes trailing a skinny young coldblood as he tripped with a box of lights. "About someone stalking him?"

I shrugged. "I've got no idea. From what Bashrik and Angie have been saying, he's a bit of a kook, but there must be a reason he's barricaded himself inside like that."

"And you're absolutely positive Queen Brisha has invited him here?" Navan pressed, his brow furrowed.

I nodded. "She caught me in the corridor yesterday,

and I asked if she'd invited all the alchemists. She said yes. I can only assume that means Yorrek, too. He's one of her best. There's no way he won't come," I reassured him, though I didn't feel as confident as I sounded. I knew there *was* a chance Yorrek could stay in his fort, refusing to come out, even if it cost him his job.

"I hope you're right," Navan said.

"Me too." I grimaced. "Can we go over the plan again, one more time?" I asked, trying to recall every point we'd discussed the night before, in the sanctuary of Angie and Lauren's chambers. The others hadn't been entirely happy about what I'd done—Bashrik had nearly torn out his own hair—but they understood the reason. At least, I hoped they did. Angie, at least, had spoken to me over breakfast, which I had taken as a good sign.

"Bashrik is going to distract the queen with his smooth moves, though Rask knows what they are, while Lauren keeps a lookout for anyone who might be after Yorrek. The last thing we want is someone else snatching him while we're trying to," Navan said wryly, making me chuckle. "Then we're going to separate Yorrek from the herd, and get him to follow us into this room, where Angie will be waiting to tie him up. I'll administer the hypnosis serum, and we'll ask him questions until we get the intel we need. After that, we erase his memory with the Elysium I so valiantly pilfered from the military surgery ward, and it's a job well done, all around," he concluded dramatically, cupping his hands over his mouth to make the sound of hushed applause.

"It sounds so easy when you put it like that," I murmured, staring out into the gardens. We were only one floor up, but nobody could see us here, though we could see everything going on below.

Navan grinned. "It will be easy. What could possibly go wrong?"

"You had to say it, didn't you?" I muttered. He put his arms around me, leaning his forehead against mine.

"Nothing like a bit of overconfidence," he said.

"Yeah, until it gets us killed," I said, only half joking. "And you're sure the hypnosis serum is finished? You cooked it all up?"

He chuckled, raising his brows with irreverence. "'Cooked it all up?'"

"Well, I don't know how you make a potion, smartass," I said, nudging him in the stomach. "I presume there's some cookery involved?"

"It's more like being a mad professor," he explained. "But yes, you can rest assured that the serum is all finished. It's a good one too, by the looks of it. Bashrik almost started spilling every secret he's ever had with just a whiff of the stuff."

I nodded, taking a deep breath. "I suppose we'd better get moving," I said reluctantly, unfurling myself from his arms.

"Can I see the dress Queen Brisha sent up for you?" Navan asked with a wink.

"*I* haven't even seen it yet. You'll see it at the party," I said, pouting playfully. We exited the annex room, locking it behind us with the key Navan had stolen, before heading upstairs to our rooms.

We parted ways in the elevator, as I stepped off at the floor with Angie and Lauren's apartment on it, while he went on up to our chambers, where Bashrik was meeting him, so they could get suited and booted.

I was eager to see my friends again, especially with such an exciting night ahead. It would also be stressful and downright nerve-racking, yes, but I couldn't remember the last time we'd all gotten dressed up to go out together, and I figured we should all try to enjoy it as much as we could. In Vysanthe, we had to take advantage of every bit of levity we could find. We'd go crazy with the pressure we were all under, otherwise.

I rapped at the door. A moment later, I heard rustling in the apartment as somebody approached. Angie opened it with gusto, ushering me in and handing me a glass flute filled with something pale and sparkling.

I sniffed it warily.

"Relax, it's not alcoholic," Angie chuckled, taking a sip of her own. Still dubious, I did the same, soon realizing that she was telling the truth. It was a sweet, sparkling drink, but I couldn't taste any hint of alcohol.

"Have your dresses arrived?" I asked, moving to the walk-in wardrobe where Lauren was waiting, her mouth hanging open as she gazed in wonderment at the gown with her name attached. It was an unusual amethyst shade that perfectly complemented her brown eyes and coffee-colored hair. On the counter beside it were two boxes. One contained a stunning necklace with a central teardrop diamond as long as my pinky finger. Tiny amethysts surrounded the teardrop, highlighting the vivid tone of the gown. There was a matching bracelet to go with it, though these diamonds were circular, with a single amethyst in the center of each one.

"Lauren, that is stunning!" Angie gushed, as Lauren continued to stare. I grinned, knowing she would look beautiful, especially as the color of the gown made her glasses look like the perfect accompaniment. Tucked away below the gown was a matching pair of shoes, glittering as though they were crafted from solid crystal.

"Which one's yours?" I asked Angie as she moved into the wardrobe.

A tag with her name had been placed above a

beautiful aquamarine gown. In a box beside it, there was an exquisite diamond necklace in the same style as Lauren's, with surrounding gems of blue topaz and aquamarine. Instead of a bracelet, she had a matching ring, with the matching shoes tucked away in a box underneath.

"You're going to look so beautiful, Angie," I said, and Lauren nodded in agreement, still speechless from the sight of her gown.

"What about yours, Riley?" Angie wondered, a thrilled grin on her face, as we moved over to mine. It had been zipped up in a protective case. As I slowly undid the zipper and pulled away the case, I understood why. In front of me was the most gorgeous dress I had ever seen in my entire life.

It was made of a fine, gauzy material, in a sort of blushing, dusky golden tone, the whole stretch of fabric glittering with tiny diamonds. A train flowed downward, intertwined with thin strands of rose gold. It looked like the wings of a butterfly, so fragile and delicate, yet holding a remarkable beauty. In the box beside it was an elegant necklace, with one large, oval-cut diamond in the center, and smaller ovals running all the way up to the clasp. In a second box lay a ring with a huge yellow diamond in the center, and a bracelet of oval diamonds, just like the necklace. Glittering shoes sat in a box below, sparkling like they belonged to Cinderella.

Angie whistled. "Never mind Brisha—*you're* going to look like the queen!"

I blushed. "Eh... You guys are going to look prettier." I pulled Lauren's dress down from the rail. "Now, I say we crack open another bottle of that sparkling stuff, and we get ready like it's the end of senior year!"

We brought the dresses and accessories into the main living space. Angie did the honors with the bottle of sweet, fizzy stuff, while Lauren undressed and stepped into the stunning amethyst gown. With my help, we shimmied it up onto her shoulders, and I set to work fastening all the buttons that went up the back. Somehow, it fitted as though it was custom made for her, though nobody remembered anyone coming to take our measurements.

"Lauren, you look incredible," I said as I took in the sight of my beautiful friend. She looked so slender and sophisticated in the gown, the straps thin on her shoulders, the neckline flatteringly cut, the waist hugging her slim frame.

Darting back into the walk-in wardrobe, I grabbed the full-length mirror and staggered to the living room with it, placing it against the wall so Lauren could look at herself. Even she gaped as she took in her reflection, turning this way and that, smoothing down the silky fabric.

"Hey, I found these!" Angie called as she reentered the room, clutching an armful of peculiar-looking objects, then freezing as she saw Lauren. "Holy crap, Lauren, you look like a movie star!"

"What are those?" I asked as Angie crossed the room, dumping the peculiar objects on the sofa.

"There was a note that said, 'Use these for your hair and face', so I'm guessing that's what they're for." Angie shrugged, picking up a strange, helmet-looking device and placing it on her head.

Lauren smiled. "Ah, so *that's* what she wanted me to write that for," she said.

Too engrossed in the device to listen to Lauren, Angie pressed a button on the side of the peculiar helmet. The whole thing lit up yellow for a moment, before fading to black. "Get this thing off my head!" she shouted, suddenly panicking.

"Hold on, hold on!" I grabbed the sides of the helmet and lifted it up, my eyes widening in surprise at the sight beneath.

"What is it? Is it awful? Oh God, tell it to me quick," Angie said.

I grinned. "Go look in the mirror."

She hurried across to it and took in her reflection, seeing the stylish up-do the machine had done with her natural curls. It had softened them slightly, making an elegant chignon with the length, so that everything was neatly and beautifully tucked away.

"Where has this thing been all my life?" she muttered.

We settled into our routine of getting ready, throwing devices to each other, and helping one another with buttons and clasps and ribbons. Angie discovered devices in the pile that could apply perfect makeup. All you had to do was flick through and pick a look, and it would put it on your face, just as requested.

My dress was the trickiest to put on, with a series of buttons up the back and ribbons dotting the sides and front, which needed to be tied shut, so I didn't end up flashing something I didn't intend to. It took both Lauren and Angie to get it fastened.

"Do you feel like you're getting ready for prom?" Angie asked.

"Yeah, I feel like Freddy Mercer should be coming to my door any minute, to stand awkwardly in the hall, while Roger goes full Spanish Inquisition mode. Poor guy." I laughed, remembering his ill-fitting tux and slicked-back hair, and our nervous slow-dancing.

"Hey, at least it wasn't Michael Russo, who seemed to think I'd given him permission to run his snaky little hands all over me," Angie said, shuddering dramatically. "I had to shower, like, twenty times after the prom, to get the grossness off."

"My date wasn't so bad," Lauren chimed in, a wistful look on her face.

I smiled warmly. "Ah yes, Seamus Barton, the love of Lauren's life."

Angie grinned licentiously. "You guys kissed for the first time, didn't you, that night?"

Lauren rolled her eyes. "Yeah. I liked him. Still do," she admitted. "We met up just before we all went to Texas, and we talked about making it work while I was at Stanford, but with him at NYU, we both realized there wasn't much point. I think about him sometimes, though... wonder what he's up to and stuff. He was supposed to be going to Europe with his brother and his brother's wife, so I guess he's probably still there, seeing the Eiffel Tower or something." She sighed. "I can't even remember how long we've been gone. Do you think our parents are worrying right now?"

It was something I'd been thinking about a lot. We'd long since passed the date we were supposed to be back from our summer excursion, and we still had no foreseeable way of returning home. That moment had come and gone—our faces would likely be all over the late-night news on Earth. We'd be the three girls who disappeared one day and never came home. It hurt like hell to think Jean and Roger were out there grieving over me because I ran off and never came back. No matter how tempting the opportunities might be, we had to find a way off this planet, before we lost ourselves in these new lives. We owed our parents that.

"You didn't tell us you'd seen Seamus before we left," I murmured, changing the subject.

She shrugged. "I didn't tell you guys about it because... Well, I was upset, and I didn't want to ruin our last month together. Plus, it didn't matter anyway; nothing was ever going to come of it. Especially not now."

"I guess things *have* taken a bit of a detour, haven't they?" I said, flashing an apologetic glance at my two friends. "I mean, you were heading to Stanford, I was supposed to be off to Michigan, and Angie was going to Paris. Now look at us."

Lauren smiled, her mood shifting. "There might be a missed opportunity back home, but to be honest, I wouldn't change *this* opportunity for the world. Who else gets to travel to another planet like this? I get to study cultures nobody on Earth has ever seen or heard of. I get to read books about things that would blow anyone's mind. I get to do things I would've never had the chance to do, if I'd stayed, safe and small, at home," she said, but the sentiment was bittersweet. It was hard to think about the lives and dreams we might have had, and how we had let them go to step into the unknown.

But Lauren was right—who else got to do what we did? Who else got to live a life of adventure, in the far reaches of the universe?

Angie nodded firmly. "I know Paris would've been amazing, but Lauren is right. We're doing something special here. Even when we have to go back, we'll have our memories, and that is worth everything we've given up to be here. Earth is good, but Vysanthe has its perks too."

"What, you mean Bashrik?" I teased.

"No, not Bashrik." Angie scoffed. "I mean, learning something new, being on a different planet."

Lauren smirked. "Come on, Ang, we know you like him. It's obvious to literally everyone but the pair of you."

"I don't like him, but I just wish the queen would leave him alone. I mean, he's not interested, for God's sake, but she keeps coming after him." Angie sighed. "Take this whole party, for example. What person in their right mind announces their love for someone who clearly has no interest, in front of a load of people? It's because she knows she's queen, and he can't say no to her, and that bugs me," she muttered.

"Do you want him to say no?" I prodded.

Angie looked at Lauren and me, then took a deep breath. "Okay, yes... I want him to say no, okay? There, I said it! I guess I do like him a bit—in a really weird way—and I... I don't want him to go off with the queen. Not that he even has a choice, so it's pointless talking about it."

With that, she sealed her lips and turned her back on us, clearly intending to reveal no more on the subject.

I exchanged a discreet glance with Lauren, who looked concerned. We moved over to the floor where Angie sat and put our arms around her. She fought us for a moment, before letting us hold her.

"What would I do without you guys?" she murmured, pulling us close.

I sighed. I, for one, had no idea what I'd do without them.

13

With our dresses on, our makeup done, our hair styled, and our heels hugging our feet, we left the apartment and headed down to the party.

An elegant stairwell led down to the foyer, where guests were being shepherded toward the gardens, their excited chatter drifting up to us. We paused on the landing, taking one last good look at each other to make sure nothing was out of place.

"You know, there's something that's been bugging me," Angie muttered as I tucked an errant strand of hair behind her ear. The chatter continued to flow around us. "Do Vysantheans have a translator installed in their heads, or what? They speak English like freakin' natives!"

That was kind of what I had been assuming. Well, either tech, or some natural, inconceivably advanced language ability. Though, I knew Navan could genuinely speak our language—he'd spent a fair amount of time in the US and Canada, and coldbloods' learning skills were off the charts in terms of speed. I suspected Bashrik and Ronad were the same, too.

Lauren smirked. "Surprised you didn't ask sooner. I read up on that, and yeah, actually, it's because of a small device they have implanted in their brains. Obviously, coldbloods have a penchant for interplanetary travel and colonization. They're always coming into contact with other species, which means they need a way to efficiently communicate with them. This brain chip... Well, I couldn't begin to tell you how it works. We might as well call it magic. But apparently coldbloods aren't the only aliens to develop such tech. Others have, too."

"How on earth could any piece of tech be capable of *that*?" Angie frowned. "When a coldblood speaks to us, we hear our language, while other coldbloods hear... their native language? And how do they understand *us*? That's insane."

Lauren shrugged. "Well, we don't know what we don't know, right? I mean, three hundred years ago, would we have ever thought the internet was possible?

Smart phones? They would have basically been magic, right?"

"Yeah, I guess," Angie mumbled, still looking bewildered as we descended the stairs.

In the entrance hall, my heart fluttered as I saw Navan standing there, waiting for us. He turned, his face morphing into a mask of amazement as his eyes locked with mine. Bashrik, standing beside him, only had eyes for Angie, his mouth open in shock. They didn't look too shabby either, with Bashrik dressed in a deep scarlet suit with a high collar and a cream shirt beneath, a peculiar maroon cravat at his neck. Navan wore something similar, though he was dressed in a suit of dark gray that highlighted the color of his eyes.

Looking around, I noticed that nobody else was wearing a suit in the same color as Bashrik, and I wondered if the queen had arranged it herself, so everyone would know who her love was, when the moment came. *Poor guy.*

"I can't put into words how amazing you look," Navan whispered, taking my hand and placing a gentle kiss on my cheek.

Bashrik looked as though he was about to offer his hand to Angie, but thought better of it. Part of me was glad, seeing that Lauren didn't have a partner, but I still felt sorry for Angie. I imagined she was wishing Bashrik *would* make a move. I resisted the urge to roll my eyes. If she hadn't been so damn passive aggressive with him till now, he probably would have. She needed to work on her flirting skills.

"Shall we?" I suggested, gesturing toward the garden exit, where everyone was being ushered.

Navan slipped my arm through his, and we set off through the arched doorway, which had been decorated with sprays of tiny blue flowers and dripping fronds of crystalline willows forged from gemstones. Miniature lights were embedded within the display, illuminating the way into the gardens.

In the distance, I could hear the beating of happy drums. The street carnival was well underway outside the palace, by the sounds of things. I still longed to be out there, immersed in some true Vysanthean culture. Instead, we had a job to do, with sparse opportunity to enjoy our time.

As I stepped down into the gardens, I marveled at the lights that filled every tree and snaked around every branch and bough, the whole place sparkling like a galaxy. Crystals dangled between the lights, catching the beams and sending a shower of rainbow luminescence down upon the gathered party. The grounds had been decorated with ice sculptures conveying strange birds and lovers entwined. Chatter babbled all around, with stunningly beautiful cold-bloods sipping scarlet liquid from expensive-looking glasses. Underneath it all, I could make out strange music, the mood somewhere between a melancholy lullaby and a pretty ballad, though it was nowhere near as exciting as the bawdy music outside the palace walls.

Waiters weaved in and out of the guests, offering vials and glasses filled with Vysanthean delicacies. As a waiter paused beside us, Bashrik took up one of the proffered drinks, while the rest of us gave a polite refusal.

"You think that's wise?" Navan reprimanded, nodding to the glass.

"Hey, you're not the one who has to pretend to be in love with a queen. Cut me some slack," he replied tersely, drinking it down in one gulp.

"Fair enough, just don't drink too much," Navan muttered.

Bashrik shot him a look. "Let me worry about that."

"So we need to find Yorrek," Lauren cut in.

"Yes. Anyone seen him yet?" Navan asked.

I shook my head. "No sign, but I'll keep an eye on the door, check for new arrivals."

"I'll hang around by the tables, see if I can spot him," Lauren added.

"I'll join you," Angie said, stealing a sly look at Bashrik, whose eyes had been discreetly wandering back to her since she'd come down the stairs.

With that, my friends disappeared into the crowd, heading for the dancefloor that had been set up on the lawn, with the dining tables arranged around it. There were a surprising number of couples already dancing, but it was the sight of Queen Brisha, sitting on a throne at the center of the high table, that caught my eye. She was dressed in a silver gown that looked like a second skin, a glittering tiara upon her head, her long, pale copper hair tumbling down in elegant waves. She looked stunning, I had to give her that, even though my hopes were firmly on Angie and Bashrik.

"How about a dance?" Navan asked, taking me by surprise.

"I need to watch the door," I replied, eyeing him suspiciously. He hated dancing.

He smiled. "We can watch the door from the dancefloor. It has the best vantage point for watching the entire garden," he explained, offering out his hand.

"What makes you so eager to show off your moves all of a sudden?" I asked, raising my eyebrows.

"Dancing with you, in *that* dress, makes it just about bearable," he said, grinning as he took my hand and led me over to the dancefloor, where Angie and Lauren were already dancing in one another's arms, much to the amusement of the surrounding coldbloods.

Turning my attention to Navan, I nestled into his

arms, feeling one hand slip around my waist, as his fingers laced through mine. I rested my head on his shoulder, my eyes on the doorway to the gardens. Even as a lookout, it didn't mean I couldn't enjoy a dance with my boyfriend.

As we made our way around the dancefloor, swaying to the slow music, I was barely aware of anything but Navan and the doorway. I saw Queen Brisha smile as we passed her by, but everyone seemed to have had enough of the novelty we presented, returning to their own conversations and partners. It was precisely what I'd hoped for.

Fifteen minutes later, I saw Angie and Lauren dance toward us.

"He's here," Angie whispered, nodding her head toward a second entrance, to the side of the gardens where two burly guards stood, their pikes crossed. Yorrek flashed them a hologram, which popped up on a device he held, and the guards let him through. Even so, he didn't appear to be in the party spirit, his eyes glancing around furtively, his manner on edge.

We broke away from the dancefloor for a moment, the five of us gathering beside an empty drinks table. From the outside, it looked like we were just taking a refreshment break after a long dance.

"Okay, everyone move into their places," Navan said quietly, and we all nodded in agreement. "Bashrik, you really need to make the queen swoon," he added with a grimace.

Bashrik cleared his throat nervously. "Good thing I'm the best dancer in this place, then," he said, forcing a smile, though his voice was strained.

"You'll be fine," I said comfortingly, trying hard not to look at Angie.

"I just wish I had a good reason to refuse her, you know?" Bashrik muttered, letting out a breath. "It just doesn't seem fair to lead her on. She's not that bad of a person... I suppose I can't just say I'm not attracted to her, can I?"

Navan smiled. "Afraid not, Brother."

"Then, swooning it is," Bashrik murmured, his expression darkening as he took off toward the queen's throne.

Taking that as our sign to move out, Angie hurried through the throngs of guests toward the secluded room on the first floor, taking Navan's key with her. Lauren, meanwhile, moved away from the dancefloor, coming to a halt beside a piece of topiary shaped like a winged wolf, where she could keep an eye out for guards, or anyone who might come and snatch Yorrek before we had the chance to.

"You ready?" Navan asked. My gaze drifted toward Yorrek, who seemed to be keeping to the high hedges of the garden perimeter.

I nodded. "Let's get this over with."

We casually wandered in Yorrek's direction, not wanting it to seem too obvious that we were making a beeline for him. His eyes went wide in surprise as he spotted us, though he stopped and waited for us to approach, evidently concluding he had nothing to fear from us.

"You—you're the one who came to see me?" he barked as we came to a halt in front of him.

"I am, though we still haven't had the pleasure of your company at the building site," I said, smiling warmly.

"In fact, it's serendipitous that you happen to be here this evening, as we've had some developments regarding the alchemy lab. We'd really appreciate your opinion," Navan added, a polite smile on his face. "Bashrik was thinking about writing to you, but would you mind coming to have a look now? If you're not busy, that is. I wouldn't want to drag you away from the celebrations, considering you're one of the honored guests."

"Don't be ridiculous. I despise parties. I would rather be home," Yorrek snapped, narrowing his rheumy eyes at Navan. "You're both Jareth Idrax's sons, correct?" he added, his tone cold.

Navan nodded. "Sadly, Jareth Idrax is my father."

"A fine alchemist," Yorrek muttered. "Shame he works for the enemy."

He didn't say it, but I heard a slight accusation in his voice that Navan might hold the same allegiances as his father. Even so, it was evident that Yorrek held Navan and his brother in some sort of high regard, given their impressive bloodline.

"It is a shame I couldn't persuade my father to switch the direction of his moral compass, as I have done," Navan replied, a sincere expression on his face.

"You say you want me to look at the latest developments?" Yorrek asked.

Navan gestured to the doorway of the gardens. "If you're not too busy."

"Bashrik seems preoccupied with the queen. I don't think his mind is anywhere near the alchemy lab," Yorrek remarked frostily, his eyes resting on Bashrik, who was leaning over the high table, speaking with Queen Brisha in a way that was making her smile giddily, her cheeks flushing. *Good job, Bash.*

"Indeed, his mind is otherwise engaged for this evening," Navan said. "In fact, it's Bashrik's assistant, Angie, who wishes to meet with you. I believe you've met her before?"

"Short one, hair like a basket of snakes?" Yorrek sniped.

Navan maintained his polite smile. "That's the one."

"What kind of developments are we talking about?"

Navan shrugged apologetically. "Honestly, I don't know. Angie just said she would rather be working on the lab tonight than mingling with people. She mentioned she had some ideas that will quicken the build, but that's all I know," he replied. "She's up in the palace studio now, drawing some designs. I'm sure she'd welcome the insight, since Bashrik is proving useless today," he added grimly. This seemed to please Yorrek, a cold smile creeping onto his thin lips.

"I admit that I respect a female with a mind firmly on the job. None of this romance nonsense clogging up the brain," Yorrek said, waggling a finger in Bashrik's direction. "If she's at work, then I should be too. Lead the way. The sooner we have that lab built, the sooner I can get back to doing what I do best, under the safety and security of the queen's protection." His small eyes glanced around, as if to punctuate the point that he didn't feel safe. His paranoia was so infectious, I almost felt like someone *was* watching us.

We led Yorrek, who walked between us, back through the gardens and into the palace, taking him up the staircase and toward the hallway on the first floor, where the annex was tucked away. I glanced over my shoulder as we hurried down the corridor, conscious of someone following. However, no matter how many times I turned to look back, there was never anyone there. Either they were very good at hiding, or my mind was playing tricks on me.

We ushered him into the annex room, shutting the door firmly behind us. As Navan reached into his pocket and took out the hypnosis serum, which had been placed into a syringe, I turned the key in the lock. Navan immediately darted for Yorrek and thrust the needle into his neck, pressing down on the plunger until there was no trace of the purple substance within.

Yorrek yelped and gaped up at Navan in surprise, before raising his fists in a fighting stance. I glanced to Navan in confusion. The serum hadn't worked!

With his fangs bared, the alchemist lunged for the door, trying to grasp the handle. Navan barreled into him, knocking him out of the way. Yorrek whirled around with surprising agility and swiped at Navan's face.

"Stop it!" I shouted as Yorrek's clawed hands reached for Navan's throat.

Immediately, Yorrek went still, retracting his hands.

The serum *had* worked—we just had to express commands. Angie looked at me excitedly, and a wave of relief crashed over Navan's face.

"Which ingredients are needed to make the immortality elixir?" Angie asked, jumping straight in.

"A pressurized combination of some kind of alien blood, extract of Morgana, a base of Vysanthean blood, liquid from the seed of a fenghazi plant, a few drops of maram root, and adrenaline distilled from a frostfang," Yorrek replied automatically, his voice a monotone.

"In which quantities?" Navan asked.

Yorrek looked thoughtful. "It is hard to say. The quantities are still being studied. I have a book of almost-successful trials, using various quantities. Queen Brisha has it. I could not tell you off the top of my head," he answered. I frowned at this news, knowing it might necessitate a trip to Brisha's chambers to see if we could get our hands on Yorrek's book.

Glancing at Yorrek, it was definitely nice to be on the opposite side of the interrogation table, for once.

"Have any alien bloods worked yet?" I asked.

Yorrek shook his head. "None, though we are hopeful of the new sample being the key."

"And how might that blood be synthesized?" Navan added.

"It has to be put in a centrifuge to separate the purest part. The plasma of many species is toxic to us, and we believe it is the same with this new blood," Yorrek replied obediently.

"What is the alchemical process in making the immortality elixir?" Navan asked, the curiosity in his eyes intensifying.

Yorrek smiled. "Each individual aspect has to be allowed to react, one at a time, in sequence."

Navan frowned. "How long does that take?"

"Ordinarily, synthesis takes weeks, and alchemical reactions can take months," Yorrek explained. "However, we have successfully completed a new compressor device and a rapid centrifuge, which work together. They are used in unison to speed up these alchemical reactions, meaning we do not have to wait for the synthesis of the blood, or the time required for reactions to occur naturally. And so, we can reduce alchemy time down from weeks or months to hours or days, depending on what we are making."

I flashed a look at Navan. That was news to me. When I'd last asked Brisha about a timeframe, she'd told me weeks. This was definitely something the rebels hadn't heard about before, either. I was sure of it. If this technology now existed, that changed the game entirely. It would allow an alchemist to trial a new elixir in super-quick time, meaning a success could be achieved faster. Not only that, I realized it would undoubtedly mean that an elixir could be produced in mass quantities, if it could be done that quickly.

Standing in the center of the room, I noticed Yorrek's sinewy muscles tense, where before they had been loose and relaxed. His rheumy eyes were still foggy and unfocused, but they seemed to be gathering some sort of clarity.

"The serum is already wearing off," Angie said, voicing my thoughts.

"One more question," Navan said quickly, leaning closer to Yorrek and gripping his shoulders. "Do you know where the new sample of blood comes from?"

The alchemist looked at him blankly, his mouth hanging open, his brow creased in thought.

Then he lunged forward and headbutted Navan, hard. Staggering back, Navan tried to grasp at Yorrek again, but Yorrek managed to dodge him. I realized we'd forgotten to tie him up, as per the plan. We'd been lured into a false sense of security by the hypnosis serum, thinking that would be enough to hold him. With it fading from his system, he shot toward the door and yanked it open with all his Vysanthean speed and strength, before tearing out into the hallway beyond. Back toward the party.

14

"We can't let him escape!" I gasped.

Navan immediately launched after Yorrek, spreading out his wings. He glided over the balustrade of the landing and dropped to the ground below, where Yorrek was already weaving through the crowds of revelers. I glanced at Angie, who hurriedly shoved the cap back on the syringe of Elysium she had just pulled out, and put it down the front of her dress. With that, we sprinted from the room as fast as our gowns would allow. I kicked off my heels and carried them under my arms as we descended the stairs. If only my wings were permanent.

Up ahead, Navan had almost caught up to the

alchemist, though he'd had to tuck his wings away to avoid hitting the faces of those around him. People were already looking at him as though he were something nasty on the bottom of their shoes, given the intrusive way he'd landed among them. Regardless, Navan's eyes were focused on his prey, who had slowed down, thanks to the after-effects of the hypnosis serum.

Yorrek paused, catching his breath at the far edge of the grand entrance hall, but within seconds he was running again, heading for the archway that led to the garden party. Navan was closing the gap, but it wasn't small enough. If Yorrek got outside and told anyone what was going on, we were done for.

Hurtling after them, Angie and I reached the steps that went down into the gardens just as Navan barreled into Yorrek, knocking him to the ground behind a row of bushes. Yorrek removed the stopper of a vial he had seemingly retrieved from nowhere and threw the contents in Navan's face. Navan dodged, and the curious liquid landed on the gravel pathway with an almighty hiss, smoke rising from the earth. I stared at it in horror, wondering what it might have done if it had hit Navan. Already, I could see tiny spots where some of the fluid had splashed against his clothes, boring holes into his suit jacket.

Taking advantage of Navan's surprise, the alchemist

got to his feet and bolted. Navan followed as Yorrek darted toward the nearest ice sculpture and toppled it with one savage push, causing the whole thing to come crashing down on Navan's head. He managed to knock some of it to the side, but the rest hit him square in the skull and shoulders, and his knees buckled as he sank down beneath the weight.

Partygoers stopped, looking at the scene in horror and disgust, their hands raised to their mouths as they tried to decipher what was going on. Was it a family dispute? A quarrel over love? Something to do with money? I heard every kind of gossip on the lips of the revelers, but my mind was elsewhere.

Feeling torn, I glanced between Navan and Yorrek. I wanted to check that my boyfriend was okay, but I knew there were more important things at stake right now. No matter what happened, Yorrek could not be allowed to reach the high table where Queen Brisha sat. Right now, the alchemist was staring down at his aggressor, apparently taking a moment to catch his breath.

Seizing the opportunity, I bolted along the sheltered pathway that led toward the dancefloor, sprinting down a narrow track sandwiched between two high walls of hedgerow. I waited at the end, knowing it was one of only two paths that Yorrek could take. I just had to hope he wouldn't take the main route, especially not after the commotion he'd caused with the ice sculpture. No, this was the way Yorrek would come if he wanted to reach the queen quickly. It had to be.

A moment later, I heard the unmistakable sound of footsteps on the gravel path, the pace hurried. Within seconds, Yorrek would pass by the spot where I stood.

Taking a deep breath, I jumped out from my hiding place and landed a savage kick to the backs of Yorrek's legs. It was an Aksavdo move I'd learned in training, though it had never worked against my fellow trainees. Now, I realized it probably worked better with the element of surprise.

Yorrek stumbled, crumpling to the ground with a heavy thud. Dipping low to the ground, I used another Aksavdo move, gripping his arms behind him and jerking them upward, right up to the back of his head. He fought hard against me, but I sat on his spine, rendering him immobile.

Fortunately, I had managed to floor him in a spot that was hidden by the hedgerows. Here, we were secluded. Yorrek tried to cry out, but with me pressing his face into the dirt, the sound came out strangled.

Turning, I saw Navan and Angie running up the pathway behind me. *Thank God.* I was holding Yorrek for now, but I knew he had greater stamina than I did, and I was already beginning to tire.

"Nice work!" Angie whispered. Navan knelt beside Yorrek and held his head, exposing his neck.

"Inject the serum, now!" Navan ordered.

Nodding, Angie whipped the syringe out from the bodice of her gown and bit the cap off, injecting the serum into the alchemist's neck before he had a chance to struggle.

For several moments, Yorrek continued to thrash around, the serum working its way through his body, until at last, the alchemist went still, his muscles relaxing, his body collapsing beneath me as Elysium's oblivion took over. Even so, I was reluctant to let him go, just in case he was pulling another stunt like last time.

"You can get off him," Navan said, offering his hand to help me up.

Slowly, I stood, keeping one foot pressed into Yorrek's spine. When he still didn't move, I relaxed, stepping away from the splayed-out figure on the ground.

"That was close," Angie muttered, putting the cap back on the empty syringe and burying it deep in the foliage of the outer hedges, where no one would find it.

I whirled around at the sound of more footsteps thundering down the narrow pathway behind me. It was Lauren, her purple dress shimmering in the dim light of the garden lanterns. Her brow was furrowed in distress.

"Guards! Coming this way!" she said breathlessly. "They saw the ice sculpture and they're coming to investigate!"

Navan flashed me a look. "Riley, you, Lauren, and Angie need to get out here and distract the guards while I move Yorrek elsewhere. We can't risk being seen with him like this, so I'm going to have to sneak him through the hedge or something. Go and buy me some time!"

Angie, Lauren, and I headed back through the narrow passageway, making a show of giggling raucously as we stumbled onto the main path that wound through the garden. I clutched my ribs, howling at some imaginary joke Lauren had just told, while Angie doubled over in hysterics, clinging to Lauren's arm. We were three ordinary girls, having fun at a garden party.

It was only when we looked up that the amusement disappeared from our faces. Pandora and two other guards, one male, one female, stood in front of us. None of them looked amused by the state of us, but that only sent us into further hysterics—real ones, this time.

"Nice to see you dressed up for the occasion!" Angie joked brazenly. Pandora was in her usual, all-black military fatigues, her hair up in the same pony-tail as always.

Pandora frowned. "What's going on down there?" she asked pointedly, gesturing down the darkened pathway, to the spot where Navan and Yorrek were.

To my surprise, it was Lauren who answered. "A run-in with a *particularly* delicious young man—said he was a soldier or something. Turns out he was one of the waiters!" she began to explain. "Anyway, you know how it is. He said he wanted to show me something I'd never seen before, so I followed him, thinking it might be a diamond tree or a glowing toad or something. Before I know it, he whips out his you-know-what, so I slap him in the face and my friends come running! We taught him a lesson, but he's fine now. I think he's gone back to whatever he was doing before, no doubt harassing some other poor soul. A shame he was a colossal asshat, but then the handsome ones always are, am I right?" She doubled over with laughter, prompting Angie and me to laugh with her.

"What did he look like?" Pandora asked, her face a blank canvas. I had no idea whether she believed Lauren or not.

Lauren shrugged. "You know, tall, handsome, gray skin, coldblood-looking."

If Pandora had been unamused before, she was downright irritated now. Fortunately for us, the unexpected arrival of Bashrik distracted her attention, her focus turning to his concerned expression.

"Is everything all right?" he asked, looking at the three of us with wide eyes.

Lauren nodded. "Just a run-in with an unruly waiter. We were just telling Pandora here what was going on. I think we caused a bit of a scene, made too much noise," she said apologetically.

Bashrik frowned, evidently trying to piece together what was happening. With Pandora there, we couldn't exactly tell him. "But you're all okay?" he pressed. His eyes fixed on Angie, who nodded, a small smile upon her face.

"What is everyone doing here?" Queen Brisha's voice cut in, silencing us all in one fell swoop. She had clearly followed Bashrik, wondering where he was headed. Now, seeing us all standing here, she didn't look too pleased. It was just a shame that her presence attracted the attention of every single other partygoer in the garden.

Bashrik turned to her, grinning. "Queen Brisha, do you remember that woman I was talking about, to whom the stars paled in comparison? The woman with more light in her soul than a thousand burning suns? The woman who held an entire universe in her eyes?" he asked, as my heart began to race.

What the heck was he doing? Was he going to kiss

the queen here, in front of everyone? It certainly looked like it. I didn't know whether to stop him or let it happen, my eyes wide in shock as the queen gazed back, adoration written all over her face.

"I remember, Bashrik," Queen Brisha whispered.

"Well, I have been waiting all night for the right moment to express my feelings toward this woman," Bashrik continued, raising his voice so everyone could hear. "I've been looking everywhere for her, but I couldn't find her in the crowds. I wasn't even sure she was here, but now I've found her again, and I am never letting her go! Love is a precious thing, and must be sought out, even in the strangest of places!" he shouted, as he whirled around and scooped Angie up into his arms.

My jaw dropped. Angie looked at him as though he had sprouted a second head, but she didn't pull away when Bashrik leaned down and met her lips in a passionate kiss. Looping her arms around his neck, she kissed him back, leaving the whole party reeling.

Tearing my eyes away from the scene, I saw the world-shattering sadness in Queen Brisha's eyes, and felt instantly terrible. True, Bashrik didn't love her, and she had become a little obsessive, but humiliating her like this didn't seem right, either. I wanted to put an arm around her, or something, but she was the queen.

How was anyone supposed to comfort the ruler of a nation?

Her gaze shot to me. I knew why. I had told her Bashrik wasn't in love with anyone else, and though I wasn't sure how much truth there was behind what Bashrik had just said, and what he was doing—given that he'd been trying to come up with a way to end the queen's advances for a while now—I knew how it looked. Even to me, their kiss seemed genuine.

"I didn't know, Your Highness," I whispered in apology, moving to her side.

"At least he saved me from humiliating myself," she hissed back. I could hear the unspoken sentiment in her words: *unlike you.*

"Your Highness, please believe me. I didn't know about this," I repeated, but she was already walking away from me, returning to the solitary throne at the far end of the garden.

It seemed the party was over for her.

She paused in her tracks as Navan came hurtling down the garden steps, his wings outstretched. He flew haphazardly, swinging from side to side, a giddy expression on his face. I'd seen that expression before, when he'd taken strong painkillers what seemed like a lifetime ago. Spiraling downward, he landed with a flourish, stretching out his hands like a gymnast who'd perfected a dismount.

"What did I miss?" he asked, feigning drunkenness as he chortled to himself.

Queen Brisha turned and shot him a sour look, but Navan seemed determined to make her laugh. I was grateful for that. No matter what the queen had done to try to woo Bashrik, she deserved to smile, and not feel like a fool for the way she adored him. I nodded to Bashrik and Angie, who were still canoodling in front of everyone.

"Bashrik, get away from her this instant! You don't know what you might catch!" Navan joked, drunkenly nudging Bashrik in the shoulder. When that didn't work, he tried to pry them away from each other, only to get a smack in the head from his brother. "I think they might be glued together." He hiccupped. "Maybe we need to get something to cut them free before they suffocate!"

A small smile lifted the corners of Queen Brisha's lips.

"Speaking of glue, Your Highness, please accept my heartiest apologies. I was trying to show off my flying moves, and I may have broken a few things in the process. An ice sculpture here, a priceless vase there, a couple of chandeliers... but who's counting? It's all in the name of a good time, right?" he blabbered, dropping to his knees in front of the queen. "Say you forgive me, Your Highness. Say I'm not for the executioner!

Say you'll let me see another dawn!" he begged, hiccupping through his words.

Queen Brisha chuckled, patting Navan on the back of the head like he was an unruly child. "I forgive you, Navan. I imagine the headache you'll have tomorrow will be punishment enough," she said kindly, before turning to me. "Perhaps you should get him to bed?" she suggested, most of her former animosity gone. I could still see the hurt in her eyes, and a heartbreak that would be difficult to shake, but she was a strong woman. She would get through it. I hoped so, anyway. There had to be someone truly worthy of her out there.

I nodded. "Of course, Your Highness."

With that, I put my arm under Navan's and pretended to help him to his feet, his body leaning against mine as I led him back toward the palace. He was still grinning like an idiot, his eyes unfocused, his wings flapping mindlessly behind him. I had to hand it to him. He was a convincing drunk.

"You are so shiny, like a bright star," he murmured, keeping up the pretense as he smothered me in kisses.

I snorted. "Come on, let's get you to bed."

"Yes, please!" he whooped.

Peering over my shoulder to check on the others, I saw that Pandora was still watching me. There was uncertainty in her eyes, but she made no move to follow us. That was the strange thing about her: no matter what lies we told, or what we got up to, it never seemed to go any further, or find its way back to Queen Brisha. As the queen's most trusted advisor, I would have expected Pandora to interrogate us, or confront us outright about our behavior, but she never did. Each time, she let it pass. And that, in and of itself, left me with a tingle of suspicion.

*a*s I led Navan back into the palace, I realized that an opportunity lay before us. I couldn't believe it hadn't come to me sooner. Then again, all we'd been thinking about was getting the information out of Yorrek. Getting the information *to* Orion had been the next step, a bridge to cross, when we came to it. But now, it seemed the ideal moment had arisen.

"We need to go to the control room," I whispered to Navan, who was still making a show of being drunk.

He frowned, his face turning serious for a moment. "Now?"

"Not many guards should be there. At the very least, it'll be a reduced team, considering everyone is at the party," I explained hurriedly. I was still thinking about the notebook Yorrek had mentioned, which was in the queen's possession, but that would have to wait. I mean, we didn't want to feed Orion everything at once. If we did, what further use would we be?

Navan smiled. "I love your mind," he murmured, kissing me passionately on the lips. For a moment, I wondered if he might actually *be* drunk.

"We can do this later," I whispered, pulling away from him.

Navan released me and took my hand with a sigh. "If I didn't already despise Orion, I'd hate him for his uncanny ability to ruin a romantic moment, even from the other side of the universe."

We hurried down the network of palace corridors, seeking out a doorway that would lead us down to the queen's underground control bunker. The secret entrance on the top floor, where Pandora had exerted her impressive might upon the emergency exit, had already been closed back up again. If we busted it open, someone would undoubtedly find it and let the queen know, which was something we couldn't risk— not after the close call we'd just had. Pandora might not have reported anything suspicious so far, but I doubted she'd be able to ignore a gaping hole in the wall of a palace corridor. No, we were already walking on a knife edge where Brisha was concerned; we needed to tread carefully.

An idea came to me. The wing of the palace that

held the ancient galleria, and all the artifacts of the former royals, was abandoned. Nobody went there. Even if we had to kick down a door, we could always cover it up and nobody would notice. A guard doing a routine check would hardly bother to look too closely.

"The old part, with the galleria," I whispered. "We should check for bunker entrances there."

"Good idea," Navan replied as we turned a corner into the main hallway of the palace. Guards were standing around, but they paid us no heed as we passed, evidently expecting us to go up in the elevator to our chambers. By now, our faces were well known in the palace, giving us the freedom to walk around relatively unhindered.

We darted down one of the side corridors, out of sight of the guards. A short while later, we entered the dusty halls of the abandoned wing. It seemed a shame that all of this had fallen into ruin, when it must have been spectacular once, but I could see how it might trouble the queen. On the walls, the old images were of united royal families, not two sisters tearing a nation apart.

"There," Navan said, pointing to a blank wall at the end of the long hallway. There was something strange about the way it had been painted, making it look almost false.

I crept forward, following Navan toward the peculiar, bare patch of wall. My eye was drawn to the galleria a short distance away, the shrouded statues and covered paintings just visible through a gap in the door. A creeping sensation shivered up my spine at the sight of the ghostly figures. I found myself half expecting one to swoop out and attack us.

Reaching the patch of wall, Navan tapped it lightly. The sound was oddly hollow, confirming our suspicions: something was hidden behind the façade. Casting a nervous glance backward, Navan turned and smashed his leg through the wall. An enormous hole crumbled inward, revealing a door beyond. With his muscles bulging, Navan tore the rest of the stone and plaster away, before kicking the door open. It swung wide, with a spiral set of stairs leading down into the dark unknown.

"Let's hope this leads to the right place," Navan said.

"Where else could it possibly lead?" I reached for a golden tassel that held back a flowing velvet curtain, dyed blood red. The curtain swung across the hole Navan had created. Whether it was a remnant from when the doorway hadn't been shrouded by plaster, I wasn't sure, but it had clearly been custom-made to cover this section of wall.

Ducking behind the curtain, we made our way down the steep spiral staircase, our path lit by the dim glow of emergency lighting. The metal was shaky, each step rustier than the last, crumbs of stone falling away with every move we made.

"How exactly are we going to send the intel to Orion?" I whispered, wanting to break the silence of our steady descent.

Navan kept his eyes dead ahead as he replied. "I have some of the hypnosis serum and some Elysium left. So we should be able to convince one of the intelligence officers to get a message to Orion, on a remote wavelength. You remember that black box I had, back at my cabin?"

"Yeah, but it didn't work, did it?"

"The *disc* didn't work. The transmitter would have worked. Anyway, they should have something like that down here that can send a message, separate from any main systems," he went on. "The queen probably uses them to get messages to her spies in the South. We just need an officer to use one of them, to bounce the message off a deep-space satellite and reach Orion."

"Why off a satellite?" I frowned, puzzled by everything he was saying.

"If we send it straight to Earth, then the transmitter will know where the message has been sent. If we send it via a satellite, the transmitter will think the message has gone to whichever satellite we've sent it to," he explained. "So, even if an anomaly is discovered in the system, they won't be able to trace where the message went."

"Will they be able to read what the message says?" I pressed, feeling more anxious by the minute.

He shook his head. "I'll get the officer to delete it as soon as it's been sent and we've received the reply we need."

"If you send it like that, how can we get confirmation that my parents won't be hurt?" I asked. It already pained me to know there was nothing I could do for the humans that the rebels would continue to kill in Siberia for their blood. But I *could* do something about the rest.

"We'll set up a connection via the satellite, and we'll ask him to confirm his end of the bargain. If we're satisfied with the answer, then we'll give him the intel in a separate message. If we don't like what he has to say, then we'll come up with something else," he said, though there was a hint of worry in his voice.

As we reached the bottom of the stairwell, he put a hand out and lifted a finger to his lips, bringing me to a silent halt. Beyond the door, the control room looked fairly empty. A few guards were wandering around, but they didn't seem to be paying much attention to what they were doing. Two stood talking in front of the doorway.

"We need their clothes," I whispered, gesturing at

my ballgown and Navan's suit. They weren't exactly inconspicuous.

"I have a better idea. Wait here," Navan said, before slipping out the door. Peering through the gap, I watched as he crept up behind the two guards. He tensed his hands, then sliced them down hard on the sides of the guards' necks. Their heads jolted, and, instantly, their eyes went blank, their knees giving way as they crumpled to the floor. I had never seen that particular Aksavdo move before, but it was certainly impressive. Casting a quick look around, Navan tilted their heads back and poured serum into their mouths, using his thumb and forefinger against their throats to coax it down without choking them. *Which* serum, I wasn't sure.

Their bodies were already limp, but their eyes took on an extra layer of fogginess as the serum took hold. Navan hauled each one backward and leaned them up against the door, making it look like they were merely slacking. Then he hurried across the control room toward the huts at the back of the bunker. He reappeared five minutes later. A guard stopped him on the way back, but whatever he said to her, she believed him, and he continued on his way a moment later.

Moving the guards to one side, Navan reentered the small space where I stood, pulling black fatigues out of his suit jacket and handing me a set.

"What did you say to that chick?" I asked as I shimmied out of my ballgown and pulled on the military clothes.

Navan smirked. "I told her my friend had forgotten something, and those guards told me I could come and fetch it," he said, zipping up the flak jacket and pulling the metal peak of the cap down over his face. I did the same, wanting to look as close to the real thing as possible.

Once we were ready, we snuck through the door and headed over to the workstations. A few officers were on duty, but Navan made a beeline for the back of the room, where a solitary worker was at his position, his station almost hidden from the rest. He looked up in surprise as we approached.

"Can I help you?" he asked uncertainly, his brow furrowed.

Before he could say anything else, Navan had poured the hypnosis serum into the officer's mouth and clamped his hand across his lips. The officer had two options: swallow or choke. Fortunately for us, the officer chose to swallow the serum, the gulp echoing outward. Even so, Navan didn't release the man's mouth until the serum kicked in. We couldn't risk him shouting out. As his eyes glazed over and his shoulders slackened, his face taking on a dopey expression, we both took seats beside the poor coldblood, making it look like we were hard at work surveying the monitors for any signs of Gianne. The hypnosis serum was working its magic, leaving him open to suggestions.

As Navan explained to the intelligence officer what he wanted him to do, I thought about the rebels and everyone's obsession with the immortality elixir. It made me furious to know we'd have to give up our intel to Orion, after everything he had done to us. I still had the scars from the device he'd put in my neck, and Galo's death still haunted me, though I'd forced myself to repress my grief for him as best I could, knowing it would only serve to stop me from functioning.

"I wish we could sabotage the rebels' attempts to create the elixir somehow," I murmured sourly. "I mean, there must be a way we could do that, and get rid of their hold on us. I hate that they have so much power over our every move."

Navan sighed. "I know. It's been playing on my mind a lot lately, too."

I watched the hypnotized intelligence officer at work, his hands moving across the translucent screen below him, working to connect us to a secret frequency. There was only one saving grace in all of this: with the two queens occupied with trying to outdo one another, neither of them knew about Earth. I wasn't sure I could deal with three factions in all-out war with one another. Not yet, anyway. Not while we were still in the middle of it all, and my species hung in the balance.

"Maybe we could figure out a way to bring the rebels back to Vysanthe," I said, my mind clawing for ideas. "If we could bring them back here without giving away their base on Earth, then we could let them fight it out among themselves. We could make sure Gianne and Brisha are prepared for the rebels' arrival, while convincing Orion that his attack will be a surprise. Then, maybe, they'll all just... destroy each other?"

"The rebels won't come back here until they have the immortality elixir," Navan said sullenly.

"What if we told them that the elixir can only be made here? That there's a certain ingredient or some-thing that can only be taken from Vysanthean soil?" I said, though I knew it was a longshot.

Navan shook his head. "They'd get us to box it up and bring it back to them one way or another. Until they have a working elixir, they aren't coming back to Vysanthe. I guarantee it," he replied, making it clear he'd already thought through most scenarios. But then, something glittered in his slate eyes, and he sat up taller in his chair. "Unless... If we could find a way to reverse the effects of the elixir, once the rebels arrive on Vysanthe, then we could destroy them that way."

"What do you mean?" I asked, frowning.

A moment later, his face fell once more, and he exhaled. "Actually, it doesn't matter. Because without knowing how a successful immortality elixir works, we can't hope to come up with a counteracting agent," he muttered, throwing his head back in annoyance. "We'd need to take a live specimen and figure out an anti-elixir from that..."

A gruff voice spoke from behind us.

"How did you get clearance to be here?" a guard asked, curling back his lips to reveal sharp fangs. My heart leapt to my throat. I glanced at Navan, but he made a subtle gesture toward his pockets, revealing that he was out of any useful serums, aside from the Elysium we'd need to knock out the intelligence officer.

"We have permission," Navan replied firmly.

Panic coursed through my veins as the guard drew closer. Unless this guy backed down, if we wanted to leave the control room unnoticed, we were going to have to kill him. But, in doing so, I knew we'd only end up drawing more attention to ourselves, the way we had with Queen Gianne and Kalvin. Someone would inevitably find his body or sound an alarm that he was missing, and then we'd be in serious trouble.

"Who gave you permission?" the guard pressed, his face stern.

"I did," a voice called from across the room, making us all whip around in surprise.

Pandora made her way through the stations, her boots thudding on the hard ground, her eyes cold and focused. "They are here under my jurisdiction, Bartok. I should have sent word earlier, but I had some misdemeanors to attend to at the party. My apologies."

The guard bowed anxiously, suddenly nervous in Pandora's presence. "No need to apologize, ma'am. I should have known better than to question guests of yours," he mumbled, before backing away, hurrying as far from her as possible.

I looked at her suspiciously as she waited for Bartok to fully disappear, her shoulders tensed, her eyes homing in on him like a predator watching prey. What was she doing here? And, more importantly, why was she helping us? Surely, she knew we were up to something, if we were down here in stolen clothes, while everyone else was up at the party.

"So," Pandora said, turning slowly back around with a knowing smile on her lips. "How's Chief Orion?"

16

"*I* don't know what you mean," Navan replied, our stunned silence dragging on a moment too long. "We were just trying to find some video footage from Gianne's attack, to see if there's anything we can do to fortify the new lab against that same kind of onslaught," he explained, leaving me speechless at the sharpness of his mind. I was still reeling from the sound of Orion's name coming from Pandora's lips.

She smiled tightly. "Relax, you don't need to lie to me," she said, peering over Navan's shoulder to look at the screen, which the hypnotized intelligence officer was still working away on. "Orion and I are... Let's just say we're close acquaintances. I had a feeling you were gathering some kind of intel out in the garden, although I had to keep up pretenses around the other guards. You ran off before I could speak with you in private."

I gaped at her. How could she be on Orion's side? She was Queen Brisha's most trusted advisor! Was she double-bluffing, trying to trick us into giving something away so she could arrest us? I couldn't tell. Her face was a confusing, blank canvas. How had she managed to reach such a prime spot in Brisha's court without alerting suspicion? A million questions raced through my mind, but Pandora spoke again before I could ask one.

"I would gladly have sent your information to Orion myself, since I am aware he's expecting news from you. You certainly did not need to go through all of this rigmarole, drugging defenseless intelligence officers and knocking out guards," she muttered, glancing back over her shoulder. "The pair of you draw too much attention to yourselves."

"If you wanted things done your way, you should have revealed yourself to us earlier," Navan replied defensively, scrutinizing her. I could sense that neither of us knew what to make of her now; she had thrown us completely off guard.

Pandora shook her head, her purple ponytail swinging from side to side, jangling the golden trinkets woven within the strands. "Get him to stop what he's doing and delete everything from the system. I'll use my own device to set up a connection with Orion. This is much too risky."

A frosty stalemate stretched between Navan and Pandora, the two of them facing off against one another, though neither said a word.

"I suggest you do it now, before your serum wears off. I know you don't have any left," Pandora said with a slight smirk.

Navan remained frozen for a moment, before he finally relented. Turning to the intelligence officer, he instructed him to delete all memory of the event in the system. The officer nodded and set to work, his hands dancing across the screen. His eyes were still blank, his shoulders slumped.

I eyed Pandora curiously, every word she said making me more and more uneasy. All those times I'd been sure I could feel the burn of eyes on me... Now, I knew why. This whole time, Pandora had been watching us. It also made sense that she had been so lenient about our suspicious activity. When she had found us creeping around the ancient wing of the palace, she'd given us the key because she had *wanted* us to leave. She might not have known where we were headed, but she would've suspected it was part of our mission for Orion. That was why word never got back to Queen Brisha. It had all been a ruse. I was glad, at least, that Pandora hadn't overheard the conversation Navan and I had been having moments before her arrival.

"If you've been here all along, why is Orion getting us to do all of this for him? Why ask us to gather information on the elixir, when he has you?" I asked, realizing it didn't quite add up.

She sighed, as if I were an idiot. "Do you honestly think I could have gained my position as the queen's most valued advisor if I snuck around stealing things from her and asking her key workers for information? I am Orion's eyes inside Brisha's court, but I cannot risk being caught as a traitor. I am important to him in a way you are not," she explained, puffing her chest out with pride. "I am here to report on the queen's movements, weaknesses, army, and explorations—anything that will aid the rebels in the war to come. *You* are here to reach the places I cannot, without getting myself in trouble," she added, with a flick of her wrist.

"Surely, the queen would've confided in you about the elixir if you're that important to her," I replied, suspicion dripping from my tone.

A haughty expression fell across Pandora's stern face. "She continues to keep that information to herself, no matter my approach," she said bitterly. "I tried to ask the alchemists, too, but they are tight-lipped, even with me. The idiots fear they'll lose their jobs if they breathe a word to anyone," she muttered. "Now, tell me, what did Yorrek reveal about the elixir?"

"We have enough information to satisfy Orion, and that's all you need to know," Navan cut in.

"There's no need to be so secretive, Navan. We're all playing for the same side, remember?" Pandora reprimanded, frowning. "I don't suppose Yorrek mentioned a book, did he, when you questioned him?"

I tried to keep my expression impassive. "He said the queen kept a collection, but he didn't mention one in particular. Should he have?"

She shrugged. "There has long been a rumor that she's keeping one of Yorrek's notebooks somewhere, one that contains all the failed trials and near successes with the elixir," she explained, her eyes narrowing in annoyance. "I don't know if it's true, as I myself couldn't get a word out of Yorrek, but I thought he might have been freer with his words to you. If you did happen to hear anything, I'm sure Orion would be *delighted* to know about it." An unmistakable warning hovered in her voice. Still, I wasn't about to confirm her suspicions, not if there was a way we could get to that notebook first. It might be just the thing we needed to develop an anti-elixir.

"I'm sure he would, but Yorrek didn't tell us anything about it," I replied confidently. "Lauren spends every day in the library, and she hasn't seen any sort of *secret* notebook," I added, putting sarcastic emphasis on the word "secret."

A thoughtful expression flickered across Pandora's face. "Hm. Very well."

The intelligence officer turned from the computer to Navan. "The task is complete," he said in a monotone. Without hesitation, Navan delved into his pocket, tilting the man's head back before administering the last of the Elysium. A few minutes later, the officer went limp.

"If you're done here, follow me," Pandora instructed. We stood and left the sleeping intelligence officer to the rest of his shift.

Following Pandora up the same stairwell we had arrived through, we passed the guards, who were still asleep against the door, though one had slumped in front of it. Pandora pushed him aside. Inside the dim interior of the staircase, I picked up my beautiful gown and heels. I brushed my hands across the exquisite material, knowing I'd likely never get the chance to wear it again.

It took ten minutes before we reached the gap in the wall, the scarlet curtain undulating outward. Feeling desperately unfit in comparison to my cold-blood companions, I paused to catch my breath before following them out into the dusty hallway of the abandoned wing.

"You managed to make an unholy mess of a perfectly good wall," Pandora remarked, flashing an accusatory glance at Navan. "This is what I mean by drawing attention to yourselves."

"Nobody comes this way," Navan replied tersely, the muscles twitching in his jaw.

"But if they do, they will see this and suspect something immediately," Pandora continued, her tone patronizing. "I'll have to get this seen to tomorrow. Yet another task on an endless list." She scowled, turning on her heel and heading through the ghostly galleria.

She didn't stop until we were back out in the frosty night air, surrounded by the twisted trunks of forgotten trees and the overgrown grass of a long-lost garden. She had brought us to the same spot we had come to the night we left for the artisan market. I still thought fondly of that strange square, with its twinkling lights and jaunty music. Subconsciously, I lifted a hand to my heart, feeling for the climpet that flashed there.

"So, this is why you were creeping around in the abandoned wing of the palace?" Navan mused.

"Not quite," Pandora remarked as she took off into the air, flying up to the shadows of the surrounding mountainside. There, she landed, perching on a ledge, hidden from sight. Navan followed, lifting me upward and landing a short distance away. Pandora took out a comm device and pressed a button on the side that made it flash red.

"I could say the same thing about you two, creeping into dark corners of the palace alone together, though you were probably trying to canoodle or something equally nauseating," she retorted, her focus on the device in her hand.

"No, we went to find the hypnosis fruit to use on Yorrek," I snapped, annoyed by her constant condescension.

"Temper, temper!" Pandora mocked. "Besides, there's no need to be coy. I understand the need for physical contact. *Believe me*, I understand it," she murmured, raising her eyebrows. There was a note of frustration in her voice that turned my stomach. She had already implied that she and Orion were in some way... close... *Could he be her lover?* To think of the two of them enjoying *any* kind of physical contact made me want to hurl.

A deep voice crackled through the device. "Pandora? I wasn't expecting to hear from you today."

It set my nerves on edge, to hear that voice again. After everything Orion had done, I wanted to reach into the comm device and tear out his throat.

"I have some special guests with me, darling," Pandora purred in response. "Riley and Navan. There is something they would like to say."

A cold laugh rippled through the device. "So, I hear from you at last? And here I was thinking I'd have to start slicing fingers off dear old Jean and Roger."

My blood ran cold. How did he know their names? Suddenly, it all felt very real. If he knew who they were, then he definitely wasn't bluffing. Rage prickled inside me. How dare he utter their names aloud? How dare he threaten me? Before I could retaliate, I felt Navan's hand circle my waist, catching me before I said something I might regret.

"Before we tell you anything, we need to know that Riley's parents are safe, and that you'll uphold your end of the bargain if we give you this information," Navan said, his arm steadying me.

For a moment, there was nothing but white noise.

"Your parents are safe, Riley. For now," Orion spoke, at last. "I am a man of my word, and I will not touch a hair on their heads so long as you continue to send intel."

My heart sank at his words. I had known Orion would do this. He had a way to squeeze information out of us. He wouldn't release his hold until he had every morsel of intel he wanted. Or maybe it would never be enough, and we'd be forced to work for him until we died—or until he did.

"I expect more information in a month's time," Orion continued. "Now, you may tell me the information you already have," he prompted, followed by a beep. He was recording the conversation.

Sighing, Navan relayed the intel we had received from Yorrek regarding the way the elixir was made, and most of the ingredients required. I noticed that he left one or two out, but I didn't know if it was deliberate or not. He also left out the part about the notebook, and the device that Brisha had, which sped up the alchemy and synthesis processes. I was glad of that, knowing what the rebels would do with that kind of information. Then again, there were no assurances that Pandora didn't already know about that machine. If she had already told Orion about it, and they got the elixir to work, then the entire universe was in trouble.

"Interesting," Orion mused. "You may deliver your next batch of intel to Pandora, who will ensure I receive it. Do not take risks, and do not betray me. You know the consequences if you do," he warned. "Until tomorrow, my warrior queen," he added softly, just for Pandora, and I cringed.

"Until tomorrow, my supernova," Pandora whispered in response, her eyes twinkling in a way I never thought I'd see. With that, he was gone, the line going dead.

"Cute nicknames," I muttered.

She whirled around, casting me a withering look. "You might be daring now, but you cannot begin to understand the bond that binds true lovers together. *This* is a falsehood," she said, gesturing between Navan and me. "It is a thing of fantasy that can never be. Your worlds are on opposite sides of the universe; you aren't meant to be together. I doubt you could even begin to know what true love is," she spat, her words somehow piercing my heart.

Navan squeezed my waist, as if to say, *Don't listen, she's wrong*, and I slowly relaxed.

Pandora's gaze turned ice cold. "Going forward, remember that I will be watching you. If you decide to do anything foolish—perhaps you'll feel bold one morning and think about telling the queen about my true allegiance—I will inform Orion, and he will see to it that your nearest and dearest die the most painful deaths imaginable." She grinned, and whatever respect I had once had for her vaporized. "Now, run along to bed. The queen has some exciting news in the pipeline for you, and you will need your strength when you hear it. Believe me, it is simply to *die* for."

With her soft laughter dying on the breeze, she disappeared from the tumbledown garden, leaving us with the looming shadow of whatever lay ahead.

eeling despondent, we returned to our apartment to find Angie, Lauren, and Bashrik sitting in the hallway outside. They looked up as the elevator doors pinged open, immediately getting to their feet. They were still wearing the clothes from the party and looked surprised to see us in black military fatigues, with my gown draped over my arm.

"Where have you been?" Lauren asked, her tone concerned.

I shared a guilty look with Navan. "With everyone distracted by the party, we took the opportunity to go down to the control room, to see if we could get the intel to Orion," I explained, feeling bad about having kept them out of the loop.

"Let's head inside, and we can fill you guys in on the rest," Navan said, unlocking the door to the apartment.

As my friends made their way to the lounge area, I noticed that Bashrik sat as far away from Angie as possible, their eyes refusing to meet under any circumstance. The sight made me smirk. I knew there was still some tension lingering between the pair of them. Now, if only they'd just look up and confront it.

"So, that was almost a colossal disaster," Angie remarked, readjusting the neckline of her dress, shifting uncomfortably beneath the tight fabric.

I gave a small smile. "Almost, but not quite. We got the Elysium into Yorrek, and nobody is any the wiser, right?" I asked, understanding the stern look in her eyes. Navan and I hadn't been there to check that the serum had worked on Yorrek, since Orion had taken precedence. Even so, the three of them were capable of handling a single unruly alchemist without Navan and me.

"He was out cold in the hedges when I left him, but that doesn't always mean it worked. Did you see him again after we left?" Navan pressed.

Bashrik nodded, clearing his throat. "He reappeared a few minutes after you'd gone, but he was pretty disoriented. I'd say the Elysium worked, though it's hard to tell. He didn't go around blabbing to anyone, at least," he replied with a shrug.

Lauren raised a polite hand. "After the debacle with the guards and the queen, and you two leaving, Yorrek ended up wandering out of the bushes toward Brisha's table. I stayed close, in case he decided to spill any beans, but all I overheard was her asking if he was feeling well, as he seemed a little woozy. He just muttered something about needing to head home," she explained, a grim expression on her face. "He left shortly after that."

"So, that's a good thing, then? His memory got wiped, and he went home. No harm, no foul," I said, relieved.

Lauren shook her head. "The only problem is, I'd say he looked more perplexed than disoriented, as if he was trying to figure out what was wrong with him. It was like he was trying to find the missing piece of a puzzle, but he couldn't remember where he left it. Being an alchemist, I wouldn't be surprised if he sensed something unusual had happened. We just need to hope he doesn't figure out what." She sighed anxiously.

"Can Elysium be traced in the blood?" I asked, turning to Bashrik and Navan.

They looked at each other uncertainly. "It depends how quickly a sample is taken. Usually, no, unless the person is very quick. It disintegrates in the blood-stream within a quarter of an hour, give or take," Navan replied. I prayed Yorrek hadn't somehow managed to take a sample of blood from himself. Sure, he was strange, but I doubted he'd have brought an extraction kit with him. If he had, and found the Elysium in his system, we'd be in a lot of trouble.

"But you'd say the Elysium worked?" I repeated, looking to the others. I just wanted confirmation; otherwise, I knew I'd never sleep again, with the worry that we were going to get found out.

"I'd say so," Lauren conceded. "He looked too confused for it not to have worked. Besides, he'd have told the queen right then and there if he'd suspected something."

"So, it was almost a colossal disaster, but we just about got away with it," Angie said. "I say we make cheers to that," she ventured, before getting up and heading to the kitchen.

The sound of clinking followed, and she returned carrying a bottle of the same fizzy stuff we'd been drinking before the party. In her other hand, she was balancing two vials for the coldblood contingent, and three glass flutes for the three of us girls. Setting the flutes down on the table, she poured the fizzy drink into them. The bubbles rose up, threatening to spill over. Once the flutes were full, she passed them to Lauren and me, picking up her own.

With a forced smile, she held it aloft. "Here's to a semi-successful mission."

"And another month of borrowed time," I added as we all clinked our glasses and vials against Angie's. Looking around, it didn't seem like anyone was in the mood for a celebration.

The trio who hadn't been in the control room looked to me, their expressions curious. With a sigh, I explained what had happened down there and where Pandora had taken us. I told them of Orion's gratitude for our intel, resulting in the extension of my parents' protection, though I did have to mention the caveat of him wanting more intelligence in exchange. Then again, that didn't come as a surprise to anyone in the room.

What did surprise them, however, was the revelation of Pandora's true loyalty. As soon as the words were out of my mouth, an audible gasp rippled around the room, their disbelief evident. A second wave of gasps spread when I told them who her lover was. Even now, it was difficult to wrap my head around.

"Orion and *Pandora*?" Lauren whispered, her face frozen in shock.

"They're... lovers?" Angie gagged.

I laughed. "I know. It's hard to imagine Pandora with anyone. She isn't exactly the cuddly type."

"So what? Everyone is entitled to love and be loved," Bashrik muttered unexpectedly, his cheeks flushing a pale shade of pink. "It's no stranger than you and Navan. In fact, it's way less strange than your relationship."

Navan grinned. "I guess that goes for you and Angie, too?"

"Yeah, what the hell happened there?" I wondered, thinking back to the dramatic kiss in the garden, Bashrik sweeping Angie off her feet. And now, their awkwardness was palpable. "Kissing Angie in front of the queen wasn't exactly part of the plan, was it? I hope you did it for a good reason, because Brisha is going to hold one hell of a grudge now." If Bashrik had kissed Angie because he truly cared about her, then I was all for it. But otherwise, I wanted to know what on earth he'd been thinking, offending the queen so callously.

Bashrik lowered his gaze, running an anxious hand through his cropped hair. "It... might not have been part of our initial plan. But it made sense in the moment. It killed two birds with one stone. It got me off the hook with Brisha, and it was the perfect distraction. That's all it was," he said tightly, the muscles twitching in his neck.

Knowing how Angie truly felt about Bashrik, I stole

a glance at her, catching a flicker of disappointment as it flashed across her face. A split second later, it was gone, replaced with her trademark show of bravery.

"It's like Bashrik says—it was the best course of action in the moment," she stated, her tone a little too strong. "I was just playing along, making it seem genuine. Although a bit of advanced notice might have been nice," she retorted.

"It wasn't like I planned it meticulously. I didn't know it was going to happen until about a minute before it did," Bashrik countered, refusing to meet her gaze.

"Yeah, well, I didn't have any mouthwash nearby. Thanks to you, I might have caught some rare brand of Vysanthean cooties." She sighed melodramatically. "You have to warn a girl if you're going to kiss her, especially if you're an alien species who only drinks blood. And you *definitely* didn't need to slip me any tongue. There's putting on a show, and then there's crossing a line. I've still got a weird metallic taste in my mouth," she muttered. With each word, Bashrik was turning a deeper shade of crimson.

"Look, can we just forget about it? The ruse worked, and that's all that matters," he said quietly, his throat constricted. I wanted to knock their heads together. It was clear they both liked each other, and yet they were holding back through embarrassment.

Angie had done her usual thing of covering her discomfort with brash humor, and Bashrik was retreating into his shell. The pair of them were useless.

"Yeah, all we have to worry about now is Brisha's retribution for being humiliated," I said with a sigh, returning my mind to the gravity of the situation. She was a queen; she would not take kindly to being made a fool of, especially not by a man she was besotted with. I could only imagine how deeply that must have stung her, to watch Bashrik kiss another woman in front of her very eyes. I wouldn't have taken kindly to it, and I was a nobody with no power. There was no telling what a woman like Brisha would do in the pursuit of payback.

Bashrik looked up, his expression blank. It was clear that he hadn't intended to do any harm. He had been swept up in the moment, doing what he thought was best... and a little extra too. Still, he wasn't a bad guy. He hadn't meant to hurt the queen.

"I had no choice. I needed her to stop obsessing over me, and we needed a distraction. If there are consequences to my actions, then we'll have to deal with them when they come," he concluded stoically. "I'll take whatever punishment she wants to dole out."

A tense silence drifted across the group, our thoughts turning to Brisha, and the kind of retribution she might bring down upon us. In addition to Bashrik's betrayal, she was undoubtedly harboring some kind of anger toward me, too. I had told her that Bashrik wasn't interested in anyone else. I had given her hope when I shouldn't have. She had trusted me, and I had let her down. I doubted I could ever win her favor so easily again.

*A*fter our encounter in the abandoned palace garden, two weeks passed without much interaction from Pandora. Despite Orion's threat and the knowledge that his lover was constantly watching us, life took on an unexpected sort of normality. Navan and I returned to our training, Lauren continued to work her way through the royal library, and Angie and Bashrik resumed their game of skirting around each other, choosing to pretend they'd never kissed. It had been discussed once; apparently it didn't need to be brought up again.

Soon, I began to wonder if Pandora had merely been toying with us, dangling a carrot of doom so we would never feel comfortable, our minds constantly on edge, waiting for the worst to happen. Even when it didn't come, I couldn't relax, fearful that bad news was just around the corner.

In fact, the only thing that had changed in the realm of Northern Vysanthe was the speed with which the alchemy lab was being built. The queen had mostly forgiven me for my indiscretion, believing I knew nothing about Bashrik's affections for Angie, but she had not been so kind to the man himself. Bashrik had well and truly fallen out of the queen's favor, with her demanding he finish the new lab quicker than previously agreed... or else. The threat, by all accounts, was the usual sort, with her promising to banish him to the polar ice caps, or send him back to her sister as a traitor, or feed him to a pack of hungry frostfangs, but I didn't believe she would actually carry any of that out. I knew damaged pride and a broken heart when I saw them.

I could tell that Bashrik truly felt bad about what had happened and wanted to make up for it by building the lab quickly. The building was coming along more and more every day. In fact, within the next couple of days, it would be finished, ready for the alchemists to resume their work.

"At least you won't be sent packing to the South," Navan teased as we stood around the building site, watching the workers put the finishing touches into place. It was possibly the most stunning creation I'd ever seen, the walls almost liquid in the way they shimmered, the sharp contours of the roof glinting in the Vysanthean sun. It looked like someone had put the ocean on its side, the frozen waves crashing at the top, while the still waters stretched below.

Bashrik grimaced. "I'm still not convinced she won't punish me out of spite. I'll finish this up, and she'll change her mind," he muttered, shielding his eyes as he watched a glazier dangle from the side of the structure, fitting a small, mirrored piece of glass.

I waited for Angie to make a smart remark at his expense, but the cutting retort never came. They'd been like this ever since the garden party, no longer sniping at or bantering with one another, but standing shyly beside each other, avoiding eye contact.

"Somebody's in love," I whispered to Lauren, who stood next to me.

Lauren rolled her eyes. "She paces around the apartment like a puppy. I wish they'd just kiss again already. Their awkwardness is making *me* awkward."

I stifled a chuckle as Angie flashed us a sharp look, her cheeks reddening.

"What are you two snickering about?" she asked, her eyes narrowing.

I tried to straighten my expression. "I was just

telling Lauren that we better get going. Otherwise, we'll be late for training."

"And I have a pile of books to get through before the end of the day," Lauren added, not bothering to hide her smirk.

"You and Bashrik enjoy whatever you plan to get up to on this fine, sunny morning, and we'll see you for dinner later," I said, relishing the embarrassed looks my words elicited from the pair of them. Bashrik was literally looking at everything other than Angie, while her cheeks went scarlet.

Navan grinned, giving his brother a pat on the back. "Don't do anything I wouldn't do," he said, leaning down to plant a kiss on my lips, as if to prove a point.

With that, I looped my arm through Navan's, and we set off toward the training center. Lauren followed as far as the palace before disappearing inside with an amused wave of farewell.

It was the first morning in a long time that I actually felt good about things. With the passing weeks, my stamina and recovery time had improved on the training grounds. Now, I barely noticed the aches and bruises, and if I did, it meant I'd taken a particularly brutal hit that deserved to hurt. The day-to-day strain of the tasks no longer affected me, and it felt glorious to be able to say that.

Moreover, I was acing my flying tasks, both with wings and in the training ships, and was managing to hold my own in hand-to-hand simulations. The only thing was, I wished my wings were more permanent. I was almost at the end of my second vial, with about a quarter left after strict training-only rationing, but I hoped I could ask for more when I ran out.

During training itself, Navan had backed off, after I'd asked him to, but he still couldn't help himself when it came to the big battle scenarios. I would catch sight of him creeping around a ruin, keeping an eye on me, believing I had no idea what he was doing. It usually ended in him getting himself killed in the simulation, but I was getting better at defending him, keeping him safer for longer in those situations. I was no longer the puny Kryptonian who only had knives at her disposal. I was formidable now, able to take down multiple enemies within a few seconds of letting my knives fly, while drawing my weapons back without it turning into a friendly-fire situation.

I was proving my worth in a hostile environment, and the other trainees were noticing. Two days ago, Iskra had offered her hand to help me up after a particularly long and vigorous sparring session. And then, yesterday, a guy named Orval had slapped me on the back after a flying fight, whooping about how awesome I'd been. The slap on the back had nearly ended with me falling flat on my face, but the sentiment had been a welcome change.

I didn't know why they were being kinder to me, and the shift in mood almost made me suspicious, but it seemed genuine enough. I had thought they'd be bitter that I was succeeding, but I had shown my determination to be part of their team, if nothing else. One of the officers had even nodded at me as he gave a speech about how a unit was only as strong as its weakest member, the others nodding along.

"You seem very smiley this morning," Navan said, putting his arm around my shoulders.

I grinned wider. "Today feels like a good one, don't you think?" I asked, slipping my arm around his waist. Things still hadn't progressed between us, physically. That moment hadn't arrived yet, but I was safe in the knowledge that it would, when the time was right. He didn't seem in any rush, though we'd had a few heated evenings, spent tangled in one another's arms. That was enough for me, and it seemed to be enough for him, for now.

"It does feel like a good one," Navan agreed, lifting his face to the sunlight.

We were still in good spirits as we headed to the locker rooms, changing quickly before getting out onto the training floor, separating to take up our positions with our sparring partners. I had Iskra again, while

Navan was facing off against a bulky coldblood whose name I could never remember. It sounded like Seth, but I knew it couldn't be something as Earthen as that.

It was an intense morning session, with Iskra challenging me at every turn. Even so, it couldn't wipe the smile off my face. I could feel myself getting stronger thanks to the training, and that was worth every move that floored me. I learned from my mistakes, remembering her body language so I didn't fall for the same trick again. Not just that, but I was learning how to read coldbloods in general. A curious thing happened when they were flagging—their veins darkened every couple of seconds, flashing like beacons. I guessed it was because the blood was pumping faster to their hearts, but it was a sure sign they were weakening, and I knew just how to take advantage of it.

In fact, Iskra's veins were doing just that as she charged toward me. Thinking fast, I sidestepped one of her favorite attacks and brought my foot down on the back of her legs, watching in delight as she sank to the ground.

"Nice counter!" she said as I helped her up, an impressed smile on her face. "You're getting good, Riley. I'm going to have to start watching my back." She chuckled, wiping a bead of sweat from her brow.

"I'm getting there," I said coyly, adrenaline coursing through my veins. Somehow, I felt like I was doing this for the human race, even though nobody knew I was anything other than "Kryptonian." This was my chance to prove we weren't puny underlings, but a scrappy, defiant species that could put up a decent fight.

We were about to start another round when everyone's heads snapped toward the door of the training room. It burst open, and Pandora and the queen strode through, flanked by a handful of guards. It wasn't like Brisha to come with such an extended entourage, and the sight of it filled my heart with dread. Had we done something wrong? Had Pandora double-crossed us? I noticed her eyes seeking me out, a cold smile on her lips.

"Gather round, soldiers. I have good news for you," Queen Brisha announced as she came to a halt in the center of the room. We did as she asked, hurrying toward her and forming a haphazard circle.

I sought Navan out and stood beside him as we waited to hear what the queen had to say. Something about her manner troubled me, even with her announcement that she had good news to deliver.

"I have a mission for you to undertake," the queen continued, lifting her chin proudly. "I have selected your particular squadron, as you are the finest of my trainee intake. However, you can't all go on this particular mission, and so I have selected the best among you to partake. This is not a decision I have made lightly, but I know you will not let me down when the time comes. Upon completion of this mission, those involved shall graduate early, earning their emblem," she said solemnly. This mission had to be the news Pandora had alluded to—the dangling carrot of doom.

"A select group of you are going to wage a counter-attack on Queen Gianne," Pandora explained, taking over for the queen at her approving nod. "You are going to infiltrate the South and place explosives in and around her famed Observatory. This will take down almost all the surveillance that she has, as well as send the message that we mean business. It will leave her vulnerable, so we can show her that her defiance of the peace treaty will not be tolerated. She can't expect to attack us without consequences. Enough time, and enough benevolence, has gone by, and now is the time for action," she boomed. The other soldiers whooped and hollered, beating their fists against their chests in a peculiar percussion. All but Navan and me.

"Queen Brisha, I must protest this!" Navan shouted above the din, silencing the room and surprising me. "That is not a counterattack; that is an act of terrorism, Your Highness. Innocent civilians visit that site every day—workers, tourists, and everything in between. If you hit the Observatory, you will kill thousands. I implore you to reconsider. After all, they didn't strike against you, Your Highness. Your sister did!"

"It is a counterattack," the queen replied curtly, "and that is the nature of war. People die, Navan. You are a soldier, drafted in to do a job. I suggest you revise your moral compass when it comes to the enemy. Do *not* forget whose side you are on." She scowled, evidently displeased at being called out in front of her militia. Plus, I had the feeling she wasn't about to let another Idrax embarrass her.

In fact, I was sure that was where this change in pace had come from. Before Bashrik had spurned her, her focus had been on obtaining his affections. Now, with him out of the picture and her heart in pieces, her desire for revenge had clearly undergone a renaissance. I cursed silently, knowing we might have prevented this if Bashrik had played along and kissed Brisha instead. Then again, how good could I say my moral compass was, if I was willing to put a man out as bait, hurting my friend's feelings in the process? No, we'd definitely been between a rock and a hard place. I just hadn't expected an all-out act of terrorism to come from it.

"Why not your sister's alchemy lab, or a military base, Your Highness? Surely, that would be a more direct retaliation?" Navan pressed. I nodded along, guessing there would be fewer civilians in those places.

"I do not need to explain my decisions to you, Navan Idrax," Queen Brisha retorted. "I have selected the Observatory because it will not only hit her where it hurts, but it is isolated, meaning a greater chance of my soldiers getting in and out undetected."

Navan grimaced. "Fewer guards, more civilians, you mean?"

"I will have you locked up if you speak another word against me!" Queen Brisha snapped, her eyes glittering with fury. With all that had happened with Bashrik, I'd forgotten just how terrifying and fierce she could be. "You are on my list to partake in this mission, Navan, and you *will* go, or you will face corporal punishment. You are *my* soldier now, but if you no longer wish to be, then I have no further need of you. Make your choice, Idrax," she barked.

My heart pounded. A tense silence stretched between the two of them, with everyone's eyes fixed on the scene. I gripped Navan's arm, hoping it would get him to see sense. Launching an attack was an awful thing, but protesting it wouldn't stop her, and I didn't want him killed.

"Is Riley on your list, Your Highness?" he asked quietly, the tension almost unbearable.

Queen Brisha smiled bitterly. "No, she is not. I would not put her in harm's way," she replied, her expression softening as she let her gaze settle on me.

"Then I will do as you've asked, Your Highness," he

said, his voice low. "My loyalties lie with you. I am a soldier, and I will do my duty."

"Good," Queen Brisha remarked. "Those who are on my list will receive details of their mission soon. Your training is complete for today. Return to your homes, refresh yourselves, and expect word to come. Be prepared. This is one of the most important missions you will ever undertake, and you do it all in my name. I thank you for your service," she said solemnly, before striding out of the room, her entourage in tow.

Navan and I looked at one another, not knowing what to say.

After changing out of our training uniforms and stowing our weapons, we took our time returning to our chambers, neither of us speaking on the walk over. His hand held mine, but we had no words. Even though it looked like Pandora was otherwise engaged with the queen's newfound focus, there was no telling who might be listening. And so, we said nothing until we were back in the safety of our room.

"I don't want you to go," I said, as soon as the door was closed. "It's too dangerous. You'll end up dead, and

I can't cope with that." Tears pricked my eyes, and I gripped his hands, afraid to let go.

He brushed a strand of hair behind my ear. "I'll be fine, Riley. I promise you, I will come back, and everything will be okay."

I shook my head. "I'll be sitting here, sick with worry, until you come back through those doors," I murmured, looping my arms around Navan's neck. He held me, holding my gaze as I stared into his slate eyes.

"I'm just worried about those poor civilians," he said, a sadness creeping into his eyes. "There has to be a way we can reduce the fallout."

"We can think about that tomorrow," I said. "Right now, I just want to commit as much of you to memory as possible, to give me something to focus on when you leave," I urged, holding his face in my hands as I leaned in to kiss him. It was a desperate, urgent kiss. A goodbye kiss.

His hands ran up my spine as the kiss deepened, his tongue exploring my mouth, his fingertips searching every contour of my skin. I shivered in anticipation as he lifted my shirt over my head and cast it to the floor, his kisses trailing down my neck and across my collarbone, moving downward. I gripped him tighter, pressing against him, wanting to feel as much of him as possible, in case I never saw him again.

He lifted me up, and I wrapped my legs around him

as he carried me over to the sofa and lay me down on the soft cushions, the fire roaring beside us. Grasping for the edges of his shirt, I practically tore it off him and sent it flying to the ground, reveling in the delicious friction of his skin against mine.

We were both reaching for the buttons of each other's pants when a knock ricocheted through the room like a gunshot, making us freeze. Not knowing who it might be, but fairly sure we didn't want to get caught in this situation again, we scrabbled for our clothes, throwing them back on as fast as possible.

More or less fully clothed, Navan approached the door and opened it cautiously, while I crept up behind him, wanting to see who had disturbed what might have been the greatest night of my life. To my shock, Queen Brisha was standing in the hallway, a stern expression on her face.

"I have further news to impart," she said, eyeing us curiously. We were still out of breath, and Navan's hair was a mess.

"What can we do for you, Your Highness?" I asked, trying not to pant.

"It's about the mission," she explained. "I've changed my mind."

"Changed your mind, Your Highness?" I felt dizzy with relief at the thought that Navan wouldn't have to leave—that he wouldn't have to fight.

"I have decided that you should also go on the mission, Riley," Queen Brisha stated, shattering my hopes.

Navan opened his mouth to object, but the queen interrupted. "If you say a word against my decision, I will banish you both to the farthest reaches of this realm."

"I'm not questioning your authority, Your Highness, but... why? Why must you do this?" Navan asked, clearly dumbfounded.

The queen's gaze flickered between the two of us, and I saw the jealousy in her eyes. "This is because of you, Navan. I want you to know that. She would have been safe, if you had not spoken out of turn," she spat, her face twisting into a bitter mask of contempt. "I expect you to be there when the rest of the soldiers leave. If you aren't, I will track you down, and I will end you both."

It almost brought me to tears, to see Queen Brisha like this. Where once our love had inspired her, now it embittered her. As she turned and headed for the elevator, I felt regret twist in my stomach. More than anything, I wished I had told her that Bashrik hadn't reciprocated her feelings, so I might have spared her the pain she felt... and the suffering she felt it necessary to inflict upon us.

It wasn't Bashrik's fault, and it wasn't her fault. It

was mine. I had broken her heart by not telling her the truth, and I knew the crazy things people did when their hearts were in pieces. I wished I could put it back together again for her, though that was the hardest task in the universe. A heart, once broken, was never the same again.

19

*W*ord came at dawn, via a holographic message that flickered to life in our chambers. I was already awake, not having been able to sleep after Brisha's unexpected visit. After the news, neither Navan nor I had felt like resuming what we'd been up to before she interrupted. Instead, we curled up in each other's arms and struggled to drift off. Eventually, I had given up, choosing to just lie there with his arms around me, enjoying the closeness while I had the chance. I was getting better in training, but I was nowhere near ready to enter a real-life mission. If it came to blows, I just hoped I could keep up—and not get Navan killed.

The message told us to meet around the back of the palace in an hour's time, at the tunnel entrance where we had first entered Brisha's queendom. It added that we should wear civilian clothes beneath our military fatigues, though it didn't go into detail as to why. With that, it cut off, leaving me to the turmoil of my own thoughts.

I had gotten so used to this part of Vysanthe that it felt strange to be going back to the South. Plus, the circumstances of our return weren't exactly great. All I could think about were the civilians who might lose their lives because of us. This was not what I'd signed up for. I didn't want to kill anyone. I didn't want anyone to die because of me.

All through the night, I'd wondered if there was a way we might prevent people from dying, but I hadn't managed to come up with anything. It seemed too vast a task for one person, or even two people to undertake, without alerting suspicion. And, right now, we couldn't risk crossing Brisha or Pandora, for fear of what they might do in retribution. Pandora in particular. She seemed to fully support Brisha's decision, for whatever reason, which had to mean Orion did, too.

"You want something to eat?" Navan asked groggily, wandering into the kitchen. I knew he hadn't gotten much sleep either.

I shook my head. "I'm not hungry," I said quietly.

"You should get your strength up. You'll need it. There's no telling when you might get the chance to eat again," he said, slicing up some fruit and putting it into a bowl. He took down a vial for himself, drinking the fluid in one gulp before handing the bowl to me.

I took it from him, grimacing at the sight. My stomach was in knots, my mouth dry, my eyes tired. The last thing I wanted to do was force breakfast down my throat, but I could see the sense in his advice. Reluctantly, I worked through the slices, chewing slowly, gulping the sweet fruit down before my body could reject it.

After breakfast, I dressed in black military fatigues, with my civilian clothes underneath, and laced up my combat boots, pulling my hair back into a ponytail before splashing cold water on my face. I looked at Navan's reflection in the mirror. He stood in the doorway of the bathroom, a worried expression on his face.

"You know, vampires aren't supposed to have a reflection," I said, trying to lighten the mood. "In all the stories, you're invisible in mirrors. I've seen enough *Dracula* remakes to know."

A hint of a smile pulled at the corners of his lips. "Your vampire stories get a lot wrong," he said. "We're supposed to be immortal already, in those tales. A stake through the heart is the only way to kill us, right?"

"That's right," I replied, coming up to him and

curving my hand into a fist, as if I were holding a stake. I raised it above his heart, play-acting, while he put his arms around me. As I plunged down the invisible stake, he made a face, but we didn't laugh. It only reminded me of what we were about to do. It might not be a stake pressed to his chest, but Navan's mortality was definitely on the line. Mine, too.

Reaching up, I kissed him tentatively on the lips, wanting to freeze the moment. I longed to rewind to the night before, or even the day before, when we were happy in our false bubble of security. I didn't want this. The moment had come for me to act, and I wanted it to go away.

"We should get going," he murmured.

I glanced up at the clock on the wall in the living room. How had an hour passed so quickly? Feeling panic begin to course through my veins, I held his face in my hands, kissing him with everything I had, and he returned my kiss with desperate passion. Only when he pulled away did I stop, knowing the time had come. There was no putting it off any longer.

"Navan, will you promise me something?" I asked, snatching up my knives and attaching them to my chest and waist. From the table, I grabbed the quarter-full vial and the last full one, and slipped them into my pocket, the glass clinking together.

He looked at me curiously. "What?"

"Promise me you won't be a hero," I urged. "Promise me you won't put yourself in danger for me, okay? If I put you in harm's way, I'd never forgive myself."

He smiled. "I'll try," he said, but I didn't believe him. It wasn't in his nature to stand by and do nothing if I got into trouble. Still, I had to ask him, just to comfort my own fears, if nothing else. "Will you promise me something, too?" he asked, strapping two blades onto his back.

"It depends," I murmured, knowing I couldn't make promises I wasn't willing to keep.

"Promise me you won't leave my sight throughout this mission," he replied, his expression serious.

"I'll try."

"I mean it, Riley. Don't leave my sight," he warned, all humor gone from his voice.

With a sigh, I nodded. "I'll do my very best not to leave your side, unless something tears me from it." It was the only compromise I could make, since I had no idea what would meet us when we got to the Observatory. There hadn't been many guards the last time we'd visited, but that didn't mean they wouldn't have heightened their security in the wake of Gianne's attack on her sister. Perhaps they would be expecting a counterattack.

We left the apartment together and headed for the

tunnel entrance, my nerves building with every step. On the ground floor, I froze, realizing I hadn't even had a chance to say goodbye to Angie and Lauren. It had all happened so quickly, with my mind so confused that I hadn't told them I was going, or when I might be back. If I died, they would never know what had happened to me. I mean, someone would fill them in, but they would wonder why I'd gone without saying a word. I didn't want to listen to it, but a small voice inside my head reminded me that, for all I knew, this *could* be the last chance I'd ever have to see them again.

"I have to go and say goodbye to Angie and Lauren," I said desperately, backing away from the palace entrance.

"There's no time," Navan said, reaching out to pull me back. "If we're late, or we don't show, you know what the consequences are. You heard the queen lay them out for us, plain and simple. Do you think she won't extend that vengeance to your friends?" His eyes were sorrowful.

"But I need to let them know where I've gone. They won't forgive me, if I don't," I said, my heart and head torn in two directions.

"They'll understand, Riley. Come on, we have to go," Navan insisted, his pull on my arm increasing, until I was helpless to do anything but stagger after him. I looked back over my shoulder, my thoughts with my friends, as his arm slipped around my shoulders, comforting me. Holding me tight, he led me out of the palace, into the driving rain. Each icy pellet stung my skin as it landed, but I lifted my face to the downpour regardless, wanting the cold water to calm me.

We made our way up to the tunnel entrance where a group of soldiers was already waiting. I recognized most of them as fellow trainees, but there were one or two unfamiliar faces. They looked older, their features grizzled, a darkness glinting in their eyes that suggested they had witnessed the horrors of war. Pandora was there, too, though Queen Brisha was nowhere to be seen.

"Navan, Riley, how good of you to grace us with your presence," Pandora announced tartly as we approached. Glancing down at her watch, she pulled a face. "On time, with three minutes to spare. I hope you won't be cutting it quite so close when it comes to laying explosives," she mocked, prompting a snicker from the assembled group.

Navan leveled his gaze at her. "Apologies, Pandora. We're here now, and that's what counts, right?" he remarked, his tone cold.

"Indeed," Pandora muttered, before turning back to the rest of the group. "Now, please take a belt each and strap them firmly to your waists," she instructed, handing out several straps that each held a row of small black orbs. These were the explosives, I supposed, taking my own belt and strapping it over the set of knives I already had, resting just above my hips.

"Do not touch this button before you are instructed to, unless you wish to blow yourselves out of the sky," Pandora warned, gesturing toward a small blue button on the side of the black orbs.

A few of the meatheads in our group chuckled among themselves, pretending to push the blue button, much to the evident disdain of Pandora, who flashed them a threatening look. Instantly, they stopped, looking down at the ground in shame.

Pandora cleared her throat. "We will be flying into enemy territory. Ships will be too conspicuous, so you're all going to have to rely on your own strength and stamina. Don't waste your energy on speed. Stealth is what we need here, on the way in," she began. "All of you will follow Commander Korbin here, who will be your ranking officer on this mission," she added, gesturing to one of the grizzled, older coldbloods who had joined us. His dark hair was streaked with white, shorn close at the sides, with jagged tattoos coiling beneath the remaining bristles. His eyes were a pale blue, his face broad and stern. I felt anxious at the very sight of him; he did not look like the kind of guy anyone would want to meet in a dark alley.

Korbin nodded, the movement tugging at a long,

silvery scar that shot up his neck, curving all the way up his skull, where it stopped just shy of his eyebrow. "In the air, now!" he yelled, startling me. The other trainees sent out their wings, taking to the skies in a rush of wind and a cacophony of leathery flapping.

Padding around my pockets for my wing serum, I quickly took out the stopper and downed the remainder of the second vial. I only had one left now. After it was finished, I would have to ask for more. Navan grabbed me under the arms, lifting me up into the air so I wouldn't be left behind. I flushed, feeling humiliated at having to be carried in front of my fellow soldiers. Still, I knew I would rather be carried than fall behind, uncertain whether I'd be able to catch up.

Navan clutched me to his chest as my face twisted in agony, the serum leaving no muscle free of pain. I gritted my teeth against it, unwilling to show weakness in front of the others. I felt the familiar razorblade sensation of the wings forcing their way out from under my scapula, before they stretched out behind me, catching a current of air beneath their silky tension.

"You good?" Navan asked.

"You'd think it would get easier at some point," I gasped.

Navan released me, letting me fly solo with the rest of the flock. He flew beside me, his wings beating steadily, my own wings copying his almost mechanical motions as we soared up the side of the jagged mountain range, the cold air whipping our faces. We came down the other side ten minutes later, flying over the spot where our Snapper still rested, forgotten about in the secret glade that stood before the tunnel entrance. It was strange to see it sitting there, abandoned, especially as we were about to reenter the domain it had come from.

Feeling the twist of fear in my stomach, I focused my eyes forward, taking in the impressive sight of the soldiers flying in formation ahead of me. Off to the sides, I could make out the glitter of Northern Vysanthe's frozen lakes, and the fanged horizon of far-off mountain ranges. In the driving rain, it looked remarkably bleak, though there was a certain type of beauty to it.

A savage beauty, I thought, reminded of Lazar's words. It had been a long time since I'd thought about Navan's uncle and what might have befallen him. As much as I resented him for keeping the tracker in my neck, I couldn't help wondering if he was okay. He had helped Navan and me escape Queen Gianne's soldiers, after all.

In the distance, the shimmering wall of the barrier between nations came into view. It was like catching the silk of a spider's web in the right light, only seen in glimpses. As we neared, however, I could hear the steady thrum of it, the energy crackling upon our approach. How we were supposed to get through it without being noticed or destroyed, I had no clue. We'd managed to get through in the Snapper, but even that had been a rocky entrance. Without anything to shield us from the barrier's energy, I worried we might explode.

Korbin came to a halt a few yards from the first patch of barrier, urging us all to hide behind a parapet of rock that jutted out from the jagged mountains. We did so, keeping our eyes on him as he took something out of the backpack he wore between his wings. I squinted for a better look, seeing that he carried a large, peculiar, net-like square in his hands.

He approached the thrumming barrier with the square, the crosshatched surface bursting into life as he placed it against the sheen of raw energy. A small explosion crackled through the air, and my eyes darted toward the Southern side of the wall, expecting ships to approach at any moment. When they didn't, I turned my attention back to the square, suddenly realizing what it was for.

It worked like a circuit breaker, as far as I could tell, the square cutting out a section of the barrier so we could all filter through without setting off the border patrol alarms. A genius move, and one we definitely couldn't have achieved in the Vysanthean ships.

"Get going!" Korbin hissed, ushering the first of us through the gap.

I brought up the tail end of the soldiers, with Navan the only one to follow. When it came to me, however, Korbin shoved me roughly between the shoulders, aggravating the tender spot between my scapula. With the sting of it searing through my chest, I glared at him, knowing he hadn't laid a finger on anyone else. He glared back, letting me know he didn't want me on this mission any more than I wanted to be on it.

Navan looked furious at what Korbin had done, but I silenced his anger with a warning look. I didn't need him starting a fight. It would only get us in trouble. I'd grown used to coldbloods looking down on me, and as long as Korbin didn't try to blow me up with the rest of the Observatory, I could handle whatever derogatory behavior he threw at me.

As I reached the other side, coming through the barrier unscathed, a thought dawned on me. What was the real reason Brisha had changed her mind all of a sudden? Why *had* she decided to send me on this mission? A shiver of dread ran up my spine as I began to doubt that she had solely been acting under the influence of her broken heart. Thinking on it more clearly, I realized that if anything happened to me,

Navan would do whatever Brisha asked to get me back —including more attacks against innocent civilians.

This was her way of showing her power over him, with the perk of making him suffer for what his brother had done. I could see it now. It was important to her that he bend to her will, with no doubt as to his loyalty. Considering his knowledge of the South and who his father was, he was a valuable asset, but only as long as he was malleable to her requirements.

I knew he would do anything to save me. And I had no doubts now that *she* knew he would, too.

20

I kept my anxious thoughts to myself as we continued across Southern Vysanthe. After creeping through the barrier, we took an immediate left, clinging to the shadows of the mountainside and taking the less-traveled route to Regium. I missed the familiar sight of the fighting pits, even though it wasn't a particularly pleasant landmark. Still, it was one that would have centered me, where I felt entirely disoriented. Everything below us looked the same, the landscape unchanging in its flat hostility, making me wonder if Korbin even knew where he was going.

An expansive plateau stretched out into the distance once we moved out of the protection of the mountain range. Barren wasteland rushed beneath us, the ground frozen and cracked, glistening with permafrost. Now and again, I'd catch sight of a twisted tree, its skeletal arms reaching to the sky as if in prayer, its leaves long since gone. There were settlements too, scattered around the flat landscape, though we were careful to give them a wide berth, knowing they might sound the alarm if they saw a squadron of soldiers approaching.

An hour later, the jagged peaks that surrounded Regium appeared in the distance. Their snowy caps glinted in the harsh sunlight, each one looking like the silvery tip of a spear, protecting the people within its guarded center. Instead of traveling toward the city, Korbin led us over a neighboring mountain range, before coming to a halt on a narrow ledge overlooking a black lake. Its frothing waves crashed against the slick cliffs that curved all around us.

Catching my breath, I stared down at the churning water and recognized the spot immediately. My head snapped up, and I felt a refreshed sense of panic as my eyes caught sight of the crystalline edge of the Observatory peering out just above our heads.

"Half of you are going to make the climb up to the Observatory to fit explosives along the underside of the building and in the joints that run along the wall," Korbin explained, keeping his tone low. "This should cause the crystal structure to collapse in on itself, but we want to ensure maximum damage. So, I want the other half of you to get into the building itself and masquerade as citizens. Set explosives anywhere you can, though ensure they are well hidden. If we are discovered, it is unlikely we will make it out alive. Do you understand?"

Everyone nodded, though I longed to shoot back up into the air and keep flying until I was as far from everything as it was possible to be. I looked at Navan, and from his grim expression, he felt the same way. And yet, there was nothing we could do. If we betrayed Queen Brisha, our friends would suffer. And pissing off Brisha could potentially piss off Orion, if it would affect our standing with her. If we didn't betray her, innocent southern Vysantheans would suffer. It was a terrible situation no matter which way we turned.

"You two need to stay outside the Observatory and stick to the outer perimeter," Korbin declared, his gaze shooting toward Navan and me. "You're too recognizable here, even in civilian clothes."

I wasn't sure if that was good news or bad news, but at least I wouldn't have to look anyone in the eye as I set an explosive I knew would inflict pain and suffering on so many. Did that make it better? For me, perhaps, but not for those whose lives it might take.

"Of course, Commander Korbin," Navan replied, while I'd lost all ability to speak.

"The explosives are self-sticking. All you need to do

is place one on a surface and press the blue button once. This will keep it in place," Korbin went on, his gaze darting around the assembled group. "Now, you need to press the button a second time to start the timer. Once you have done that, a light will flash. That means the explosive is primed and will detonate after a set amount of time. I have set the timer on each one. You have an hour to get out once the light starts flashing. Any questions?"

The group shook their heads, though I could see a glimpse of fear on each of their faces. It comforted me slightly to know they weren't eager to do this either. And yet, nobody was mounting a rebellion, nobody was calling for it to stop, and I knew nobody would.

"Right, then get going!" Korbin said, separating the team into two groups. "Civilian team, make sure you fly up to the main entrance, so you look like you've come from the city. Outer team, keep yourselves hidden!" he added, ushering our group up the side of the slippery cliff face, while the others removed their military fatigues, revealing the civilian clothes beneath.

Our group was the smaller of the two, but I could sense the relief coming off my fellow trainees as we flew upward at a slow pace. I realized they were probably thinking the same as me—if they didn't have to look their enemy in the eye, then surely that made it easier? I couldn't entirely convince myself that was true, but I could understand the comfort that might come from it.

A few of the soldiers stopped at the underside of the Observatory, the steel base jutting out over the water. I grimaced as they removed a few of the explosives from their belts and fixed them to the outer surface of the structure, pressing the buttons in twice, as Korbin had instructed.

"Shall we head up?" Navan murmured, taking my hand.

I nodded, feeling wretched.

We clambered over the edge of the clifftop and crawled along the grass until we reached the outer wall of the Observatory. Through the transparent crystal, I could see all the people milling about inside. There were hundreds, if not thousands. At the very far corner, staring out at the choppy waters of the black lake, I saw the faces of coldblood children pressed to the glass, pulling faces and pointing out at the horizon. Nothing about this was right. Gianne had attacked her sister, and lives had been lost, that was true, but that didn't make retaliation fair or just. Brisha was supposed to be the better one, the one whose side I thought I could take. But not now. Definitely not now.

"They're all going to die," I whispered, tears welling in my eyes. "There are children here, Navan!"

"There are so many coldbloods," he breathed,

seemingly in a world of his own as he gazed in horror at the building. "I... I didn't think there would be this many."

"There has to be something we can do," I urged.

His hands balled into fists. "I want to save them, Riley. I want to save all of them. But how can we? You know what's at stake. She knew that when she sent us here. She knew we would have to watch, even if we didn't participate. She's punishing us," he said through gritted teeth, his eyes glittering with hatred.

Just then, my gaze caught a familiar face in the crowd, and I raised a hand to my mouth in abject horror. Seraphina, Navan's fiancée, was making her way toward the side exit, which led out into the gardens, close to where we were crouched. It was a wild sort of display, with gnarled trees and sparse bushes, but there was an observation deck in the center that gave the best view of the lake. With the brutal winds battering the clifftop, nobody was out there at the moment, but Seraphina seemed to be heading straight for it.

A call to action echoed in my head: I needed to warn her. Once upon a time, she had saved my life by telling Lazar about the chip in my neck—I *owed* it to her to return the favor. Besides, it wasn't only her life at stake. Seeing her served as an even more painful reminder that these were real people, with lives and families and hopes of their own. If I allowed the explosives to go off, then the blood was on my hands for not stopping it when I had the power to.

I couldn't take it any longer.

Before Navan could pull me back, I jumped up and ran toward the observation deck, ducking behind the trunk of a twisted tree and crouching down as I lay in wait for Seraphina. Across the garden, I could see Navan's horrified face, but he stayed where he was, evidently unsure what the heck I was doing. In truth, I wasn't sure either. I just knew I had to do this.

She appeared a moment later, her head down, her expression thoughtful.

"Seraphina," I whispered from behind the tree trunk, catching sight of Navan's expression as the pieces fell into place for him.

Her head snapped up, a frightened look in her eyes. "Who's there?" she demanded, her gaze darting around the garden. Navan ducked down before she could see him, but I poked my head out from behind the tree.

"It's me, Riley," I hissed.

Her face morphed into a mask of shock. "What are you doing here?! If anyone finds you, they'll take you away, and... I don't even want to think about what they'd do to you," she said sharply, making sure she didn't draw too much attention to me as she faced out toward the horizon.

"*You* are the one in danger, Seraphina," I urged, knowing I was running out of time.

She frowned. "What do you mean?"

"You need to listen to me very carefully," I replied, keeping one eye on the cliff edge for any of my fellow soldiers. "The Observatory is going to explode in less than an hour. Explosives have already been set and primed to detonate. I need you to help me evacuate this place without raising any alarms about the explosives or the soldiers who have infiltrated it," I continued, praying she wouldn't panic and start shouting. To my relief, she didn't, her brow furrowed in thought.

"This is an attack by Queen Brisha?" Seraphina asked.

"It's a retaliation for the destruction Gianne caused when she brought down Brisha's alchemy lab," I said quickly, feeling the weight of the task ahead on my shoulders.

For a moment, Seraphina didn't speak, her gaze set upon the distant sky. I worried she was about to out us, or raise the alarm anyway. I wouldn't have blamed her if she did, since it was likely the quickest way to evacuate a building of this size. And then, she glanced toward me.

"I'll figure something out, Riley," she promised. "If anyone finds out about this counterattack, it will prompt the breakout of actual war between the sisters.

We need to make the explosion look like an accident. They have been seeking a reason to shatter the treaty, but *this* will not be it."

"You're... not on Gianne's side?" I asked, genuinely curious.

She shook her head solemnly, her glossy hair gleaming in the sunlight. "I desire peace across Vysanthe, as it was before the sisters tore it in half. My loyalty lies with neither queen. In fact, if I had my way, there would be no queen at all, but a true democracy, appointed by the people, for the people. As that seems unlikely to happen anytime soon, I will be happy with a world without bloodshed instead," she stated firmly, though there was uncertainty in her eyes. "Are you sure there is no way to stop the explosion altogether? Even if we come up with an excuse, Gianne will suspect foul play, and this is such a beautiful building. I would hate to see it crumble into the water."

"If the explosion doesn't happen, then Brisha will know it had something to do with Navan and me," I explained, wishing I had a different answer for her. "She already doubts us, and has warned that if we try anything, then we will be punished. Not just us, but our loved ones too."

She grimaced, flashing me a look of apology. "Who does she have?"

"Two of my friends, and Bashrik," I replied, her eyes going wide in shock.

"Then we must try to protect everyone," Seraphina said, after a short, tense pause. "If we can save the people here without raising an alarm that would result in the deaths of others, then we must do it. I will not see a drop of blood spilled, if I can help it," she added, with a defiant nod.

I smiled inwardly, wishing more coldbloods could be like her. Unlike Navan, Seraphina seemed to understand the potential that still resided within the heart of Vysanthe. There was good to be found in this world, if people would only open their eyes to the positives, instead of scrapping over land like dogs over a meager bone. Indeed, she seemed more queenlike to me, in her diplomacy and grace, than Gianne and Brisha put together. Where they sought war, she sought peace.

"Thank you, Seraphina," I whispered gratefully.

"Is Navan with you?" she asked, looking around.

"He's hiding nearby," I replied, though I'd lost sight of him after he ducked down in panic.

Seraphina smiled wryly. "It is strange that the pair of you should come here, as I have been visiting this place every day in the hopes of finding news of Navan. I have been peering over the shoulders of security officers, hoping to catch a glimpse of something that

might tell me where he went, and now here you are."
She chuckled.

"Why were you looking for him?" I asked, not
unkindly.

"Queen Gianne has decreed that she is willing to
pardon him if he returns. I wanted to get the news to
him so he might come home without fear of
retribution," she explained, a sorrowful look on
her face.

I frowned, puzzled. "Why would she do that? She
was pretty mad last time we saw her," I remarked,
recalling how she tried to shoot us out of the sky.

"It's his father. Jareth told Gianne that Navan was
forced into working for the rebels, and has vouched for
his character. It would seem Gianne believes her most
trusted advisor, since it's not every day that someone
like her offers forgiveness to apparent traitors,"
Seraphina said, though I could sense she was holding
something back. There was a sadness in her eyes that
didn't make sense. Nobody had died because of Navan's
indiscretions, as far as I could tell, so what was there to
be so distressed about?

"Is something else troubling you?" I asked.

She smiled, but it didn't reach her eyes. "It's nothing, honestly."

"There's something else, I can tell," I pressed,

wanting to know what could bring such despair to a woman like her.

Seraphina sighed, visibly steeling herself. "Queen Gianne has also decreed that, if Navan doesn't return to Southern Vysanthe, then I am to be wed to her advisor, Aurelius, in two months' time."

My stomach sank as I recalled the hunched old skeleton that followed Gianne around everywhere. I remembered the look of jealousy in his rheumy eyes when he spoke to Navan about Seraphina. I'd had an inkling about the reason behind his envy, even then, though I'd never gotten my suspicions confirmed. Now, it made sense. All this time, Aurelius had had his eye on Seraphina, desiring to have her for himself. And, if Navan didn't come back, he would get exactly that.

I felt sick, realizing what it might mean. And yet, I didn't know whether I had it in me to sit back and watch another woman endure that—be passed around like a prize instead of a person—especially one as good as Seraphina. Once this mission was complete, and the building had been evacuated, I knew I would have a difficult choice to make.

Right now, however, other lives mattered far more than my own.

"The clock's ticking," I said, trying to push thoughts of Navan and Seraphina to the back of my mind. "We need to get these people out of here before it's too late. How can we evacuate without causing a panic?"

A grin spread across Seraphina's face. "I've got the perfect idea," she whispered. "Don't worry. You should head back before anyone misses you. Leave the evacuation to me," she insisted. Ordinarily, I would have been wary about trusting a coldblood I barely knew, but there was an honest quality to everything Seraphina did that was hard to ignore.

"Thank you," I whispered, eager to return to Commander Korbin and the others. Peering through the crystal exterior of the Observatory, I could pick out one or two of our comrades, but the rest seemed to have dispersed, their job done. The fact that nobody else had come up this way made me think they had finished up with the outer surfaces too, leaving this side to Navan and me.

Leaving Seraphina, I crept around the tree trunk, readying myself to dart back to the clifftop where Navan was hiding.

Then Seraphina called out to me again. "Could you do one favor for me, Riley?" she asked.

I stalled, turning to look at her. "What... What would you like me to do?" I asked, frowning.

A sheepish expression passed across her stunning features. "I hate to ask, but... would you be able to persuade Navan to return to the South, if he finds a way to come back?" she wondered, not meeting my gaze.

The underlying meaning of her words pierced my very soul. I couldn't believe she'd actually asked it out loud, considering what it would mean for Navan and me. More to the point, she *knew* what it would mean for us. I pitied her for how she had been forced into an engagement with Aurelius, but to be so blunt about getting Navan to return—I wasn't sure how I felt about it. It left a sour taste in my mouth, and a tangled web of confusion in my mind.

"If we make it back, I'll see what I can do," I promised. Right now, it was all I could give her.

"That means a lot, Riley. Believe me, it does," she said, lifting her gaze to mine, a sad smile on her lips.

Why does she have to make it so difficult to hate her? I wondered silently. It would have been easier if I could look at her and despise every part of her being. But I couldn't. She was kind and gentle, with a sharp intellect. Plus, right now, my gratitude toward her was immense. She was going to get the civilians out, without putting Navan's or my life at risk. It was a task I couldn't do alone, and I trusted Seraphina's ability.

"I'd better get going," I said, creeping back across the gardens. I was almost at the other side, when she called out again.

"One last thing," she ventured, her hand on the door handle that led inside, and I turned back, anxious at what she might ask of me next. "I heard news that Queen Gianne is building a new weapon in the underground hangar. I believe you know the one? If the mood struck you, perhaps you might take a look?" she suggested, before pulling her coat tighter around her and stepping back into the warmth of the Observatory, disappearing from sight.

I let out a breath, relieved that it hadn't been another request involving Navan, then turned around, expecting to find him on the other side of the row of bushes. But he was nowhere to be found. Puzzled, I lay flat on my stomach and crawled over to the edge of the cliff, my mind racing with thoughts of what Seraphina had just said. A weapon? What kind of weapon? Part of me wished she hadn't said a word about it, knowing we would have to check it out before we left. There was no way we could ignore something that big. I was certain Navan would agree with me, once I found him.

Before I could lower myself over the cliff edge, I heard a commotion coming from the building. I lifted my head sharply and peered through the crystal surface of the Observatory, watching as the crowds streamed out in an orderly fashion. Nobody was running, nobody was screaming, though they were all covering their heads with whatever fabric they could find. I smiled, noting that the high-tech sprinklers were spraying water across the inside space, the droplets cascading down in a vigorous downpour. Lights were flashing a warning on the walls as the enormous screens that displayed the goings-on of Southern Vysanthe blinked sporadically against the damp intrusion.

A few officers sprinted around, frantically tapping several panels that were fitted into the walls in a vain attempt to get the water to stop, but nothing they did seemed to make a difference. Whatever Seraphina had done, she had made it impossible to stop. In fact, their actions seemed to make it worse. The officers shielded their eyes as the water increased in its volume, pouring down from the ceiling like a monsoon, a significant pool rising upward with each moment that passed. A few crackles and glittering sparks jetted out of one of the biggest screens, prompting the officers to give up, their eyes fearful of further explosions while they headed for the exits. With the screens out of order and the water lashing down, there was no point in them staying to try to fix it, until the water ran out.

It was simple, but perfect.

Thankful for Seraphina's quick, skillful work, I flattened myself back down on the ground and shimmied off the edge, opening out my wings to catch myself. Navan was waiting below, his wings beating impatiently, his face looking deeply worried.

"Why did you run off like that?" he hissed, pulling me down toward him.

"There's no time for that now," I replied quickly.

My mind turned to the cascading water in the building above. With the crackles and sparks exploding from the screens, perhaps it would cover the cause of the imminent explosion as some sort of electrical fault. I clung to that hope as I grasped Navan's hand and pulled him in the opposite direction to the ledge, where Commander Korbin and the others would be expecting us.

"What's going on?" Navan demanded, as I struggled to drag him along.

I paused, letting out an exasperated sigh. "Seraphina pulled it off. She managed to get the civilians out without raising any kind of alarm. A stroke of genius!" I said, taking his hand again. "But, right now, we need to make a little side trip. Seraphina heard about something important that Queen Gianne is building in the underground hangar, and I figured we should take a good look before we head for the North. It might be just the thing to get us back in Brisha's good books," I explained with a wink, leaving out the part about him returning to the South fulltime. That conversation could wait.

He frowned. "What is she building, exactly?"

"That's what we need to find out," I said, pulling him along. This time, he didn't resist me, allowing me to drag him along in the shadow of the slippery rockface. I paused in the darkness for a moment, casting a glance back at the ledge where the commander had dropped us. From here, I could see him yelling into the face of one of our comrades, who was trying to attach a bomb that refused to stick.

It was now or never. We needed to move before he realized we'd gone. Clinging to the shadows, allowing them to swallow us up like camouflage, we headed for the underground hangar.

My memory was a little hazy where the city layout was concerned, but Navan took the lead when I began to flounder. I took another small sip of the wing serum on the way, to keep them from fading, while we kept to the outskirts for as long as possible, sticking to the shadows. On the way, I encouraged Navan to unbuckle his explosives belt, and we dropped mine and his into a deep pool of melted ice that glinted on the mountainside. I didn't want anything to do with them now that the evacuation was underway, and it seemed Navan didn't either.

"Was it really this far out?" I asked dubiously, following Navan past the perimeter of Regium.

"They keep it outside the city on purpose," he said, leading us downward toward an inconspicuous-looking patch of frozen grass, the earth hard-packed beneath my feet as we touched down.

I looked around, partially recognizing the wall of stone that rose up ahead of us. Then again, I was pretty sure most mountain ranges looked the same. Turning my head this way and that, as if inspiration would suddenly come, I noticed Navan giving me a strange look.

"What are you doing?" he asked, half amused.

"Figuring out where the hangar is," I retorted.

He chuckled. "It's this way," he said, gesturing toward a section of the mountainside.

"You're in good shape, Navan, but I doubt you can tear through solid rock," I muttered, hurrying after him. Wherever he was headed, he seemed determined.

As we neared the spot he was gesturing to, I swallowed my words. There, in the mountainside, was a crack about the size of two people standing side by side, though nature had camouflaged it with a tangled mass of vines and brambles that crisscrossed over the opening, hiding it from plain sight.

"This isn't the way we came in when we first arrived on Vysanthe," I said, utterly confused. Part of me wondered if Navan had hit his head while I wasn't looking.

He smiled, a knowing look on his face. "It's not, but I know this place well from my younger days. Me and my brothers used to sneak around these parts all the time, watching the engineers and making notes on each exploration ship that left the hangar. It's what made me want to be an Explorer, watching those ships leave. Well, that and wanting to get the hell out of Vysanthe." A curious smile pulled at the corners of his lips. "Over the years, I've discovered a few hidden treasures, where the guards don't go. This is an old air vent, though it doesn't look like it's been doing much lately," he said, chuckling to himself. He began to tear away the tangled roots and crumbled rocks that kept the opening so well hidden.

"Wait, we're going through a sketchy gap in the wall of a massive mountain?" I raised an eyebrow in disbelief, fearing it would all tumble down around us the moment we set foot inside.

"There's a ventilation shaft inside. It's not just rock," he said as he pulled away the last of the twisting vines and stamped them down on the floor of the fissure, covering his tracks. This place wouldn't stay secret for long if someone came by and discovered a pile of torn-away weeds.

Still dubious about the structural safety of the crevice, I let Navan lead the way, holding on to his hand as he led me through the darkness beyond. Using my free hand to cling to the walls, I shuddered each time something fell around me, stone clattering to the ground. However, after a moment or two, the ground became more solid, the shadows lightening to a barely discernible dimness. Just as he'd said, the rock gave way to a secure, square tunnel of sheet metal. Our footsteps echoed as we walked along. It was tall enough to walk through in a standing position with my shoulders a little bit hunched, but Navan was bent over.

"Did Seraphina say anything else?" he asked as we moved on through the ventilation shaft.

I contemplated telling him about her request, but I

couldn't get the words to come out. It was like my heart was reaching up and grabbing at them, pulling them back down into my voice box, leaving them unspoken. I had to tell him, but now didn't feel like the right time. I was still processing what she'd said myself.

"She told me she'd trigger the evacuation, and that Gianne was building a weapon of some kind," I replied, even as I felt bad for delaying Seraphina's request. The more I thought about it, the more I understood her perspective. She wasn't asking to be cruel to me. She was asking because she feared for her own happiness. And, if I were being forced to marry a man like Aurelius, I'd probably be desperate for *any* other option, too.

Navan's head snapped back to look at me. "You didn't say it was a *weapon!*" he whispered sharply.

"Didn't I?" I murmured, realizing I should have mentioned it. "I guess I thought it would have been obvious. I mean, what else is a queen going to build after she's obliterated her sister's prized possession? She's got to expect payback of some sort. I presume she's preparing for it."

"You really have to tell me these things, Riley." He sighed.

"Miscommunicator Riley," I mumbled, shrugging. "I'm sorry."

He gave me a wry look before continuing ahead.

Ten minutes later, with my brow dripping with sweat from being smothered in the surprisingly stuffy vent, we reached the end of the tunnel. A grate faced us, looking out on the underground hangar where we'd arrived on that fateful first day. A twinge of sadness rippled through me as my mind drifted toward Kalvin and the rest of his team, whose fates were still unknown. Kalvin had been loyal to the end, giving us a chance to survive by offering up his own life. Yet, here we were, back in the lion's den, putting ourselves in danger. If he could see us now, I was fairly sure he'd be rolling his eyes or making a cutting comment about Navan's "ineptitude."

I squashed in beside Navan, and we knelt on the floor, peering out at the hangar. What we saw chilled me to the very core.

Scattered across the vast, cavernous space was a fleet of brand-new ships gleaming like smooth pebbles at the bottom of a riverbed. One of them had its hood popped open, revealing the inner mechanics of the shiny new ship. An engineer tinkered with the interior, making notes as he worked.

A harsh breath surged from the back of Navan's throat. "No... it can't be," he whispered.

"What?" I asked, my mouth dry. Mechanical engineering was my forte, but my experience didn't exactly extend to alien technology. I had no idea what I was looking at, and the panic in Navan's eyes alarmed me.

"She's figured it out," he breathed, his voice catching. "There—that's the engine required for deep-space travel. I'd recognize it anywhere." He gaped at the open ship, its metal innards gleaming ominously.

I gasped in horror as my eyes settled on something else, tucked away in the farthest corner of the hangar. It was a pile of scrap metal that looked out of place among the sleek new ships. There, on the side of one of the discarded panels, was the word *Asterope*.

I realized with a crushing feeling what had happened. Gianne had used the *Asterope* to figure out how to conquer deep-space travel.

If what Navan said was true, the engine was noticeably different. An engineer must have been working on the *Asterope* and spotted the discrepancy, reporting it back to their queen. Through trial and error, they would have figured out what the difference entailed, by dissecting the technology used in their own ships and adding this extra element. In opening up that gateway in technological advancement, they had evidently realized the untapped potential in their own fleet, prompting Gianne to build a new one entirely.

If that were the case, then it was only a matter of time before Gianne found Earth. It would be mapped on the *Asterope* somewhere. If she didn't understand the significance of my small, seemingly weak little planet now, she soon would, and the thought of that filled me with gut-wrenching dread. Why did human blood have to be the stuff that worked? Was it because of our position in the universe, on practically the exact opposite side from the Vysantheans? I had no idea, but it angered me regardless.

"We need to get this back to Brisha, pronto," I muttered bitterly, my eyes narrowing with rage.

Navan nodded. "We need to stop this before the fleet is fully functional."

I glanced at him. "It's not yet?"

"Not by the looks of it. They have some kinks to work out, but it will be finished soon enough. We need to get Brisha to step in or we're all doomed. With that number of ships, there's no telling what Gianne could do. That sort of armada could take over the universe," he said through gritted teeth.

"Then there's no time to waste," I whispered, taking his hand. We rushed back through the ventilation shaft, bursting back out into the bitter Vysanthean landscape.

I pictured the explosives we'd abandoned, their electrics frazzling in the icy water, and sighed. Maybe we could have damaged these ships. Then again, the hangar was crawling with coldbloods. We'd never have managed to pull it off without being spotted.

No, we needed to get back to the North as soon as possible. We couldn't risk a moment longer here. Seraphina and her wedding would have to wait, too. There were more important things at stake... like the entire universe.

22

"Should we head straight for the border or go back to the others?" I asked, aware that the rest of the soldiers would likely be done planting explosives by now. They wouldn't know what had caused the sprinklers to malfunction, I hoped, but they would've hurried to complete the mission if they thought the authorities sensed any suspicious activity. The bombs would still blow, regardless of whether or not any people remained inside.

"We have to rejoin the others," Navan said heavily. "Commander Korbin will think we've deserted the troop if we don't get back soon. We can tell him we've found important intel for Brisha," he added, stretching out his wings. I mirrored the motion and took to the sky, Navan soaring beside me.

With the wind whipping at our faces, we sped away from the mountain range that surrounded Regium. I glanced back to witness the twin behemoths that guarded the entrance to the city—the old king and queen, I remembered, from Navan's personal tour, the last time we were here. They really were impressive, towering over both settlements and mountains, keeping watch over those beneath. I wondered what Vysanthe might have been like back then, before the sisters tore the planet in two. Had it been a better place? All kings and queens had their faults, but I had to wonder which the Vysanthean people preferred, the past or the present.

This time, we didn't veer off toward the barren wastelands that flanked the main route from Regium to the neighboring districts. There was no time for caution, not if we wanted to meet up with the other soldiers before Korbin questioned our prolonged absence.

As we drew closer to a settlement, the pretty houses ringed by a glimmering river, the trees more luscious here, I became aware of a sound behind us. It was almost like a kite flapping in the breeze.

Turning sharply, I thought I saw a figure disappear behind a dense canopy of treetops. However, with the clouds rushing across the sky, trailing in front of the sun, it was hard to tell what was real. It was only when the creeping sensation refused to leave me alone that I realized my mind wasn't playing tricks on me.

"I think we're being followed," I whispered to Navan, flying in close to his side.

He frowned, casting a subtle glance over his shoulder. "I can't see anyone," he replied, though he looked uncertain.

My pulse quickened as I was reminded of our nerve-wracking journey from Alaska to New York. "Whoever it is, they're good at hiding."

Passing across the icy flow of the river, Navan took my hand and led me off toward the left, straying from the central route that led back to the Observatory. Using the shadow of the nearby trees to shroud us, we peered through the gaps in the boughs to see who was on our tail. My anger pricked as I spotted the skeletal frame of Aurelius, his single wing flapping double speed to keep him in the air, while a fake wing trailed hopelessly, rising up and down only when it caught a current of air. Despite his disability, he seemed like an adept flier. His rheumy eyes scanned the landscape, narrowing as they glanced into the forest below.

Why had he followed us instead of sounding the alarm? After all, he wasn't exactly a prime specimen of strength. *Could he be working for the rebels, like Pandora, reporting from Gianne's side?*

Suddenly, he took out a gun, the metal barrel

glinting in the sunlight. A moment later, a projectile shot through the air, whizzing past us before exploding into a tree behind. The wood burst outward in a flare of splinters. I clutched Navan's hand, confident now that Aurelius was *not* working for the rebels. If he were, he wouldn't be trying to kill us. Maybe Aurelius was just trying to use a heroic deed to impress his beloved queen—or even Seraphina.

Swooping low, Aurelius hovered on the outskirts of the forest, his gun raised to the dense canopy. "Who goes there?" he called, firing another shot into the darkness.

He didn't know whom he had been tailing. Pulling the hood of my jacket farther over my head, I signaled for Navan to do the same. If Aurelius hadn't spotted who we were already, I certainly didn't want him finding out.

"No one of concern," Navan replied, altering his voice to a higher pitch as he spoke. "Allow us to leave, and we will say no more about it. We are harmless merchants, come to visit Regium on business!"

I realized the only way to escape was to keep the advisor talking, so we could rocket past him unawares. Already, Navan was gesturing for me to brace against the tree trunk behind us, to increase my momentum outward. Meanwhile, he was doing the same on a neighboring tree.

"You are trespassers!" Aurelius bellowed, though his voice wavered. "You are trespassers, and you will be punished!" With that, a round of bullets peppered the surrounding area.

"Go!" Navan urged.

I bent back as far as I could, before pushing forward with all my might. I shot up through the trees like a bullet, perfectly streamlined, my wings tucked flat against my body. Navan followed straight after, and we stretched out our wings only as our momentum faded. As we'd hoped, the sudden burst of movement took Aurelius by surprise, causing him to tumble downward before he regained his composure.

We flew away as hard and as fast as we could, but Aurelius twisted his body around, aiming his gun straight at us. I could hear the unmistakable whistle of the projectiles as they surged past, one narrowly missing the tip of my ear, the screech of the bullet deafening me for a moment. Even so, I pressed on, desperate not to be shot out of the sky. Navan was just up ahead, leading the way, letting me know where to go. With my heart thundering in my chest, I kept my eyes on him, my wings beating hard, churning the wind behind me.

On the steep incline upward, I tried to find camouflage in the cloud cover, but a sudden twinge of pain made my blood freeze. It was a dull ache, just below my scapula, leaking forward into my chest cavity. It was a sensation I immediately recognized. The wing serum was starting to wear off. I could feel it in the way my wings were slowing, my body struggling to keep hold of them.

In a panic, I pawed at my pockets, trying to find the one that held the last vial of wing serum. I delved into my jacket pocket and pulled out the vial, but my hands were too sweaty, my fingers too shaky. It almost slipped from my grasp, but I held on tight, determined not to drop it as I took out the stopper and lifted it to my lips. The liquid was almost in my mouth when a shot tore through my right wing, knocking me off balance, sending the vial plummeting toward the ground. I watched, horrified, as it hit a stretch of stone below me, the glass shattering on impact.

A moment later, I followed the vial, my wings disappearing completely, leaving me exposed and helpless. I flailed my arms, as if it might miraculously keep me in the air, but there was nothing I could do to stop myself from falling.

I closed my eyes, bracing for impact, when I felt Navan grab me under the arms, holding me up. Lifting my gaze, I saw him above me, his wings beating steadily as he lowered me carefully to the ground. Shots were still firing all around us, but his focus was entirely on me.

"Meet me at the house with the silver archway," he said hurriedly, before dropping me down into what looked like a Vysanthean garden, the landscape too manicured to be naturally made. Letting go before I could say a word in protest, he flew upward once more, his expression determined.

From my vantage point, I watched as Aurelius approached, forcing Navan to feint away from the projectiles that were firing from the barrel of the advisor's silver gun. Twisting around in the air like a tornado, Navan drew the two blades from his back, using them to deflect the projectiles as they hurtled toward him. With each explosive impact, a shower of sparks erupted into the sky, looking like fireworks on the Fourth of July.

I had always known Navan was skilled, but seeing him fight in a true battle was as impressive as it was terrifying. The blades whistled through the air, cutting through the shots, whipping across his body like ever-moving shields. I could tell that Aurelius was growing frustrated by the sudden turn of events, as his sole wing flapped vigorously in Navan's direction. Fortunately for me, this frustration meant that Aurelius didn't bother to look down. Each swipe of Navan's blades edged Aurelius farther and farther from the spot where I stood. He was drawing Aurelius away so he could fight him without having to worry about me getting hit by a stray bullet. I wished I could be up in the air with him, but I was entirely human again.

As the ache of the lost wings pulsed in my shoulders, I began to feel nauseous, clutching at my stomach as the last of the serum worked its way out of my system. Black spots danced in front of my eyes. My knees buckled, and I stumbled backward, trying to find something to grab onto. My foot caught on a twisting root, sending me careening backward into what felt like a bush. Fortunately for me, it was surprisingly soft, the leaves velvety, the branches spongy. As my vision and clarity returned, I struggled to wriggle out of the bush I'd fallen in, but the more I moved, the more I could feel a hot prickle bristling along my arms and legs, like brushing against a nettle. Only, this was far worse. This was like searing pins and needles, all the way along my body. Peering closer, I saw small, ice-blue flowers embedded within the leaves. At their very center, each one was blowing out a glittering white mist, which seemed to soak through the fabric of my clothes, burrowing to the flesh beneath.

I managed to wrangle free of the burning bush, brushing away any of the remaining mist by pulling my sleeves over my hands. I pushed up the cuffs of my jacket to see a rash emerging, the skin blistering as if it had been near a naked flame. It stung like hell, but I hoped it would end there. The last thing I needed was to be infected by some alien bush.

Feeling utterly disoriented, I wandered through the Vysanthean garden, taking in the striking flowerbeds scattered with blooms of unusual colors and sizes. In one, there was a rose-like flower as big as my head, each petal the size of my palm, the color almost holographic in the way it shifted with the light. In another, I noticed a twisting tree bearing blue fruit similar to the one Gianne had fed me in my first few days on Vysanthe.

Hearing the approach of voices, I hurried out of the gate at the back of the garden, taking off down the forest road at a sprint. Gradually, it stretched out into a much wider, cobbled street, with elegant sidewalks that seemed hewn from gleaming marble.

On either side, enormous buildings came into view, making me realize I was on a residential street of some sort, only it was filled with some of the most extravagant mansions I had ever seen. They towered above their endlessly rolling lawns like castles from a fairytale, spires glinting in the sunlight, and a thousand windows staring out at me as I passed. Some were built from an exquisite dark stone that I had never seen before, while others were pure opaleine, the pale marble shot through with veins of sapphire.

Now, where the heck is this silver arch?

I wandered along, hoping nobody would notice me. I still had my hood up, but, in a place like this, I had a feeling that made me even more conspicuous.

Something glinted in the distance, the cold sunlight catching a metallic object. Squinting toward it, I realized it was indeed an arch. Seeing as there weren't any other garish archways along the street, I figured that had to be it. I ran toward it, hoping Navan would escape and meet me there soon. If they had a garden, I could keep myself hidden for a while, but without the wing serum, the bitter cold of Vysanthe was starting to creep into my bones. If Navan didn't come for me soon, I would likely shiver to death.

Slowing to a walk, I paused in front of the silver arch. All around it, metal vines twisted and turned, while Gothic wings stretched out behind engraved figures frozen in poses of war and peace. Shielding my eyes from the glare of the sun, I caught sight of a name engraved in the metal:

Idrax.

I was so distracted by the name that I didn't notice the imposing, dark-haired coldblood walking toward me until I barreled straight into him.

23

"Who are you?" the coldblood growled, his dark blue eyes glinting furiously.

Judging by the name above the archway, I guessed Navan had sent me to one of his family member's houses, though I doubted he'd meant for me to run into one of his brothers. This coldblood *had* to be one of Navan's brothers. The hair, the build, the striking eyes, the angry demeanor... The resemblance was uncanny.

"Navan sent me," I managed, finding my voice, though my throat was constricted by fear. "He's in a... bit of trouble, but he'll be back for me. He sent me here," I added, though I knew none of it made much sense.

The coldblood's eyes darkened. "I ought to kill you right here, to teach that traitor a lesson he'll never forget."

I gulped. This wasn't exactly going the way I'd hoped. Then again, just because Navan and Bashrik tolerated outsiders, it didn't mean any of their other family members would. After all, their mother and father had ignored me outright, which, I had to say, was preferable to the threatening look this Idrax was giving me.

"What's your issue with Navan?" I asked, desperate to buy myself some time. Surely, Navan couldn't be too far away. There was no way Aurelius could overcome someone like him. However, a lingering doubt remained. If Navan never made it back, I was as good as dead.

The coldblood snorted derisively. "Other than the fact that he betrayed our queen and tarnished our family name?"

"Seems to me like you've got a more personal grudge, though," I said. It was a shot in the dark, but I had to keep the conversation going.

"To have a grudge against him would imply that I care, and I do not care about that scumbag. Navan means nothing to me; I do not even allow him into my thoughts," he retorted, his tone dripping with contempt.

It was a defensive tactic I'd seen before. Those were words of hurt and abandonment.

"It sounds like you do care," I said brazenly, hoping it didn't result in my head being detached from my body. "Come on, I'm curious. What did he do to make you hate him so much? Did he get a better job than you? Your parents love him more than you? What?" I pressed, feeling his irritation rise, his shoulders tensing in anger. I gritted my teeth, steeling myself, praying I hadn't gone too far.

The coldblood snarled. "You know nothing about him, and you know nothing about me, outsider. What are you, anyway?" he asked sharply, reaching out a hand to snatch up my wrist, his eyes scrutinizing my veins.

"Kryptonian," I lied, my body trembling. The fragile skin of my wrist was so close to his mouth. One bite with those sharp fangs, and I could bleed out.

He grunted. "Let me guess, he picked you up on one of his famous explorations? You his new pet, or something?" he said bitterly, surveying the length of my arm.

"Something like that," I said quietly, realizing their parents must not have said a word about me after they met me at Gianne's celebrations. It didn't exactly surprise me. They had barely acknowledged my presence at the time. Maybe they were even embarrassed by Navan bringing an outsider into Vysanthe, given the South's distaste for such things. It appeared I was the dirty little secret, kept from those who didn't need to know.

"That's all he ever does, you know? He just runs, all the time. He gets up and he goes, and he doesn't care about anyone else but himself." A morose look rippled across the coldblood's face for a moment, before anger replaced it.

"Why do you think that is?" I wondered, sounding more and more like a therapist. Next, I'd be asking how it made him feel.

He shrugged angrily. "He thinks he has more of a right to run away than any of us. Every time we confront him about it, he says he can't bear to be here, in Plentha, where *she* was. It's ridiculous. He's always acting like he was the only one who suffered after our sister's—" He stopped abruptly, casting me an odd look. It was somewhere between suspicion and surprise. Even so, he didn't continue, probably realizing he'd revealed too much to a total stranger. Worse than that, an alien stranger who was traveling with a much-despised brother.

The rustle of wind distracted my attention as a figure landed in the street behind me. Navan folded up his wings with a grimace and walked toward us, his face bruised and swollen, his arms covered in welts from Aurelius's gunshots. He was moving unsteadily, as though walking brought him immense pain. Without a word, he put his arm around me protectively, pushing me slightly behind him, forcing the coldblood to let go of my arm. A wave of relief washed over me, but Navan's eyes were fixed on his brother.

"Sarrask, you know that's not true," Navan whispered. "I know you all suffered when Naya died, but not a single one of you stood up to our father, or came to see Ronad after he lost her. She loved him, he was part of the family, and you all pretended he never existed, even though his heart was torn out that day. He held her as she died, Sarrask. He fed it to her as a gift, thinking that's what it was. Do you have *any* idea how that must have felt?" he continued, his voice rising in anger.

Sarrask pulled a sour face. "He didn't deserve her in the first place. He was low-born, sponging off our family for years. Who's to say he didn't make it all up, to frame our father?" he countered, his fangs flashing.

"If you believe that, you're more of an idiot than I thought you were," Navan snarled. "Naya loved Ronad, and that's all there was to it. Our father is a psychopath. If he hadn't done what he did, Naya would still be alive, which is a fact you all seem far too eager to forget!" he added savagely. "What, you scared he'll cut off your credits if you defy him?"

"I don't need Father's charity," Sarrask sneered, "but at least I value everything he's done for us, unlike you. You wouldn't have gotten that Explorer job if it wasn't for him, but you look down your nose at him every chance you get. Not to mention the fact you keep dragging our name through the mud! Do you know what our father had to go through to claw back his position when you betrayed everyone?" He glowered at Navan. "No, I bet you don't. You don't care about us. You never have. It was always you and Ronad, off in your own little tribe, roping Bashrik in because he was too stupid to see you were trouble."

"You leave Bashrik out of this," Navan warned.

Sarrask gave a tight, bitter laugh. "Oh, you'll be pleased to know our dear uncle managed to evade capture, too. That must be where you get your traitorous blood from, because you definitely didn't get it from Father!"

I glanced at Navan, reaching for his hand. Lazar was alive? With his body drenched in blood, the soldiers swarming into the room, I had been sure Lazar was a goner. How could he have evaded capture? How could he be alive? It didn't make any sense.

Navan kept his focus on his brother, though I could see a twitch in the muscle of his jaw, his teeth gritted. He was just as surprised as I was to hear that his uncle had escaped. I could sense it in the way he squeezed my hand tighter.

Without missing a beat, despite his surprise, Navan replied, "Lazar would betray anyone and anything to get what he wants. Don't you dare tarnish me with the same brush as him," he said sourly. "I am *nothing* like him. If I see him again, I will be first in line to end him," he added, casting a knowing look in my direction. After the trick he'd pulled with the tracker chip, I supposed Navan still hadn't forgiven him. In many ways, I hadn't either, though it was hard not to thank him for what he'd done in helping us escape Gianne's soldiers. Without his assistance, there was no telling where we'd be right now. For that, and that alone, part of me was glad he'd evaded capture, though I still had no idea how he'd managed it. Lazar had been half dead already when we'd left him, but the crafty old fox was still alive, hiding out there somewhere.

"Then why are you here?" Sarrask asked, a touch confused. "Aren't you back to find out where he is?"

"No, of course not!" Navan replied, before speaking a string of seemingly random numbers. There were seven of them, with Navan repeating the order, as Sarrask stared at him in wide-eyed surprise. "Now that I've given you the code as a show of my goodwill, I need you to promise you won't inform Gianne of our presence here. It's essential we leave without anybody knowing we were here. Do you understand?"

Several moments passed before Sarrask offered a reply. "I will keep your presence a secret this time because of what you've given me in return, but I will not be so generous next time I catch you here. If I find you trespassing in our nation again, I will deliver you straight to *Queen* Gianne, and I will kill this pathetic specimen on sight. Do *you* understand?" he muttered, irritation flickering across his dark blue eyes.

"Thank you, Brother," Navan replied, holding out his hand for Sarrask to shake. Reluctantly, his brother reached out and gripped him by the arm, with Navan mirroring the gesture. The two of them shook hands like warriors.

"This doesn't mean you're forgiven for any of it," Sarrask said tersely as they released one another.

Navan shrugged. "I didn't think it would."

"Get out of here before I change my mind," Sarrask barked, his face twisted in disgust.

"Gladly," Navan muttered, placing his arms around my waist before he took to the skies, carrying me upward with him. I didn't know what it was like to have brothers and sisters, but I could picture the petty conflicts between the Idrax siblings as youngsters, especially with so many of them. Naya must have felt so protected and loved with a team of burly brothers around her. With a smile, I realized Ronad must have been a brave man, to fall in love with a woman who had so many brothers.

"The soldiers have likely left without us by now," Navan said. "We'll have to head over the border on our own and explain the situation when we get there."

I nodded, wanting to ask what those numbers were that Navan had spoken to his brother. They were definitely powerful. Turning up to gaze at him, I opened my mouth to ask the question, but the sad, faraway look in Navan's eyes told me that now wasn't the time. He didn't say much else as we flew toward the barrier between the South and North, his eyes fixed on the horizon. It seemed both of us were lost in thought.

Halfway to the border, an earth-shattering boom shook us out of our reverie. We turned toward the epicenter, Navan pausing in flight, his wings beating slowly. A flash of light hurtled upward in the distance, sending smoke and debris rocketing into the sky. The very air seemed to vibrate with the heat and force of the explosion, the sound trembling toward us, rattling my teeth.

My heart sank at the sight. It wouldn't be long before Gianne found out the truth of what had happened. Electric faults definitely didn't cause that sort of destruction.

I knew this was one of those unforgettable

moments, where nothing could be altered, the road taking one direction only. There was no going back from this. *This* was the true beginning of war. Here we were, watching the break in the treaty that both queens had been looking for, all this time. All that remained to be seen was how each sister would respond, now that the fragile balance had been shattered.

I looked up at Navan, surprised by the grimace I saw there. Clearly, it pained him to witness the loss of one of his homeland's greatest structures. It was a prized focal point for Southern Vysantheans, and now it was gone, quite literally in a puff of smoke. It couldn't have been easy to watch, yet I wondered if it was how the Northern Vysantheans had felt, watching their alchemy lab razed to the ground. In war, nobody won. And, at the end of it all, the prize was death and destruction, holding a throne over rubble and ruin.

"We should go," I said softly, knowing he was suffering. His current distaste for his home planet didn't take away the years he had spent here, growing up, making friends, becoming the man he was now.

He nodded, tearing his eyes away from the plume of thick black smoke that rose from the horizon. Picking up speed, we headed for the border, Navan's mouth set in a grim line.

"What did you give Sarrask?" I asked, wanting to distract him. Plus, I was still eager to know.

He smiled sadly. "It was a passcode. It unlocks a safety deposit box, with all of Naya's belongings inside. I've kept it from them for years, but Sarrask made me realize I don't have a right to keep it to myself anymore. She was their sister, too," he explained, his voice thick with emotion.

"You did the right thing," I told him, recalling the genuine hurt in Sarrask's voice when he'd mentioned his sister. Even if it hadn't bought us our freedom, it would still have been the decent thing to do. "Can you believe that Lazar is still alive?" I remarked, changing the subject, wanting to take the sadness away from Navan's face.

He smiled wryly. "It's a miracle, that's for sure. It seems that traitorous bastard can wriggle his way out of death itself," he mused, half angry, half impressed.

"I was sure he was dead," I murmured, remembering the gory sight of him slumped in the armchair.

Navan nodded. "Me too."

As we charged toward the border, I wondered what kind of reception we might receive in the North. The others would have noticed our absence by now, unless they thought we'd been caught up in the blast. Given that we'd come from the South in the first place, I doubted their thoughts would be positive ones. They would think we'd betrayed them.

But whatever they blamed us for, it didn't matter

now. What mattered was that we got to Brisha and told her about Gianne's new fleet, before Gianne could use it. With the newfound deep-space technology, Earth would have no hope.

There was just one problem.

"We can't tell Brisha what the ships can do, speed-wise," I said, the thought coming to me on a wave of dread.

Navan frowned. "The engines?"

"If she finds out about them, she'll just go after the technology herself. We need to lie," I said. "We need to tell her Gianne is building a fleet of super-powerful ships, but they're powerful in their weaponry only. We have to persuade her to destroy the fleet instead of seizing one ship for study. No matter what happens, we leave out any intel about the deep-space engines, okay?"

"Understood. I just hope she listens," he replied, a flicker of nervousness in his eyes.

I stared toward the horizon, praying she would too.

*W*ith the shimmering gleam of the barrier rising in the near distance, a worrying thought dawned on me. How would we get through without the square patch Commander Korbin had used? Would it still be there, forging a hole in the defenses?

"What if the gap isn't there anymore?" I asked anxiously, the jagged mountains still too far away to see in detail.

A frown furrowed Navan's brow. "I have an idea," he replied, his wings beating faster. Five minutes later, we descended toward the fighting pits. "Pull your hood up and keep your face hidden," he warned as we headed for the tall, wooden entrance. This time, a different guard was on duty, though she looked no less grisly than her male counterpart, with scars crisscrossing over her broad face and muscular arms.

She smiled an almost toothless grin as Navan walked up to her. "Thought you were public enemy number one?" she remarked, in a high-pitched voice that didn't quite match her face.

"That's why I need the help of some old friends," Navan replied warmly, slapping her on the back. "It's good to see you, Nisha."

"You too, Idrax," she chuckled, pulling him into a hug. "This the reason you're running?" She whistled, flashing a wink in my direction.

Navan grinned. "Something like that. You know how Gianne feels about interspecies relationships," he said with a roll of his eyes.

"So, it has nothing to do with *that*?" Nisha asked, nodding toward the plume of black smoke just visible on the horizon.

"Nothing to do with us," Navan replied, not missing a beat. "Although, with the way things are going, Gianne will probably blame me for it anyway."

Nisha chuckled and shook her head. "You do attract trouble, don't you? Well, if Gianne's minions come looking, I'll tell them I haven't seen you," she promised. "Now, what can I do for you, troublemaker?"

"We need to get through without setting off the

barrier. Is the underground pass still in use, or did you end up closing it?" Navan asked.

"Still operable, though it's not particularly stable these days. A few of the guys tried to reinforce the support beams, but they gave up after one too many cave-ins. We don't use it so much, unless there's a Northern fighter who *really* wants a shot at a Southern warrior." She chuckled.

Navan grimaced. "You still get a few coming through this way, then? I thought they'd have given up after Mako punched that Northerner's head clean off."

"Apparently, they still want to prove they're better than us." Nisha sighed.

Navan frowned. "I thought *you* were a Northerner, originally?"

"I am, but don't spread it around," she whispered back, a coy smile on her lips. "It was simpler when the planet wasn't split in two. Legendary fights, like you wouldn't believe! Every warrior an equal—no North, no South, just Vysanthean. Ah well, that's what happens when you put nobles in charge of things. We'd be far better off with a government taken from the people, voted for by the people." She sighed, then gestured for us to follow her.

"Careful, Nisha, you're starting to sound like a revolutionary," Navan teased, though I could see a glimmer of respect in his eyes. I felt it myself, too. These were

the kinds of people who should be running things—
the ones who saw a brighter future for Vysanthe, like
Seraphina.

Nisha grinned. "Perhaps I am one! That's the thing
about revolutionaries: they look the same as everybody
else," she said, chuckling to herself as we pressed on
through the grim sight of the fighting pits. There
weren't many people crowding the floor today, with
most of the betting stalls closed up, and only a few
clashes of metal to be heard from the edge of the actual
pits.

"It's quiet," I said absently, casting a glance over the
miserable faces of the gamblers. They didn't seem as
animated as the ones we'd seen the last time.

"It's still early," Nisha replied, leading us around
the pits to a doorway cemented in the side of a sheer
rockface. "This place doesn't liven up until the sun
goes down."

After opening it with a set of rusty keys, she urged
us forward into the darkness beyond. Dim light flickered from emergency lamps, but the ground was slippery underfoot, the walls dripping with cold moisture.
It was treacherous, to say the least, and I almost lost my
footing a few times. Had it not been for Navan's hand
gripping me tight, I'd have fallen on my butt more
times than I cared to count.

"This is where I leave you," Nisha said apologetically as we reached a fork in the tunnel. "Head down this passageway, and you'll come out in the North. Tread carefully. As I said, the walls are crumbling."

"Thank you, Nisha," Navan replied, pulling his old friend into another tight embrace.

"What are pals for? Don't wait so long until you visit again, okay?"

Navan smiled. "I won't."

With that, Nisha disappeared back up the tunnel, headed in the direction we'd just come. Meanwhile, Navan and I took the path that led directly in front of us, walking side by side, until the tunnel thinned out, forcing us to walk single file through the dark, narrow space. I wasn't ordinarily claustrophobic, but the passageway was almost making me wish we'd risked the barrier. I could feel the walls pressing in on me as a thunderous roar boomed above my head. All around us, things cracked and creaked, making me dread each step, in case the whole thing fell down. Reaching out to touch the walls didn't help either, given that each time I felt a vibration ripple through the stone, fragments of rock crumbled downward, covering my face and hair in a layer of damp dust.

Still, we pressed on, knowing it was the only way to reach the North without being detected by the barrier's sensors. If Korbin caught us, I was fairly sure he wouldn't stop to listen to what we had to say. We had to reach Brisha before the rest of our troop so we could explain to her what had happened. She might not be our biggest fan, but I knew she would at least hear us out.

"You okay back there?" Navan asked as particularly violent thunder ricocheted through the passageway, making everything tremble. My teeth juddered.

"Still in one piece," I murmured, fearing that any kind of volume might cause the support beams to break.

"It shouldn't be too much farther now," he said reassuringly, though there was no way he could have known that, unless...

"Have you been this way before?" I asked, curious.

"Once or twice, to collect fighters from the North. That was a long time ago, though," he replied. The thought comforted me. If he'd been this way before, then perhaps he *did* know where the end was.

"How can this tunnel exist?" I wondered, knowing it went against the split between North and South. "Do the queens know about it?"

"It's one of those don't ask, don't tell scenarios," Navan replied. "The guys who run the joint make sure no spies get through, and in return Gianne lets them keep the pits open. They only let fighters through. They've always been pretty strict on that. Although, it doesn't look like there have been many fighters through this way in a while. Besides, it's not like you could fit an army through without it falling to pieces. Hell, you probably couldn't get more than two or three people through without it falling down," he mused, setting my nerves on edge. Just the mention of it falling down made my heart race.

"Are you sure we're nearly there?" I asked, imagining a horrible death, crushed beneath the rubble of an entire mountain.

"Almost," Navan promised.

True to his word, I noticed a glimmer of light up ahead. At first, I panicked, thinking it was a flashlight in the hands of someone trying to scout us out. But then I realized it was the cold light of day, and never had I been happier to see it. With a final blood-chilling boom of rock crumbling behind us, we surged out into the crisp air. I crouched low to the ground, drawing every icy breath deep into my lungs, wanting to get the stale heat of the tunnel out.

Turning, I saw that the tunnel entrance had held, though it had felt like it was going to cave in around us. Miraculously, we had made it without alerting anyone to our presence. Navan offered his hand, helping me up. I smiled, seeing the streaks of dirt and grime all over his face, looking like war paint.

"You've got muck on you," I teased.

"So do you," he remarked, brushing some of it away with his thumb.

Feeling relieved, I glanced around at the harsh landscape. I could see the mountainside rising up beside me, but there was no hint of the barrier. It was too far up. Still, I had Navan, and he would be able to lead us back to Nessun.

Just then, I heard a familiar sound in the distance. My head whipped around, snapping in the direction of the noise. Navan's eyes were already fixed on the jagged teeth of the mountain range up ahead. Across the snowy peaks, figures were appearing, swarming toward us, their wings outstretched.

The image made my blood freeze.

"They must have been monitoring this whole barrier area," Navan muttered.

"What do we do?" I asked, panicked, dreading the thought of being forced to run back through the tunnel.

"We let them take us to Brisha," Navan said stoically, his gaze unwavering. "She'll listen to what we have to say. And I doubt they'll hurt us until we've been put before her."

I didn't feel confident of that. I knew what cold-bloods were like, and if I didn't come out of this bruised and battered, it would be a miracle.

Commander Korbin was at the head of the

squadron, though none of our fellow trainees were present. Instead, he was flanked by an elite force, their faces bearing the scars and tattoos of seasoned soldiers. There were ten, in total, which seemed like overkill considering there were only two of us, but I supposed it was meant to send a message.

"Don't move!" Korbin bellowed as his team descended. "We will shoot you without hesitation if you so much as twitch!" The soldiers carried guns that flashed tiny green lasers across our bodies.

We did as we were told, staying perfectly still, while the task force approached. Two females came up behind me, yanking my arms behind my back, fastening cuffs roughly around my wrists. With my hands bound, they shoved me in the back, getting me to stagger forward.

"Careful with her!" Navan yelled, his eyes furious.

"One more word, and I will take your blade and slice her head off. Do I make myself clear?" Korbin spat, getting nose-to-nose with Navan.

He fell silent, gazing in my direction. One of my guards forced my chin down to my chest, so I couldn't look at him any longer. She kept her hand on my neck. The muscles there were screaming in pain, but there was nothing I could do. To fight back would mean certain death against soldiers like this.

"Blow it up!" Korbin ordered, and I caught sight of

two other soldiers planting bombs around the tunnel entrance. When it blew, the passageway would be sealed for good.

A moment later, the two coldblood females gripped an arm each before hauling me up into the sky, dragging me along behind them as we soared across the bitter landscape, the frozen lakes glinting in the distance. I tried to turn, to make sure Navan was following, but each time I moved, one of the coldbloods forced my head back down.

Half an hour later, we reached the unmistakable layout of Nessun, the squadron of elite soldiers bringing us right down in front of the palace before clapping more chains on our ankles. For good measure, they clamped a peculiar device down over my mouth, the solid metal preventing me from speaking. When I tried, it pinched my skin, the pain increasing with each attempt I made.

Panic coursed through me. If neither Navan nor I could speak, how were we supposed to explain the truth to Brisha? I flashed a look at Navan, who had been dragged up beside me, a metal device clamped across his mouth too. I could tell he was trying to calm me down, but there was only so much he could say with his eyes alone.

With our bodies rattling with chains, the soldiers pushed us roughly inside the palace, leading us down the echoing hallways toward the throne room. It was a far cry from the way we had arrived at Nessun that first time, when we had been welcomed as guests, not prisoners. Now, we were definitely meant to feel like traitors to Brisha's crown.

The queen was waiting for us at the top of the plinth where her throne stood, her arms folded across her chest. She was dressed in a plain, flowing black gown, her pale copper hair tied up in an elegant style, black roses woven into the tresses. Somehow, it felt like she'd dressed up for the occasion—her style best suited for an execution. I shuddered at the thought, my eyes flicking up to hers. They were fixed upon us, her expression one of deep disappointment.

"Would you call it coincidence that all the civilians happened to be evacuated from the Observatory, right before the bombs went off?" she asked coldly, pacing across the top of the plinth, her long train sweeping across the marble. "Would you call it coincidence that the pair of you disappeared shortly after you were due to report back?"

I shook my head, opening my mouth to speak, but the device bit into my face, prompting me to grimace instead. A whimper of pain echoed from my throat. Brisha's expression changed slightly as she heard it.

"Take those ridiculous things off, Korbin! How are they supposed to speak, if they have a bar of solid metal across their mouths?" she snapped, bringing me an instant wave of relief. Now we would have the chance to tell the truth, and hopefully regain her favor.

The guards removed the devices, though they were by no means gentle about it. As mine came away, I licked my dry lips, tasting the metallic tang of blood.

"Was this your doing, Idrax? I know you objected to my course of action before you left to complete your mission," she accused, her eyes narrowing. "I thought the threat of my punishment might be enough to sway your hand, but clearly I was wrong," she added sourly.

Navan nodded stiffly. "I admit it. I was the one who caused the building to be evacuated," he said, thankfully mentioning nothing of Seraphina. "However, I did so without raising any alarm. I didn't want innocent people to die, but my loyalty remains with you, Queen Brisha. If I were not on your side, I would have stopped the explosion entirely. I did not. I merely stopped the killing of innocent people," he explained, his voice calm.

Queen Brisha looked thoughtful for a moment, mulling the words over. "Perhaps you have done me a favor by acting this way. The thought of so many deaths on my conscience is not something I relish, and you have saved me from that," she said, then paused again. "However, whatever your reasoning, I must still banish you to the farthest tundra of the North, where you will struggle to survive past a week. Mercy is a noble trait, Navan Idrax, but you defied me, and I will *not* tolerate that under any circumstances," she continued, her expression icy. "Moreover, your absence is still unaccounted for. Where did you go, traitors?"

As a tense silence stretched between them, my mind raced. Our options were narrowing by the second, but there was still hope; it was just a case of figuring out which option would cause the least destruction. If we told Brisha about the advanced ships, then we would regain her favor, but there was a risk in that. We could lie and tell her they were super powerful in their weaponry only, just as we had planned to, but there was no way we could ensure she didn't capture one of them to study for herself. If she did get hold of one, and discovered that they were powerful in terms of speed, instead of weaponry, then that put us back at the beginning, with the possibility of both queens finding Earth opening up once more.

Then again, I figured it was better to give Brisha a reason to attack Gianne, destroying lots of the ships in the process. Not only Gianne's ships, but Brisha's too, reducing the forces on either side. Besides, if either sister learned about Earth and traveled toward it, they would be hit with competition from all sides. The rebels' growing forces would annihilate anyone who made it there, especially if the approaching party had a reduced number of ships. At least, I hoped.

It was definitely a gamble to put my faith in the queens weakening each other before they even got to finding Earth, but it was one I was willing to take. Plus, I was pretty sure Brisha had spies working in the South. If she didn't find out from Navan and me, she would likely find out one way or another. We might as well use the intel to our advantage while we still could.

"The reason we were absent, Your Highness, is because we came across something interesting—some information you might want to know," I said boldly, finding my voice. "In return, we would ask that you reconsider your punishment. By the time we had discovered this information, the troop had left. We were forced to return by ourselves."

Brisha frowned. "Information, you say?"

I nodded. "Please, promise you will reconsider our punishment, and I'll tell you what we know."

"Very well, go on," she prompted, her tone softening.

Taking a deep breath, I leveled my gaze at the queen. "Your sister is building a new fleet of ships, which is nearing completion. Each one is a weapon, in the true sense of the word. They are fitted with advanced technology, to gain advantage in battle. Navan recognized some of the mechanics. These are machines of war and death, Your Highness, and your sister intends to use them. They are in the underground hangar just outside Regium."

A small smile crept onto Brisha's lips. "A new fleet? This is excellent information, indeed, if true," she purred. "But... how did you come across them?" There was a hint of suspicion in her voice.

"It's where they do all of their fleet-building, Your Highness, though the location is supposed to be secret," Navan explained. "I know of it through my father, and remembered seeing them building something impressive the last time I was there. I suggested to Riley that we scope it out, as I knew a side entrance where we wouldn't be spotted."

I looked to him, hoping he wasn't giving too much away. "Yes, Your Highness. I thought it might be good to bring you something useful back," I added, knowing how lame it sounded. I felt like the teacher's pet.

"I have a military mind, Your Highness. After the attack on the lab, I knew Gianne would be up to something. As it happens, I was right," Navan cut in, covering my statement.

Queen Brisha's features softened, her eyebrow lowering. "In that case, perhaps I was too hasty when it came to your punishments. In return for this, I shall grant you amnesty for your previous actions, as I believe they were done with my cause in mind. If we

arrive at this hangar and there are no ships, however...
Well, we shall cross that bridge if we come to it." She
gave us a warning look. "As you have knowledge of
these mechanics, Idrax," she continued, "I will send
you with more soldiers to scope out the technology and
return your findings to me. We must ensure my sister
never gets a single one off the ground."

I swallowed. Those were the words I had been
dreading to hear.

"If it is not too much to ask, Your Highness, might
we rest and refresh ourselves first?" Navan asked, his
tone bleak.

"Of course." She smiled coldly. "Guards, remove
these chains and let these two return to their quarters.
We shall send a squadron out the day after tomorrow.
Perhaps we shall make a second attempt at getting you
to blow something up," she added, with a sly wink
at Navan.

As the guards removed our shackles, I cast Navan a
nervous glance.

We were back in Brisha's good graces, but at
what cost?

On the way back to our chambers, we made a detour, stopping at Angie and Lauren's apartment. I was eager to tell them we'd returned safely.

I knocked on the door, listening for the sound of feet shuffling in the room beyond. A moment later the door was wrenched open, and Angie's face stared out into the hallway. She jumped on me as soon as she saw me, wrapping her arms around my waist.

"Don't you *dare* go running off like that again, without saying a word! Bashrik told us what happened. We've been worried sick!" she exclaimed.

"I'm so sorry for worrying you. I wanted to come and tell you, but I ran out of time," I sighed, squeezing my friend tight.

Lauren appeared in the doorway, a wave of relief

washing over her face. "Riley! You're back! Thank God you're safe. When Bashrik said you'd gone to the South on a mission, we didn't know if we'd ever see you again," she gasped, joining the huddle.

Navan moved past me into the apartment, where Bashrik was pacing across the far side of the room, running an anxious hand through his dark hair. His expression calmed as he saw Navan, a wave of relief rippling across his face. The poor guy looked frazzled, like he hadn't sat down or allowed himself to relax the whole time we'd been away. Without a word, the brothers hugged each other. It was a sweet moment, but my attention immediately returned to my friends.

"What the hell happened?" Lauren asked, releasing me, her brow furrowed with worry.

"It's a bit of a long story. Let's go inside, and I'll explain everything," I suggested.

We ventured into the warmth and sat around the fireplace on the sofas and armchairs that were scattered around. It felt almost like the first day everyone had been together in Northern Vysanthe, though the tension in the air was thicker.

I told the tale of where we'd been and what we'd been up to. I told them all about Seraphina, and the role she'd played in the evacuation of the Observatory. Even now, I struggled to tell Navan what she'd asked. It wasn't that I didn't trust him, or believed him to be incapable of making the right decision. If anything, it was the opposite. I knew he would do everything in his power to protect my heart, but I couldn't bear the thought of Seraphina enduring a life with that wrinkled, ancient old man, in exchange. No, I would have to tell him about it very soon, but I had to fully process my own thoughts and feelings on the whole matter first... as well as gather the courage. Because he *had* to return to the South, even if only for a fake marriage. There was no alternative, not if that alternative meant the suffering of someone to whom I owed my life. After all, if Seraphina hadn't arranged for Lazar to take Orion's deadly chip out of my neck, who knew if I would be standing here now. Besides, I liked her as a person. She was a friend.

As I came to the end of my story, recounting the new ships, the scrap with Aurelius, and the return through the mountain pass, I glanced around, my eyes resting on Navan.

"What happened to Aurelius, by the way?" I asked, realizing I had no idea. Things had gotten so crazy that I'd forgotten to find out what his fate had been, against Navan's blades. I had just assumed Navan to be the victor, since he'd returned in one piece. Then again, if Navan had killed Aurelius, then surely that meant Seraphina was off the hook? *That* would sure solve a lot of problems.

Navan smirked. "He ran off with his tail between his legs."

"So, he's still alive?" I murmured, sighing.

"As far as I know... Why? Do you think I should have killed him?" Navan asked, frowning.

I shrugged. "I was worried he might have seen your face. It wouldn't be good for us if he told Gianne he'd seen you," I reasoned.

He shook his head. "I kept my hood up the whole time and kept my face turned away from him. I'm pretty sure he didn't realize it was me."

"So, if Brisha thought you betrayed her, how come you're not dead?" Angie asked. I was grateful for the distraction.

"We explained we didn't really betray her, we just got sidetracked. The information about the new ships bought us back her favor, for now," I replied. "She wants to send Navan back the day after tomorrow to scope out the technology. I imagine she'll want to blow a few ships up, too."

"I'll request to come with you," Bashrik announced abruptly, prompting a worried glance from Angie.

Navan frowned. "Don't you have the alchemy lab to finish?"

Bashrik shook his head, a pleased grin curving up his usually tense mouth. "We put the final touches in place today. It's finished and raring to go. The alchemists are already back at work." He sighed happily, a weight evidently lifted from his shoulders. "I think there's supposed to be an unveiling ceremony in the morning, to officially open the building. However, as soon as I'm done schmoozing, I am at your disposal. I'd be more than happy to come to the South with you and scope out some ships. Besides, I can always cover for the deep-space engines. If Brisha doesn't send anyone else with engineering knowledge, we might just get away with it, and encourage her to blow everything up instead!" he said, a boyish glee in his eyes.

"What is it with boys and blowing things up?" Angie muttered, and I could see it came from a place of concern. She didn't want Bashrik to get mixed up in this any more than I wanted Navan to.

"Bashrik has a point, though," Lauren chimed in, adjusting her spectacles on the bridge of her nose. "The more people we have who can vouch for the ships not being capable of deep-space travel, the better."

Bashrik's face softened slightly as his eyes rested on Angie. "Look, we don't have to worry about it until after tomorrow. We can enjoy the unveiling ceremony and take pride in what we've achieved," he said. "It's not every day you build a whole lab in under a month!" I noted he kept using the word 'we,' the sound of it bringing a smile to my lips. They'd make a good couple, despite their mutual stubbornness.

"Wait, the alchemists have gone back to work already?" I asked, realizing what he'd just said.

"I'm afraid so. They were straight back on it, as soon as the last piece was in place," Bashrik murmured, his expression turning grim.

If that was the case, then our human blood was on its way to being synthesized. And, with the device Yorrek had spoken about, that gave us less time than anticipated. Still, if we could get the two sisters in a position where they were fighting one another, that might buy us more time, with Brisha's focus drawn elsewhere. The immortality elixir would remain important to her, for obvious reasons, but she might put it on the backburner while war was underway. After all, she wouldn't want her sister stealing it from under her nose during the conflict.

"Speaking of the lab, we were just congratulating Lauren when you knocked on the door," Angie said, distracting my attention. "In fact, I think it might be the best news you've heard all evening."

Lauren smiled as I glanced in her direction. "The alchemists have offered me an apprenticeship. I sent them an essay discussing the different ways in which elixirs can be stabilized, and they asked to have me on board," she explained, excitement bristling in her voice. "I thought it might be a good idea to have someone in the lab keeping an eye on things. Brisha trusts me, thanks to our evenings spent in the library, and I'm pretty sure I'll be able to slow down any work they might be doing. Just a hint of a mishap here, too much soren root there, that sort of thing." Her cheeks flushed slightly as everyone's eyes turned proudly in her direction.

This was perfect news, and Lauren had done it all of her own volition. I could understand that. Had she told us of her plans, we might have tried to talk her out of it, or stick our own oars in, but this was the perfect cover. The alchemists' desire for her knowledge had overcome their suspicion of her being an outsider. I doubted any of us could have planned it better if we'd had weeks.

After the gamble we'd taken earlier, it was just the sort of positive news I needed. With Bashrik and Navan figuring out a way to keep the deep-space engines secret, Lauren keeping an eye on the alchemists, and Brisha reinstating our good name, removing the weight of imminent punishment, things were looking brighter than they had seemed mere moments before. They were small victories, of course, since we would still be forced to send intel to Orion via Pandora and her little device, but it was something.

Even so, the thought of Earth drifted back to me. I kept wondering how a little, relatively primitive planet in the far reaches of the universe could be causing so much trouble. How could we be so important? More than that, I wondered if we'd ever see its beautiful green-and-blue surface again, or set foot on its precious soil. With each day that passed, it seemed to be getting farther and farther away.

"I'm going to turn in for the night," I announced, feeling suddenly drained. It was too much for one day. "We'll no doubt be expected at this grand unveiling tomorrow, so we should probably look as bright-eyed and bushy-tailed as possible. Although, I think I'm going to need a miracle." I laughed dryly, rising up from the sofa.

"Will you come down for breakfast tomorrow morning?" Lauren asked with a hopeful smile. "I start at the lab, and it'd be nice to get a pep talk before I go —the way we used to before our big exams."

"I wouldn't miss it for the world," I promised, hugging my friends before heading for the door.

"It's good to see you safe and sound, Brother," I overheard Bashrik say as I stepped out into the hallway.

"It's good to be back in one piece," Navan replied, pulling his brother into another tight embrace. "The two of us have much to discuss, but it can wait until the morning. Sleep well. You've earned it. I'm sure the lab looks incredible," he said, before releasing his brother and following me out into the corridor.

As the door closed behind us, we set off toward our chambers, everything seeming so quiet without the energy of the other three. However, it was a silence I liked the sound of. It was a particular sort of peace, enjoyed only by a couple in love, the tension bristling between us. Truthfully, my body was tired, but there was another part of me that wanted to kiss Navan until I had no energy left, relishing in the fact that we were both still alive after everything that had gone down today.

Reaching our bedroom, all I wanted to do was curl up beside Navan in our bed, falling asleep in his arms. It seemed that was what he wanted, too, as we settled in for the night, going about our oddly domestic routine. Once Navan had showered and teased me about my smelliness, I took my own thorough shower, letting the cool water run across my skin and sloughing off the dust and dirt from the mountain pass. I dried off and changed into my nightdress, detangling my wet hair with my fingers. Navan came up behind me and slipped his arms around my waist, gazing at me through the mirror. Gently, he leaned in and kissed my neck, his eyes closing in desire, the touch of his lips thrilling my senses.

"War is coming, isn't it?" I asked quietly, hating that I might be about to ruin the moment.

He paused in his kisses, his eyes seeking out mine.

"It is, but we'll find a way to escape it, Riley. I promise you, when the worst of it comes, we will be far from here," he murmured against my skin. "You won't have to watch anyone suffer. You won't have to witness the horrors that come with it."

All this time, escape had been at the forefront of my mind. Everything we'd done was leading to getting away from Vysanthe, but now that Navan's words had made it seem real, I wasn't sure if that was what I wanted anymore. Perhaps Vysanthe needed something else. Perhaps it didn't need another battle between embittered sisters, it just needed someone better equipped to steer it toward a course of peace and harmony. Seraphina's vision for the planet seemed like a good place to start, though I wasn't an idiot. Maybe that ideal was even more impossible than a fragile balance between two halves.

"I'll be in soon, Navan. I just need a minute," I whispered.

"I'll be waiting," he said with a smile. Pulling his t-shirt over his head as he went, he turned and walked away, leaving me alone in the bathroom to sift through my endless thoughts.

I caught sight of a box on the bathroom counter, tucked away in the corner by the sink. The queen's emblem was embellished in gold upon a label, trailing down from a perfectly tied ribbon. Curious, I reached out and lifted the top off the box. There was a small brass pot inside, engraved with birds and insects, each creature entwined. I didn't recognize the animals, but the craftsmanship was exquisite. Next to the pot was a card. Excited by the prospect of a gift, I lifted the note and read the words upon it: *Enjoy. From, The Queen.*

It certainly seemed as though we were back in Brisha's good books, though the handwriting looked oddly familiar. With a wry smile, I realized it was Lauren's bubbly letters upon the card. Queen Brisha must have asked her to write out the words in our language so she could surprise us. A sweet touch.

I unscrewed the lid of the pot and lifted it to my nose, inhaling the deliciously sweet scent of the concoction within. Moving it beneath the bathroom lamps, I noticed that the cream seemed to sparkle, the iridescence catching the light in the most remarkable way. I grinned, dabbing my finger into the rich, delicious-smelling cream before rubbing it across my hands and neck—all the places that felt dry and uncomfortable after the strain of the day. Everything felt immediately better, as though my skin had taken a huge sip of water.

Rubbing it across the rest of my body, wherever it felt like I needed some help, I inhaled the sugary scent, the aroma lifting my spirits. I'd never believed in aromatherapy before, but this was changing my mind.

With my skin refreshed and a smile on my face, I stepped back into the warmth of the bedroom.

Immediately, I became aware of Navan behind me, his arms sliding around my waist, his lips caressing my skin, his hands gripping at the fabric of my nightdress. Amused, I turned to face him, catching sight of his flushed cheeks and glittering eyes.

"Well, someone's eager," I whispered huskily, running a hand through his hair. "Not that I'm complaining."

His voice caught in his throat. "It's that scent... It's a... Vysanthean aphrodisiac. It makes the wearer...irresistible to their partner," he murmured, his hands finding my face, his lips grazing mine with an almost desperate passion.

He sat down on the bed and pulled me onto his lap. My legs wrapped around his waist, and his hands slid beneath my nightdress, exploring the curve of my spine, each touch making me shiver. All I could see and feel was him, his body cool to the touch. I could feel his hunger in the way he kissed me, in the way his hands moved across my skin, taking in every curve and contour. This wasn't like all the other times.

It was infectious, his desire setting my body alight. I kissed him back, hard and passionate. He gasped against my neck, growling in the back of his throat, as he lifted my nightdress over my head and threw it to the floor, leaving me naked in his arms. This time, there was no hesitation. I didn't want to wait any longer. I wanted him, and I wanted him now.

He reached for his waistband, then paused, leaning over to the bowl that Brisha had previously left for us. He picked up two of the strange herbs, putting one in his mouth and placing the other on the tip of my tongue. I let the herb dissolve, the process feeling alien to me. In his arms, however, I felt safe and secure, knowing he would lead me.

Hurriedly, he wrestled free of his pajama bottoms. Drinking him in with a sense of surprise and excitement, I realized things were not quite as dissimilar as I'd feared they might be. We could definitely make this work.

Relaxing, I moved back onto the bed, drawing him down with me, my hands running over his smooth skin, my mouth hungrily kissing every inch of his body it could reach. My fingertips explored him cautiously, discovering things I'd never experienced before. His did the same, making my back arch against him, my breath coming in short, sharp gasps as he held me to him, guiding me through. A ripple of pure pleasure bristled through every cell in my body, setting my nerves on fire.

"I love you," he murmured in my ear, as his hands parted my legs and he pressed himself against me.

"I love you," I gasped back, realizing it was the first time we'd ever said the words aloud.

My breath caught in my throat as I bucked against him, wanting more, wanting all of him. My nails raked against his back, his breath mingling with mine.

No matter how hard he kissed me, or how his fingertips danced across the most sensitive parts of my body, or how his lips moved when they caressed my skin, I couldn't get enough. In that moment, nothing else mattered. It was just him and me, entwined together, our bodies moving in perfect rhythm, everything else lost in the wake of his addictive touch.

I awoke to the dawn sunlight glancing in through the window. I was enveloped in Navan's arms, his wings folded around me, his breath tickling my neck. I grinned, wriggling against him, giggling as he stirred in his sleep, scooping me closer against his body.

I could have lain like that for hours, but it seemed as though the world had other plans. Across the room, the holographic comm device was flashing red, notifying us that a message had been left. Not wanting to wake Navan just yet, I extricated myself from his loving embrace and padded over to the device, pressing the button to make the message play.

Pandora's face shot up in front of me, and I scowled. This wasn't the sight I wanted to see, especially after the best night of my life—when I'd been able to pretend none of this existed. She began to speak.

"You are invited to a special private ceremony at the alchemy lab, which is to take place before the official, public unveiling," she said sternly. "Queen Brisha demands your presence on this historic day, when we shall trial the first immortality elixir. This may well be the day that Northern Vysanthe triumphs. The ceremony will begin at eight. The queen is expecting you. Do not be late," she warned, before the message clicked off, leaving the hiss of white noise and the sight of a blank screen.

Checking the clock on the wall, I saw that it was just after six. Even so, I hurried to the bed, rocking Navan gently to wake him. He blinked his eyes open slowly, shielding them from the light. He gave me a goofy smile as he saw me, reaching out his arms to scoop me back into a tight embrace. I tried to struggle, laughing as he clung onto me, before giving up and snuggling against him. I figured I might as well enjoy the comfort while I gave him the bad news.

"I've just checked the message machine," I said, as he trailed kisses down my neck. "Queen Brisha asked us to meet her at the alchemy lab at eight for a 'special immortality elixir ceremony.' They want to test the first batch."

He stopped kissing me. "How can they have synthesized your blood so fast?"

"The device Yorrek told us about—it must have helped them speed up the process. None of us had access to the lab yesterday, which means Queen Brisha could be sure we couldn't tamper with anything. Now, she wants us to see the results," I muttered.

"That woman has sapped all the enjoyment out of me," Navan remarked, though his body told a different story. He grinned against my neck, flipping me around to face him. "Maybe we could remedy that, if you feel up to it?" he whispered, kissing me softly on the lips.

"It might have to wait," I murmured, knowing Angie and Lauren would be expecting us for breakfast. "We can definitely try to coax that enjoyment back once this morning is out of the way," I promised, returning his kiss.

Reluctantly pulling myself away from him, I wandered into the bathroom and closed the door. I took a long, hard look at myself in the mirror, staring at my naked reflection, trying to see if I looked any different. Although nothing had changed on the outside, I felt strange on the inside. It was as if I'd unlocked something that had always been there, waiting for the right person to come along. With Navan, I didn't feel the need to hesitate or hide. I could be wholly me in his arms, and he loved me all the same. I grinned at the memory of the previous night, and the things we had done. Even with the aphrodisiac spiking our desire for each other, it had been the right moment for it to happen. In the cold light of day, nothing felt wrong, or like it shouldn't have happened. In fact, it felt the opposite.

Running the hot water for the shower, I stepped in and let the soothing liquid calm my aching muscles, reviving my spirits for the day to come. A few moments later, Navan peered in through the bathroom door, grinning mischievously as he saw me standing under the cascade of water. Without waiting for an invitation, he hurried over and stepped in behind me. Restraining himself, he kissed me deeply before reaching for the jar of shampoo, which sat on a ledge carved into the wall. He took out a small amount and lathered it between his hands before running it through the damp tresses of my hair. When my whole head was smothered in suds, he gently tilted my head back into the running stream and washed it all out, planting delicate kisses on my face as he did so.

After quickly washing his own hair, he plucked a fluffy towel from the rail and wrapped me in it, drying me off as I struggled not to laugh. It was so sweet and unexpected, brightening my mood immeasurably. That was the thing about Navan—it wasn't often that he showed his playful side, but when he did, it was the best thing in the world.

Ten minutes later, we were dressed and ready to head downstairs for breakfast at Angie and Lauren's apartment. However, when we arrived, everyone seemed way more on edge than Navan and me. I could practically feel it even before I knocked on the door, the tension flooding out when it opened. Part of me wished I'd stayed curled up in the warmth of our bed, instead of venturing into this anxious atmosphere, and from the look on Navan's face, he felt the same.

"This wasn't supposed to happen!" Angie cried. "This could ruin everything!"

"Angie, you need to calm down. It's a test run. It might not even work," Lauren reassured her, but I could see doubt on her face, too.

"I'm guessing you got the message?" Angie asked, whirling in my direction.

"I did, but I don't think we need to worry until we see how it goes," I said, following Lauren's line of comfort. "They might have synthesized our blood, but there are a lot of other factors that go into making a successful elixir. We know that from everyone we've spoken to. This will likely just be a work in progress, to show how far they've come," I reasoned, hoping I was right. If we got to the lab and the elixir worked, we were doomed. Not just us, but the whole universe and everyone in it. Immortal Vysantheans were a terrifying prospect. It could not be allowed to happen.

"You better be right," Angie muttered, chewing her bottom lip nervously.

She only calmed when Bashrik entered, ten minutes later. Her eyes darted straight to him, his eyes already on her. In any other situation, it would have been a sweet sight, making me wonder when the pair of them were going to resume their garden party antics, but right now I just wanted Angie to calm down. Her fear was infectious, and it wasn't what we needed.

Bashrik took her to one side, speaking in a low voice, while the rest of us paced the room. I tried to eat some of the fruit that Lauren had put out, but my appetite had vanished. I kept wondering if last night had dulled my senses, making me oblivious to the severity of the situation. I had presumed it would all be okay, but then, I was basking in the glow of newly discovered passion. Of course I thought everything was going to be okay. It was a truth, universally known, that new lovers thought themselves invincible.

"Do *you* think it'll work?" I asked Navan quietly.

He gave a light shrug. "I don't know. I honestly don't. Even with synthesized blood, they'll have a long way to go before they crack the code of the elixir. My father always said that experiments mean years of trial and error. I find it hard to believe that they have the right mix already," he replied, though it didn't really calm my nerves.

"But Queen Brisha has something nobody else has," I reminded him, recalling Yorrek's personal scribblings on the subject. "She has Yorrek and his book of near-successes. Surely, that must narrow down the options a bit?"

A worried frown crossed Navan's brow. "I'm sure it'll be fine," he said, but the confidence had gone from his voice.

At half past seven, we left the palace together as a quintet and made our way toward the site of the new alchemy lab. Bashrik and Angie led the way, and the rest of us followed close behind. The streets were surprisingly empty, with only a few passersby wishing us a good morning.

With ten minutes to spare, we arrived at the alchemy lab. My eyes drank in the majesty of it. It really was impressive, the glass elements glinting in the morning sunshine, looking like a waterfall frozen in time. Pandora was waiting for us on the steps, though there didn't seem to be anyone else around. Perhaps the crowds would come later, at the official unveiling. Even so, I doubted the legitimacy of this meeting. After all, it had been Pandora who'd sent the message, not Queen Brisha herself. Was this some sort of ruse to get us where she wanted us? Had we said too much to

Brisha? Had Orion decided he no longer needed us? Or was I just being paranoid, spurred on by the anxiety of my friends?

Probably.

"Welcome," Pandora said coolly as we approached. Holding the door open for us, she ushered us into the building beyond before bringing up the rear, the door shutting with a very final slam.

We paused in the central atrium, staring up at the dynamic skylight Bashrik had implemented, the intricate glasswork casting a rippling ocean of blue light downward to greet us. It was stunning, the radiance moving in an almost liquid manner across the ground, the light dancing off the neighboring windows in a spectacular show of rainbow refraction. Meanwhile, Pandora walked past us, her boots echoing on the sleek floor. As she reached the door on the opposite side of the atrium, she turned, barking at us to follow her.

Drawing our eyes away from the pretty lights, we hurried after her, traipsing down a long, beautifully decorated hallway, the windows looking out on the city. I kept my gaze on the now-familiar buildings and skyscape, allowing it to ground me while keeping my thoughts away from what was to come. Whatever the conclusion, we would figure something out. We always did. Surely, our luck hadn't run out yet?

We arrived at a large circular auditorium with

raked seating, a prominent stage and a vast screen behind it. Queen Brisha was standing on the stage, an excited grin upon her face. She was certainly dressed for the occasion, looking like the Vysanthean version of an eccentric college professor, clad in a checkered gray pantsuit, her hair tied up in a bun.

"Welcome!" she announced. "Please, sit in the first row!"

She hurried across the stage and brought out five coldbloods, a mix of men and women. Behind them, two male coldbloods and one female followed, their lab coats singling them out as alchemists. Yorrek was notably absent, which surprised me somewhat, though he was probably still locked away in his cottage after the events of the garden party. Even with the Elysium in his system, he'd have known something was up. He, more than anyone, would know the peculiar effects of a mind-wiping serum.

We sat down tentatively in the front row of chairs, though it felt strange with the other seats empty behind us and to the sides of us. This really *was* a private ceremony.

"Good morning," Queen Brisha continued, resuming her spot in the center of the stage, while the test subjects lined up behind her and the alchemists stood awkwardly to one side. "I am so delighted you could make it on this momentous occasion. After all, none of this could have been possible without the generous donations that you gave to us." She smiled, her eyes seeking out me, Angie, and Lauren. We smiled back politely, though it wasn't like she'd given us much choice.

Before anyone could say a word, she continued, pacing across the stage as she spoke. "Here, we have five test subjects, who will be given the first batch of immortality elixir that has just come out of our laboratory this morning. Once it is in their systems, our alchemists are going to run tests on the cells to see if there is any change," she explained, gesturing at the corresponding individuals. I had to admit, the test subjects looked even more nervous than we did.

I faced forward, not daring to look at the others on either side of me. On my right sat Navan, while on my left sat Angie, and I could feel the animosity rippling off them both. I understood it completely. After all, if this elixir worked, would the queen then want regular samples of our blood to make more? It seemed like the only rational thing to do, if it was a success. A shiver of dread shot up my spine as another thought crept into my head: what if she wanted *all* of our blood? I mean, would she ever truly be satisfied with a small amount? If there was a chance she could offer her elixir to every single coldblood in the North, surely she would take actions against us, to make us take her to Earth, where she could harvest every drop she needed.

I gulped, reaching out to take Navan's hand. To my left, I noticed Angie doing the same to Bashrik, though she was careful to keep the movement from Brisha's watchful eye. I almost felt sorry for Lauren, who was sitting on Navan's other side. She had no one's hand to hold, and yet she seemed to be the calmest out of all of us. Her face was oddly a picture of serenity, not a trace of fear on her features. I envied her for that.

"Shall we begin?" Brisha asked, clasping her hands together. "Alchemists, administer the elixir," she instructed, sounding oddly like a gameshow host. Unfortunately for me, I'd always found gameshow hosts unbearably creepy, and the sound of her voice ramped up the thunder of my heart. With every fiber of my being, I prayed that the elixir failed.

I held my breath as the alchemists moved forward with a tray of hypodermic needles, each tube filled with a bluish liquid. Deftly, they lifted the needles to the arms of the test subjects and pushed down on the plungers, the blue fluid disappearing beneath their ashen flesh.

One.

Two.

Three.

Four.

Five.

Each injection had been administered, and now all we could do was wait. My pulse was racing, the blood rushing in my ears, my mouth dry as a bone. I couldn't bear the silence, or the prospect of success. And yet, I knew it was a possibility. That was the worst part about it, that I knew there was a chance this could work.

"The elixir has been administered to our five test subjects. Now, we must draw their blood for analysis," the female alchemist announced, her voice ringing out across the empty auditorium. It was the moment of truth. Taking out much larger needles, they moved toward the subjects.

But before they could get near, the five individuals spasmed wildly, blue froth gathering at the sides of their mouths, their eyes rolling back into their heads. Beneath their ashen skin, their veins expanded, colored a deep purple that pushed against the underside of their flesh, threatening to burst through.

As the first of their agonized cries ricocheted outward like a gunshot, I realized that their faces were aging at a rapid pace, their skin shriveling up, dark spots splattering across their features, everything collapsing in on itself. It was as though the very bone beneath was decaying, their bodies crumpling with it.

It was horrifying to watch, and yet I was helpless to tear my eyes away. After all, it was my blood that had been used in this experiment—it was my blood that was somehow doing this to them. I didn't understand it, but then there was no way anyone could wrap their head around what was happening. These people were decomposing in front of us, with no hope of a reprieve. There was no antidote, no anti-elixir, only a painful death.

As Queen Brisha's gaze locked with mine, it was clear she felt the same. Her fury was written all over her face... And I realized with a sinking feeling that she blamed *me* for this. *My* blood had done this.

From the rage in her eyes, I couldn't help but feel there would be no amnesty this time.

"Seize them!" Queen Brisha roared into a comm device taken from her hip.

Black-clad soldiers barged in from the side doors of the auditorium, evidently having been there to guard against outsiders trying to enter the building during the event. They surrounded us within seconds, but we were on our feet, ready to fight. It may have been my blood that had caused this reaction, but it wasn't our fault it hadn't worked! It seemed that Queen Brisha did have a streak of Gianne in her, after all, when the right buttons were pushed.

"Tell me you didn't have anything to do with this," I breathed to Lauren, knowing she'd had access to the alchemists and their findings.

She shook her head, her face a mask of horror. "I

didn't touch the test batch. I didn't even know it was ready," she whispered back. Given her calm demeanor throughout the trial, I had wondered if she'd done something to tamper with the elixir, but I could tell when Lauren was lying, and she definitely wasn't lying now.

The soldiers thundered toward us, their boots pounding on the hardwood floors. The fast percussion matched the beat of my heart, adrenaline pulsing through my veins. We had to try to get out of here before Brisha could punish us for something we didn't do. Ordinarily, I would've tried to talk my way out of it, but the queen no longer seemed in the mood to listen. I had *never* seen her this furious.

In a way, it was understandable. If I'd thought myself close to cracking immortality, only to have success snatched away, I'd be pretty pissed too. Even so, that didn't give her the right to punish us for her failure.

"Head for the fire exit!" Angie hissed, gesturing at a narrow side door tucked away in the shadow behind the stage. The path to it was clear, but there were soldiers running down the aisle toward it.

I sprinted for the door, bursting through it to the blare of a siren going off. The others followed close behind, the sound of their footsteps bringing me comfort. Beyond the door was a flat expanse of gravel and underground lighting, with a few saplings reaching skyward, leading up to the slope of the mountainside. My eyes darted around to find an escape route. There were buildings on either side, and slim passageways that cut back through to the city. I headed for the passageway on the right, picking up speed. It was only as I reached the entrance to the alleyway that I turned over my shoulder to make sure my friends were following.

Bashrik and Navan had just launched into flight, while Angie and Lauren were about twenty yards away, running hard in my direction.

"Come on!" I screamed, holding out my hand as though we were in some death-defying relay race. "Help them!" I bellowed up to the brothers, seeing the horde of winged soldiers pursuing my friends, the sky turning black as they filled the outside space. Without hesitation, Bashrik swooped out of the sky, his arms outstretched to grab Angie. He managed to get hold of her arms, pulling her upward. He was almost at the rooftop of the building where I stood, when three soldiers shot forward and took him out, shocking him in the neck with an electric spear. It stunned him for long enough that he lost his grip on Angie, and her body fell from the sky.

I screamed, watching her plummet, but another soldier arced downward, plucking her out of harm's way. She flailed as he held her fast, her legs kicking wildly, her arms doing everything they could to land a punch, but the soldier was too experienced and too fast.

Meanwhile, Bashrik had circled back around, rubbing his neck, trying to bring his limp arm back to life, while Navan rocketed toward Lauren, who was trying to feint around a group of soldiers that had landed directly in front of her, blocking the path between her and me. She was surprisingly fast, darting this way and that, but she stood no chance.

Navan managed to grab her by the waist and haul her upward, evading the soldiers and heading for the mountains instead of the city. They could lose their assailants in the icy landscape, and I could hide among the buildings and alleyways of Nessun. But if I kept running, what would happen to Angie?

Bashrik answered my question a moment later, when he barreled toward the soldier that held her. In the cold sunlight, I saw the flash of a blade, though I wasn't sure who held it—Bashrik, or Angie's captor.

A moment later, I realized that they were each holding a blade, and each of them knew how to wield it. The soldier and Bashrik swiped at each other with incredible speed, Angie dodging out of the way. One false move, and it would pierce right through her, and yet her eyes didn't move from Bashrik's face. She trusted him innately; I could see that. She knew he wouldn't let her come to harm.

Bashrik twisted around the side of the soldier and, catching him off guard, sank his blade into the soldier's hand, then knocked him out with a blow to the back of the neck. He put his own arms around Angie as the soldier tumbled to the ground, lying in a crumpled heap at my feet. Around his waist, I recognized the familiar belt of explosive devices, their orb-like exteriors glinting black in the sunlight. Suddenly, I had an idea.

Turning my gaze back toward Navan, who was growing smaller in the distance, I realized I would have to make a decision. Hidden in the shadows, the soldiers couldn't see me, nor was their focus on me, considering everything else going on around them, but I knew it wouldn't be long before they came this way to figure out where I'd gone. Queen Brisha would see to that.

It felt awful to admit, but I wanted to run. I didn't want to face another trial, not knowing the outcome. This time, the queen had no reason to be lenient. She could take every drop of blood we had to keep working on the elixir, and we would be helpless to stop her. I had seen the unmerciful look in her eyes when she had turned to me. All potential alliances had gone out of the window the moment those poor test subjects had crumbled in front of us.

And then, the soldiers caught up with Navan, who seemed to be struggling up the mountainside. He looked like he was flagging, the endurance of the last few days catching up with him. He still bore the bruises of his fight with Aurelius, and he'd carried me for hours the day before, not to mention what we'd gotten up to last night. There was no energy left in him to make such an extensive climb.

Even so, he struggled onward, his grip firm on Lauren. I watched as he glanced over his shoulder, seeing the soldiers advancing behind him. He knew it, and I knew it: they would catch him, and there would be nothing he could do to stop them from taking Lauren. *That* was what worried me most. The soldiers didn't seem bothered about capturing Bashrik and Navan. Their focus was solely on the human contingent—and that meant Brisha wanted our blood.

The soldiers tore Lauren out of Navan's hands, smashing the end of a spear into his head. I gasped, my stomach sinking. I had to stop this before they could hurt him more or take my friends away.

Lunging forward, I snatched the explosives belt from the unconscious soldier's waist and sprinted down the alleyway. I didn't stop until I reached the front of the alchemy lab again. Hurtling through the doors, I skidded to a halt in the atrium, seeking out the emergency stairwell. Finding the signs that led in the right direction, I hurried through the halls of the alchemy lab, barreling through each door, seeking out the stairwell. With the siren already going, it did nothing to sound the alarm as I burst through the fire door and hurried up the floors until I reached the roof. The door to the outside was locked, but that didn't matter. I had the makings of an explosive lockpick in my hands.

Sticking one of the orbs to the door, I turned the dial until it read twenty seconds, and pressed the button down twice. With that, I sprinted back down the stairs, taking shelter a few floors down, until the entire building trembled beneath me, a boom ricocheting through the walls.

Tentatively, I headed back up to the top floor. There was no longer a door standing in the way. Where it had been, there was a smoking hole. Spurred on by the explosion, and knowing the bombs wouldn't let me down if I needed them, I stumbled out onto the slick roof, the roar of the blast still ringing in my ears, while I prayed I didn't fall and break my neck.

At the top, just as I had remembered from Bashrik's model, were the hexagonal greenhouses—and a row of enormous generators. Without these huge units, every single specimen they had within the alchemy labs would become useless.

"Let them go, or I will blow these generators to pieces!" I roared, my gaze fixed on Queen Brisha, who had come out to see how her soldiers had fared. Angie and Lauren were on their knees in front of her, with soldiers pushing their heads down, while the rest of the attackers raced through the skies, trying to grapple with Bashrik and Navan, who were managing to evade their clutches, despite their injuries.

The queen was already looking up at me, no doubt drawn by the blast of the door, her face horrified. In that moment, everyone froze. I plucked a bomb off the belt and held it aloft as I approached the first of the generators, seeking out the control panel. It was locked inside a glass case, but I knew that would be nothing against an explosive, not after I'd seen what it could do with the door. And, by the looks of it, so did Queen Brisha.

"If you so much as touch that generator, I will have your friends executed!" Brisha shouted back, her voice booming up through the still air, but I was past the point where threats could frighten me. She wouldn't risk her lab being destroyed for a second time, not now.

"I *will* blow this generator sky high unless you release my friends. You won't kill them—you need their blood to be fresh and living. Otherwise, your precious elixir won't work!" I yelled, making it up as I went along.

She frowned. "What do you mean?"

"The second a Kryptonian dies, their blood begins to decay and fill with toxins! You need to take it from a live specimen if you want the elixir to work!" I shouted. I just hoped she took the bait.

"Don't touch that generator! Come down here, and we can discuss this like adults!" Brisha replied, her voice echoing up.

I shook my head. "You need to let my friends go. They had nothing to do with this. *I* had nothing to do with this, other than the fact that you used my blood!" I bellowed, standing my ground. "I know you're disappointed that the elixir didn't work, and you lost some of your people today, but that isn't our fault! You have to admit that!" I moved to stick the explosive on the control panel's box.

Instantly, her hands shot up in a gesture of surrender. "Okay, okay, you've made your point, Riley!" she shouted, her voice anxious. "I was upset that it didn't go as planned, and I took it out on you. I can see that now. I overreacted, and I apologize for that! Please, step away from the generator, so we can talk about this properly!"

Navan landed on the ground beside the queen,

with Bashrik following close after. The soldiers all landed a short distance away, the chase evidently over in the wake of Brisha's unexpected apology. Even the soldiers holding my friends' heads down desisted, taking a step back so Angie and Lauren could breathe, although it didn't stop Angie from shooting her guard the dirtiest look I'd ever seen.

"Your Highness, if you would just listen to us, we might be able to explain what happened to the elixir," Navan spoke up, loud enough so I could hear. "Threatening us like this will do no good when we might be the ones who can help you to move on from this failure and succeed the next time."

What are you up to? I wondered, lowering the bomb.

"I'm listening now, Navan," Queen Brisha remarked tersely, evidently disliking the way he was speaking to her in front of her soldiers.

"Of course, Your Highness. The thing is, from what I know about elixirs from my father, every single ingredient has to be correct, and in the precise quantity needed," he went on, garnering an unimpressed look from the queen. "Bear with me, I'm getting to the point. It's just, I think there might have been an ingredient missing. Something small, but very significant—that's the way it always happens with these things. Jethro and Ianthan thought there was something special about Kryptonian blood. Now, Jethro knew blood better than anyone, and I would believe his word over a whole planet of alchemists, which is what makes me think there must be another issue. There has to be something else that we're missing," he reasoned, a tightness coming into his voice as he mentioned Ianthan.

The queen sighed. "Your thoughts reflect my own, Navan, but what might this ingredient be? If it's not something we can seek out then we are back at square one," she muttered.

"Then allow us to go in search of it for you," Navan offered. "Send us on an official mission for you, and we will deliver the missing ingredient right into your hands. I already know where to start our search."

Ah, so *that* was what he was up to.

Queen Brisha glanced at Navan. "Before I agree to anything, will you please remove your beloved from the roof of my alchemy lab?" she remarked, flashing a look in my direction.

A grin spread across Navan's face as he launched himself upward, landing gracefully at my side. "Time to put down the bombs, Riley," he teased, pulling me toward him and tossing the belt of explosives over his shoulder.

"But she might be bluffing. She might arrest us as soon as we touch solid ground," I whispered, still feeling uncertain.

"If she does, she will have gone back on her word in front of her soldiers. That's not a good look for a leader," he reminded me. I peered over the lip of the rooftop, noting the frozen soldiers standing uniformly with their hands behind their backs. Like this, they didn't look nearly as threatening.

I sighed. "Fine, but put me down elegantly. I don't want to go stumbling around in front of the queen," I replied with a small smile.

"Of course," he murmured. The air rushed out of my lungs as he scooped me up and carried me down to ground level. He handed the belt of explosives to one of Brisha's soldiers with a dramatic bow.

"So, you were about to make a suggestion, Navan," Queen Brisha continued, barely offering me a glance. It seemed she was just relieved that I was weaponless and down from the roof, away from her precious generators.

"It's a thought that occurred to me very recently, Your Highness. You see, my father always taught me that, where serums and elixirs are involved, there needs to be a baseline, a reactive, and a stabilizer. In your elixir, we have Vysanthean blood as the baseline, Kryptonian blood as the reactive, but we have no stabilizer. At least, I don't think we do?" Navan enquired, raising an eyebrow.

To my surprise, it was Lauren who answered. "There is no stabilizer, Your Highness. In all the books I've read on the subject, there has never been a mention of a stabilizing blood added to the mix. There are stabilizing elements from elsewhere, but none are in blood form," she explained, rubbing the back of her neck, where the guard had roughly shoved her.

Lauren's words seemed to convince Brisha in a way nobody else's could. There was trust between them, though I hadn't understood the extent of it until now. I supposed it was inevitable, given the amount of time they had inadvertently spent in one another's company during long evenings in the library. It was only natural that a bond would form, and now we could use it to our advantage to persuade Brisha of the need for this extra element.

"How did none of my alchemists see this missing part, if Navan's father knew of it?" Brisha asked, her tone sharp as she glanced back at the lab.

"My father doesn't know of it. It's just a structure I've seen him use in other elixirs. Most of the time, a stabilizing element will do, such as a root or a compound, but considering that this elixir has to alter the genetic makeup of an individual, and seeing what it did to your test subjects, I figured it must need a third blood to stabilize the reactive and the baseline. Mere elements wouldn't be enough," Navan went on confidently. "I wouldn't have known that unless I'd seen the test with my own eyes. A genetic element is missing."

Queen Brisha turned to Lauren. "Is this true?"

She nodded. "I believe it's why the body decayed

instead of immortalizing, Your Highness. There was nothing to counteract the potency of our blood, mixed with the Vysanthean blood, and the other ingredients. To make it viable, you'd need a blood that could slow the reactive process, giving cells a chance to morph and adapt, instead of exploding and decaying the way they did today," she ventured, her intellect shining through. I believed every word she said, and I knew everyone else did too.

"What kind of blood?" Queen Brisha pressed eagerly.

"Draconian blood is ancient—far more ancient than ours. It has natural combative qualities, which I think would slow the reactive process down, allowing the elixir particles to infiltrate and alter cells instead of destroying them. In fact, I believe it could be the link we're missing," Navan explained, a hopeful look on his face. "My father once said that Draconian blood is some of the hardest to synthesize in the entire universe, but with your facilities, it would be possible. It might take time, once we have it back to you, but it would be perfect for your needs. I am quite certain of it."

I looked to Navan, wondering what he was playing at. I remembered him telling me about the plague on Zai that was deadly to coldbloods. It was the reason they no longer mined for opaleine there, given the virus that spread rapidly through Vysanthean systems. I still suspected the Draconians had implemented the virus themselves, since it was a reasonably pacifistic way of getting rid of their planet's exploiters. Why would Navan want us to travel to a plague-ridden place?

The queen pulled a sour face. "I will not send soldiers on a death mission to that Rask-forsaken place. We lost an entire mining colony the last time we sent Vysantheans there. I won't risk it again, and I won't risk you bringing it back here," she muttered bitterly, the hope fading from her face.

Navan smiled. "You wouldn't be sending a team of Vysantheans, Your Highness. We have Kryptonians to help. The virus shouldn't affect them in the way it affects us," he said. "With Riley, Angie, and Lauren on our side, we will have a far better chance of infiltrating Zai, and obtaining the Draconian blood without bringing the plague back with us. Just to be sure, we can take a test kit with us, so Riley, or one of the others, can check us for any signs of the virus on the return trip. If we're infected, they can leave us in the quarantine center between here and Zai."

"Who will fly the ship?" Queen Brisha asked, though the light had come back into her eyes. I could see that Navan's words were getting to her, filling her with a renewed sense of possibility.

"Riley has been excellent during flight training. If either Bashrik or myself is infected, she can fly us to the quarantine center and return the sample to you afterward," he suggested, barely missing a beat. It seemed he had thought of everything, taking up the role of Explorer once more. My only concern was, what if Queen Brisha demanded we leave before we could ensure the continued secret of the new fleet's deep-space tech?

For several minutes, Queen Brisha did not speak as she mulled over what Navan was suggesting. I tried to get his attention, but his gaze was fixed on her face. Besides, even if I had managed to get him to look at me, I wouldn't have been able to ask him about the ship's tech. Hopefully, he had a plan for that, too.

"I agree to your offer, Navan Idrax, and I will provide all the resources you require," Queen Brisha spoke at last. "However, I have one proviso to ensure your loyalty. Pandora will accompany you to Zai and keep an eye on you throughout the mission. If you do not agree to these terms, then you will not go. It is as simple as that."

At the mention of Pandora, I realized we might have an opportunity after all, to kill two birds with one stone. If we told Pandora that Gianne had managed to gain the deep-space technology, then, perhaps, Orion would be able to suggest something to prevent either sister from utilizing it. I hated involving Orion in any way, but I knew it might be the only choice we had.

"That seems reasonable to me, Your Highness," Navan replied sincerely, making me wonder what his real plan of action was. He couldn't seriously want to assist Brisha in completing the immortality elixir. He definitely had something else up his sleeve, though he was doing a stellar job of hiding it from the queen—and everyone else, for that matter.

Originally, we'd been hoping to pit the two queens against one another, to distract them from finding Earth, but now it felt like we were moving off on a tangential path. Somehow, we were turning away from Earth. If we left Vysanthe, heading toward a distant part of the universe, that meant we were leaving Earth vulnerable. It would take one discovery within the stolen ship tech, and Gianne or Brisha, or both, would know the location of my home planet. The weight of that knowledge rested heavily on my shoulders, but I prayed Navan had a solution.

"Then I suggest you return to your quarters, all five of you, and pack your things. Be ready to go at a moment's notice. I will send word when preparations are complete, though you can expect it to be soon. After all, there is no time to waste," Queen Brisha said. "I trust you will not let me down. Indeed, if you achieve this, and your hunch turns out to be correct, you can be assured that you will return to Vysanthe as national heroes," she promised, a grin spreading across her face. I could see how delighted she was at the prospect of finding the missing piece in the puzzle, the piece nobody else had found yet. Without it, everyone was doomed to fail, where she would succeed.

"Thank you, Your Highness," Navan said politely, taking my hand and walking with me back toward the alchemy lab. Angie and Lauren stood up, brushing the dust and gravel from their clothes, before following after us, with Bashrik bringing up the rear, standing close to Angie. A strange look passed across Queen Brisha's face as she saw him move toward Angie, but my time for feeling sorry for her was over. There was only a certain number of death threats one could take before realizing that someone wasn't a friendly presence. Brisha was a young woman at heart, but she was also a ruler with an enormous amount of power, and she wasn't afraid to use it. Never again would my heart go out to her.

Upon returning to the palace, Navan ushered everyone upstairs to our apartment, sitting us all down in the living room. I cast a glance at the rumpled sheets as soon as I entered the quarters, feeling my cheeks flush as I rushed to make the bed. Angie raised a knowing eyebrow in my direction, but I ignored it as I took a seat on the sofa. I was impatient to hear what Navan had to say.

"I realize you probably all think I've lost my mind, helping Brisha with the elixir. And, honestly, I'm starting to think there's some truth in what I said, especially when Lauren backed my theories up with real knowledge on the subject," he said wryly, a half-amused smile on his lips. "But, even if there is some truth in it, I have no intention of bringing a sample back to Vysanthe. You see, I want to reach Zai so we can contact the Fed outpost there."

"You want to alert them to Vysanthe's quest for immortality?" I asked, things falling into place.

"Precisely," Navan replied. "With their help, we'll be able to protect Earth. Even if the sisters wanted to use the deep-space tech, the Fed would stop them. As soon as they know what's going on, they'll step in."

"They didn't do much on Earth," I remarked, remembering the skeleton crew of lycans that had been placed on our planet. There had been no force or power in that Fed outpost. A rebel base had managed to set up beneath their noses, and they hadn't had enough power or surveillance to notice.

"The Zai outpost is far stronger than the Earth outpost. They have a proper militarized force, able to assist in universal conflicts," Navan replied hopefully. "The Fed at the outpost near Zai aren't strong enough to combat Vysanthe's entire army, but if we can persuade them to forge alliances with the planets that the queens have abused over the years, then we might stand a chance of overthrowing them, once and for all."

"What if they reach Earth before we can do all of this? What if Brisha scopes out Gianne's ships and discovers the deep-space tech?" I asked, the thoughts pushing at the forefront of my mind.

Navan sighed. "We tell Pandora what we found in the underground hangar and let her figure it out with her beloved Orion. I'm sure they'll find a way to send more rebel spies here," he said grimly. "In the meantime, we ensure she suspects nothing on our mission to Zai. As far as she knows, we're getting a sample of Draconian blood to bring back to Brisha. We persuade her that we're doing it for Orion's benefit, too, as it may be the missing piece in the puzzle."

"And then, we find a way to rid ourselves of her... for good," I cut in sharply. Orion had held an axe over our heads for long enough. Now, it was time for revenge.

READY FOR THE NEXT PART OF RILEY AND NAVAN'S STORY?

Dear Reader,

Thank you for reading *Renegades*.

Continue the journey in Book 4: **Venturers**, releasing on <u>**March 11th, 2018**</u>!

Visit: www.bellaforrest.net for details.

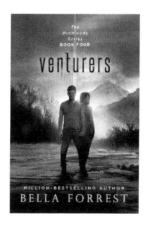

I'll see you there!

Love,

Bella x

P.S. Sign up to my VIP email list and I'll send you a heads up when my next book releases: **www.morebellaforrest.com**

(Your email will be kept 100% private and you can unsubscribe at any time.)

READ MORE BY BELLA FORREST

HOTBLOODS

Hotbloods (Book 1)

Coldbloods (Book 2)

Renegades (Book 3)

Venturers (Book 4)

THE GIRL WHO DARED TO THINK

The Girl Who Dared to Think (Book 1)

The Girl Who Dared to Stand (Book 2)

The Girl Who Dared to Descend (Book 3)

The Girl Who Dared to Rise (Book 4)

The Girl Who Dared to Lead (Book 5)

The Girl Who Dared to Endure (Book 6)

THE GENDER GAME

(Completed series)

The Gender Game (Book 1)

The Gender Secret (Book 2)

The Gender Lie (Book 3)

The Gender War (Book 4)

The Gender Fall (Book 5)

The Gender Plan (Book 6)

The Gender End (Book 7)

A SHADE OF VAMPIRE SERIES

Series 1: Derek & Sofia's story

A Shade of Vampire (Book 1)

A Shade of Blood (Book 2)

A Castle of Sand (Book 3)

A Shadow of Light (Book 4)

A Blaze of Sun (Book 5)

A Gate of Night (Book 6)

A Break of Day (Book 7)

Series 2: Rose & Caleb's story

A Shade of Novak (Book 8)

A Bond of Blood (Book 9)

A Spell of Time (Book 10)

A Chase of Prey (Book 11)

A Shade of Doubt (Book 12)

A Turn of Tides (Book 13)

A Dawn of Strength (Book 14)

A Fall of Secrets (Book 15)

An End of Night (Book 16)

Series 3: The Shade continues with a new hero...

A Wind of Change (Book 17)

A Trail of Echoes (Book 18)

A Soldier of Shadows (Book 19)

A Hero of Realms (Book 20)

A Vial of Life (Book 21)

A Fork of Paths (Book 22)

A Flight of Souls (Book 23)

A Bridge of Stars (Book 24)

Series 4: A Clan of Novaks

A Clan of Novaks (Book 25)

A World of New (Book 26)

A Web of Lies (Book 27)

A Touch of Truth (Book 28)

An Hour of Need (Book 29)

A Game of Risk (Book 30)

A Twist of Fates (Book 31)

A Day of Glory (Book 32)

Series 5: A Dawn of Guardians

A Dawn of Guardians (Book 33)

A Sword of Chance (Book 34)

A Race of Trials (Book 35)

A King of Shadow (Book 36)

An Empire of Stones (Book 37)

A Power of Old (Book 38)

A Rip of Realms (Book 39)

A Throne of Fire (Book 40)

A Tide of War (Book 41)

Series 6: A Gift of Three

A Gift of Three (Book 42)

A House of Mysteries (Book 43)

A Tangle of Hearts (Book 44)

A Meet of Tribes (Book 45)

A Ride of Peril (Book 46)

A Passage of Threats (Book 47)

A Tip of Balance (Book 48)

A Shield of Glass (Book 49)

A Clash of Storms (Book 50)

Series 7: A Call of Vampires

A Call of Vampires (Book 51)

A Valley of Darkness (Book 52)

A Hunt of Fiends (Book 53)

A Den of Tricks (Book 54)

A City of Lies (Book 55)

A League of Exiles (Book 56)

A SHADE OF DRAGON TRILOGY

A Shade of Dragon 1

A Shade of Dragon 2

A Shade of Dragon 3

A SHADE OF KIEV TRILOGY

A Shade of Kiev 1

A Shade of Kiev 2

A Shade of Kiev 3

THE SECRET OF SPELLSHADOW MANOR

(Completed series)

The Secret of Spellshadow Manor (Book 1)

The Breaker (Book 2)

The Chain (Book 3)

The Keep (Book 4)

The Test (Book 5)

The Spell (Book 6)

BEAUTIFUL MONSTER DUOLOGY

Beautiful Monster 1

Beautiful Monster 2

DETECTIVE ERIN BOND (Adult thriller/mystery)

Lights, Camera, GONE

Write, Edit, KILL

For an updated list of Bella's books, please visit her website:
www.bellaforrest.net

Join Bella's VIP email list and she'll send you an email
reminder as soon as her next book is out:
www.morebellaforrest.com

SNEAK PEEK OF BOOK 4:
VENTURERS

CHAPTER 1

My hands were covered in blood. It oozed between my fingers, snaking down my wrists and pooling across the floor of the small room. No matter how hard I scrubbed, I couldn't get it to budge, the viscous liquid turning everything a sickening shade of scarlet.

I flinched as something bit into my skin, and looked down to see a shard of glass sticking out. Cursing under my breath, I pulled the fragment out and tossed it into the trash, listening for the clink of it as it fell. I reached for yet another damp cloth, desperate to get everything cleared up as quickly as possible. The sooner I was done, the better. I'd already worked my way through a considerable stack of cloths, most now piled high in a laundry bag to my right, which looked like the remnants of a murder scene.

The stench was overwhelming, filling my nostrils with an acrid, metallic tang. Had it been normal, human blood, it would have been horrifying, but at least I would have known where it came from. This was something different entirely. Several shades of red, a patch of blue, and a funny streak of black melded together to make one nauseating puddle of grossness. I didn't want to touch it, let alone clean it up, but here I was, stuck in the stuffy confines of the ship's store room, crouched down in a pool of alien blood, wishing every kind of pain imaginable on the woman who had caused this mess.

Pandora had dropped a tray of vials earlier, and though she claimed it was an accident, I suspected foul play. Naturally, she hadn't bothered to clean the aftermath up herself, but had demanded I get down on my knees and do it instead; no doubt she thought herself too important to do any grunt work. That was certainly the way she was acting, strutting about the ship like a peacock, keeping us all busy to the point of exhaustion, while she messed around with a few dials and controls.

We'd been on the *Vanquish* for a week already, heading for Zai, and it felt like the longest week of my life. Around every corner, there was something else Pandora wanted us to do, never giving any of us a moment to ourselves. Each morning, there was an enormous list to plough through, but we knew there'd only be more jobs if we ever reached the end of it. Not that we ever did.

I understood why she was doing it, but that only served to make me more annoyed. Pandora was keeping all five of us—Navan, Bashrik, Angie, Lauren, and myself—as busy as possible, to prevent us from congregating in secret, stealing a moment to discuss plans with one another. She wasn't an idiot; she had to know we had other reasons for wanting to be away from Vysanthe, and she was making sure we didn't get a single second to put those reasons into action.

After all, we'd been shipped off in such a hurry, the five of us had barely had the chance to speak with one another about what we might do when we reached the Fed outpost near Zai. Queen Brisha had demanded we leave the day after my stunt at the new alchemy lab, perhaps fearing another manic attack involving an explosives belt and her beloved generators. It wasn't ideal, since it meant we had to miss out on the mission to Queen Gianne's underground hangar, to destroy her new fleet, but there was nothing we could do about that. Navan tried to persuade her to let us complete that mission first, but Brisha wasn't having any of it. With guards flanking us, we'd been frog-marched from our quarters, down to the waiting *Vanquish*.

And now, we were far away from that world, piercing through the eternity of space, headed for Zai.

Much to our irritation, we'd been forced to tell Pandora about the deep space tech in the underground hangar, knowing her rebel resources might be our best bet at keeping it secret. With surprising solemnity, she had promised she would get Orion to see to it—whatever that meant. Even so, I couldn't help worrying about what might happen if Brisha discovered the technology and the lies we'd told before Orion could do anything about it.

It was funny, the way my mind settled on certain things while I was in the middle of some menial task, set by Pandora. In solitude, scrubbing for hours, it was hard not to dwell on fears and errors.

Still, at least I wasn't in the engine room, polishing the thousands of pipes, big and miniscule, that criss-crossed all over the thrumming chamber, running in labyrinthine tracks across the ceilings and walls, and even under the floor. Navan and Bashrik had been sentenced to that particular duty today, and I knew they'd come back at the next mealtime shouting at the tops of their voices, their hearing muffled by the roar of the engines. The *Vanquish* was not a sleek, state-of-the art machine like the *Asterope*, with silky smooth, purring engines—it was a military beast, built for might and power, not deep space speed.

Sometimes, Navan and I would pass in the corridor, on the way to our next tasks, and I would tap the spot just above my heart, where my climpet still flashed, the light showing my love for him was still as strong as ever. He would smile and tap his, or lift his shirt to show me, if he was feeling particularly defiant to Pandora's surveillance. I usually preferred the latter, though I wasn't all that keen on Pandora looking in, getting a cheap thrill out of it. Besides, knowing her, she'd probably think we were communicating in some peculiar Morse code, though she hadn't said anything about it just yet.

Drawing my mind away from Navan, I thought of Lauren, who was in the supply closet down the hallway, making an inventory of every little thing the ship had, while Angie was stuck in the laundry, cleaning every scrap of material for the dozenth time. I could already visualize her emerging from the humidity of the laundry room, her already-curly hair frizzed up into an unruly blonde mass, her face deeply unimpressed. The inventory would go missing at the end of the day, meaning someone would have to do it again tomorrow, but we'd grown used to that annoyance in our lives. Pandora saw to it that every task needed repeating, purely to keep us away from one another. "The devil makes work for idle hands," and all that.

I know what I'd like to do with my idle hands, I thought bitterly, wondering how it would feel to smack Pandora hard across the face. Delightful, I imagined.

She just would not leave us alone, to the point where she'd taken to sleeping in the same room as us. Not only that, but she was monitoring our every move with recording devices that were dotted all over the ship. Wherever I walked, I could see the devices moving to follow me, their camera lenses glinting like eyes, surveying every corner, every walkway, every room. There was one watching me right now, at the far end of the store cupboard, peering down over my shoulder. I thought of Pandora sitting in her control room, chuckling to herself as she watched the camera feeds, and felt my hands tighten around the damp, blood-soaked cloths. She really was insufferable.

Just then, the alarm on my wristband beeped, telling me it was almost three o'clock—not that time had much purpose or meaning out in space, where there was no sunlight or moonlight, only the endless expanse of stars stretching through the darkness. Even so, it felt nice to have something routine, to keep my grasp on earthly, normal things.

Hurling the last of the sodden cloths into the laundry bag, knowing Angie would hate me for dropping off so many, I threw it over my shoulder and headed out of the store cupboard. There were still a few unsightly streaks of crimson on the ground, but they would dry. Besides, if Pandora didn't like it, she'd just get me to do it all over again.

Keeping my head down, I walked briskly down the hallway towards the observation deck, leaving the sack outside the laundry room on my way. I rapped on the door to let Angie know it was there, but I didn't stay to see her irate face. It was almost my turn to check for any updates on the Note, and I was determined not to be late because of Pandora's spillage.

Picking up speed, I had just reached the main space of the vessel, when a jolt vibrated through the ship. With the gravity drives enabled there was no graceful floating, just the hard impact of being weighted to the ground, as though we were on land. Stumbling to one side, I knocked into the wall, grasping for a handhold to keep me upright as a second shudder rippled through the vessel, shaking it violently. Still gripping the side of the wall, I peered into the main space, trying to see what was going on. There were no windows in the main chamber of the *Vanquish*, but the cockpit was just across the other side of it, the door wide open, revealing Pandora in the captain's chair, her hands darting across the control panel, struggling to steer the ship.

I turned as the sound of erratic footsteps echoed in the passageway behind me. Navan, Bashrik, Angie, and Lauren were all running towards me, swaying from side to side with the jarring movements of the ship.

"What's going on?" Navan asked, as we moved into

the main space and headed for the cockpit.

"We're passing through a field of metal debris—it came out of nowhere!" Pandora yelled, her fingertips moving so fast they were almost a blur. "Bashrik, take the second set of controls and help me navigate! Lauren, Angie, secure any loose items in the cockpit— the last thing we need is something crashing down and hitting one of us while we're trying to steer! Riley, Navan, man the force guns—we need to push this debris away from the ship before it does too much damage!" she barked, her eyes never leaving the screen in front of her, where objects kept popping up, flashing red when they got too close.

"I don't have any training with weaponry like this. I'm used to two-man fighting vessels, not giant military gunships!" I replied anxiously, while the others hurried to their posts. Only Navan hung back, waiting for me.

"Just figure it out, Riley! We don't have time for your pathetic insecurities!" Pandora bellowed back, her eyes narrowing as she took us past a particularly aggressive block of compressed metal.

With my cheeks flushing angrily, I turned and took off through the main space of the ship, with Navan in hot pursuit. We were headed for the weapons control section on the floor beneath the one we were currently running across. Turning down the corridor, we sprinted to the end, where a stairwell disappeared into the metal ground. With our booted feet clanging on the winding, steel steps, we reached the bottom of the ship, sprinting in the direction of the gun-pods, the vessel still jolting back and forth, knocking us off-balance. Well, knocking me off-balance; Navan seemed to be able to run in a straight line, regardless of the jarring movements.

Reaching the reinforced glass gun-pods, which stuck out beneath the belly of the ship like transparent eggs, we sat next to one another, staring out at the debris that floated across the landscape in every direction. The weapons panels lit up, showing the targets that surrounded the vessel, each one beeping a bright red as it got too close to the ship, much like the panel Pandora was using.

"Where the heck did all of this come from?" I asked, as I selected the button that showed the symbol for force guns. There were five, dotted down the side of the screen, each holding the key to a different weapon.

Navan shook his head. "It's hard to say—it could have come from any direction. This stuff could've been floating across space for years, but nobody bothers with a clean-up unless it's in their jurisdiction. Even then, most don't bother," he replied grimly, tapping his own force-gun button.

"Do we just fire?" I wondered, feeling nervous. I had excelled in my fighter-pilot training, but this was a whole different field of weaponry. The ship was bigger, the guns were huge, and there was a lot at stake. Unlike on the training field, where everything was a simulation, there was no restart button here.

"Yes," Navan said, as his hands moved across the panel, targeting blocks of debris, the pulse of his force gun sending it hurtling away from the vessel. I guessed it looked simple enough...

Looking down at my panel, pretending I was back in the fighter-ships, I took a deep breath and told myself to focus. This was no different than the way we had practiced, back on Vysanthe. Steeling myself, I let my hands do the work, moving deftly across the panel. It was only when I targeted a large chunk of ominous-looking metal that I realized Navan's button was in a different position to mine. By then, it was too late.

Without warning, an enormous blast made the *Vanquish* tremble as a trail of blinding white light shot outwards, slicing the chunk of metal clean in two. Everything beyond the ship played out in silence, but I could tell the impact on the metal was huge. A moment later, the two halves veered off, with one jagged shard heading straight for us. Navan scrambled to rectify the situation, his hands darting against the screen, but the metal was too close, and too quick. It was going to hit us, and there was nothing we could do to stop it.

It collided with the *Vanquish* head-on, the force of

the collision sending me flying forwards, straight out of my seat. Had Navan not stuck out his arm to catch me, I would've smacked into the solid glass of the pod wall, no doubt breaking my neck in the process.

"Are you okay?" Navan asked, putting his arm around me.

I nodded, the air knocked clean out of me. I didn't get the chance to say anything else as the sound of thundering boots ricocheted down the hallway behind us. Pandora charged through the underbelly of the ship, her eyes glittering with fury.

"What are you playing at down here? You almost got us killed!" she snarled, glancing at the control panel. I noticed she didn't look at Navan while flinging her accusations. It was clear it was my fault this had happened. "You selected the cannons, you idiot! I told you to use force-guns!" she shouted, pushing me roughly to one side and sitting down in my seat. Immediately, she set to work, skillfully sending the debris away from the ship, her hands moving expertly.

"I've never used this panel before!" I tried to defend myself, but it fell on deaf ears. She wasn't interested in what I had to say.

"Damage report?" Pandora asked, pressing the comms button on the control panel, while the force-guns continued to push the debris out of our path.

Bashrik's voice crackled through. "Minimal

damage. The hull took a beating, but there are no breaches. Guns are operational, engines are operational, shields are operational. It's just a cosmetic issue —the old girl won't look as pretty again," he remarked, offering a tight laugh.

"Very good, keep running diagnostics—if anything *has* been damaged, I want to know about it immediately," Pandora insisted.

"Will keep you updated," Bashrik replied. A click signaled his return to running checks on the ship, the conversation over.

"Navan, go and help navigate while your brother runs diagnostics," Pandora instructed, still not looking up from her work.

"Of course," he said, flashing me an apologetic glance. I could sense the rage rippling off Pandora in waves, but surely there was something I could do to help? I had made a simple mistake—anyone could have done it. The only problem was, it wasn't anyone who had done it...it was me. I waited for her to give me something to do, but the words never came.

Taking me by the hand, Navan led me out of the gun-pod and up to the main deck, where Bashrik was darting between several panels, a frantic look on his face. Ahead, the debris still floated across the vast windscreen of the *Vanquish*, but Pandora's skillfully placed force-blasts were sending each one out of our way, keeping us on a steady course to safety. I hated that I had let the team down. More than that, I hated that she had seen me do it. Undoubtedly, she would have a few savage words with me later, once she had finished saving our skin.

With the prospect of a verbal lashing glaring like a beacon in my mind, I wondered if getting split apart by a giant shard of metal might be more pleasant, after all. At least, that way, I would never have to see the anger and derision in Pandora's eyes again.

Standing back, I watched as Navan helped his brother on the controls, feeling stupid and useless. Angie and Lauren had finished fixing all the loose items into place, but they were too busy watching the path of the *Vanquish*, as it weaved through the remainder of the debris field. And so, I stood there, doing the same, waiting for the moment when we were out of harm's way.

Eventually, the last few pieces of debris disappeared, the rest of it drifting along behind us. As soon as that last chunk vanished into the darkness of space, I heard the ominous sound of heavy boots on the metal walkway once more. It was like hearing the executioner, coming towards me.

Pandora stormed into the cockpit, her furious eyes seeking me out. We might have navigated out of a treacherous path, but I was in deep trouble now.

64090621R00236

Made in the USA
Middletown, DE
09 February 2018